ONE FETA IN THE GRAVE

The Kitchen Kebab Mystery Series
by Tina Kashian

Hummus and Homicide

Stabbed in the Baklava

One Feta in the Grave

ONE FETA IN THE GRAVE

Tina Kashian

KENSINGTON BOOKS
www.kensingtonbooks.com

KENSINGTON BOOKS are published by

Kensington Publishing Corp.
119 West 40th Street
New York, NY 10018

All Kensington titles, imprints and distributed lines are available at special quantity discounts for bulk purchases for sales promotion, premiums, fund-raising, educational or institutional use. Special book excerpts or customized printings can also be created to fit specific needs. For details, write or phone the office of the Kensington Special Sales Manager: Kensington Publishing Corp., 119 West 40th Street, New York, NY, 10018. Attn. Special Sales Department. Phone: 1-800-221-2647.

ISBN-13: 978-1-4967-1351-3
ISBN-10: 1-4967-1351-6
First Kensington Mass Market Edition: March 2019

ISBN-13: 978-1-4967-1352-0 (e-book)
ISBN-10: 1-4967-1352-4 (e-book)

10 9 8 7 6 5 4 3 2 1

Printed in the United States of America

For Laura

Never stop reaching for your dreams.
I love you.

CHAPTER 1

"It looks like a giant nose."

Lucy Berberian's lips twitched at the words her longtime friend Katie Watson whispered into her ear.

"No. I think it's an oversized ear. Wait, it's a . . ." Lucy bit her lip, afraid to voice what other body part she thought was displayed, then suddenly realized the artist's true intent. "It's a big snail!"

Both women looked at each other, then burst out laughing, drawing the attention of a group of serious-looking men and women holding clipboards who were gathered around a sand sculpture a few yards away.

Lucy scanned the beach, noting the dozens of impressive sand sculptures. It was Sunday, the opening day of the Ocean Crest sand sculpture contest, the first event of many to celebrate the weeklong beach festival in the small Jersey shore town. The festival offered numerous activities on the boardwalk and on the beach. Surfing, beach volleyball, and soccer competitions would thrill tourists and beachgoers alike while a wine and food tasting event would offer delicious morsels from local restaurants to satisfy adventurous palates. Visitors would wander among the temporary tents set up on the boardwalk while local musicians performed beneath the bandstand. And all during the week, shops would continue to sell beach clothing, boogie boards, pails and shovels, hermit crabs, and dozens of other summer-themed knickknacks. The amusement pier's old-fashioned wooden roller coaster and Ferris wheel operated late into the evening, and spectacular fireworks ended the festivities Saturday night.

The festival was important for the local merchants and the town. It was mid-August, and soon after, the season would wind down and the small town that could easily swell to triple its population during the summer months would shrink to its after-season size following Labor Day.

The sand sculpture contest kicked off the festival, and local artists had molded unique creations. Mermaids, Greek and Roman gods and goddesses, intricate castles, and a variety of marine life including sea turtles, horseshoe crabs, and fish fascinated onlookers. A lifelike sculpture of C-3PO alongside R2-D2 from *Star Wars* drew kids of all ages.

Clipboards in hand, Lucy and Katie walked from creation to creation and marked their scores on their judging sheets.

Katie chewed on her pencil as she stared at the snail sculpture. "I'm not sure how to score this one."

Lucy cocked her head to the side and squinted at the sculpture. "It's very detailed. I'm giving it a high score for creativity."

"I suppose." Katie didn't look convinced.

A flash of red on the beach caught Lucy's eye. A pretty, blond teenager in a fire-engine-red bikini flirted with a lifeguard sitting in his guard stand. Her brunette girlfriend stood next to her smiling.

"The one in the red looks like you did in high school," Lucy said. Katie was tall and slender with straight blond hair and blue eyes.

"You think so? I don't remember being that flirtatious, and the curvy brunette looks like you now."

Lucy rolled her eyes. "My bikini days are long over. And you always flirted with the lifeguards."

"The good old days," Katie said.

They burst out laughing. They'd been best friends since grade school, but were physical opposites. Lucy was shorter with dark, curly hair that never cooperated in the summer humidity, and her eyes were a deep brown. The two women came from different cultural backgrounds as well. Lucy was a first-generation American—a mix of Armenian, Greek, and Lebanese—and Katie had discovered, after recently putting together a family tree, that one of her ancestors fought under General Washington in the Revolutionary War.

Their differences never mattered. They were like sisters, and when Lucy had quit her job as a Philadelphia attorney and returned home, Katie had welcomed her back with open arms and offered Lucy her guest bedroom in the cozy rancher she shared with her husband, Bill, an Ocean Crest police officer.

They marked down their scores and turned to the next sculpture—an adorable sand snowman with shiny black shells for its eyes and a small conch shell for its nose—when angry voices drew their attention.

"You're biased and everyone knows it! How the hell did you get to be a judge?"

Lucy recognized the man as Harold Harper, a boardwalk business owner. Harold was stocky with reddish hair parted on one side and the beginnings of a goatee on his square chin. He wore a striped tank top, wrinkled khaki shorts, and sandals.

"What's it to you? Mind your own business."

Lucy didn't know the second man. Tall and thin, he had a shock of white hair, bushy eyebrows, and a tattoo of Wile E. Coyote on his right bicep. His untucked, white, T-shirt and army green shorts emphasized his height and lankiness.

"I'm also a judge. I'm making it my business," Harold said.

Lucy turned to Katie. "What's going on?"

"That's Harold Harper and Archie Kincaid," Katie said. "Archie came to town a year ago and opened Seaside Gifts, a store on the boardwalk. I issued his mercantile license at the town hall."

Katie worked at the Ocean Crest town hall and handled real estate taxes, zoning, pet licenses, and business licenses.

"Archie's going at it pretty good with Harold," Lucy said.

"They own shops next to each other on the boardwalk. Sparks fly whenever they're within five feet of each other."

Their combative stances reminded Lucy of the TV commercials advertising a big mixed martial arts fight at one of the large Atlantic City casinos. Was it all bravado or could they really pack a punch?

Katie vigorously fanned her red cheeks with her clipboard. "If it has something to do with the judging, then I have to get involved."

Katie was the head judge on the judging committee for the sand sculpture contest. The committee appointed six additional judges and everyone's scores would be anonymously tallied. Lucy was one of the appointed judges.

Lucy had also been recruited to oversee the food and wine tasting event, which was part of the festival and would take place on the boardwalk. As the new manager of Kebab Kitchen, her family-owned Mediterranean restaurant, Lucy had been the perfect fit for the job. She'd also wanted to give back to the town who had warmly embraced her after she'd returned home months ago.

Harold and Archie glowered at each other and were starting to cause a scene. Several tourists had stopped on the beach to watch.

Lucy eyed them warily. "Maybe you should call Bill." A man in uniform carrying a gun could quickly calm down a fight between two idiots.

"I can handle it," Katie said, stiffening her spine as she approached the pair. "What's the problem, gentlemen?"

"He should be disqualified as a judge," Harold said, pointing his pen at Archie.

"Shut up, Harper! No one wants to hear your opinion," Archie countered.

This wasn't going well. If things escalated, then Lucy would call Bill on her cell phone.

"Why do you think he should be disqualified?" Katie asked.

"His nephew created that." Harold motioned to a sand sculpture of a sea serpent attacking a castle. "I glimpsed at his scores. He gave everyone lower scores and his nephew a ten. A ten! No one should get a perfect score."

Lucy had already judged the sculpture in question, and she tended to agree. The face of the serpent was not detailed, and one wall of the castle was starting to crumble. It was average, certainly not a ten—not when the competition was stiff and there were a lot of spectacular sculptures.

"Is this true about your nephew?" Katie asked.

Archie shrugged. "Neil is an aspiring artist and happened to enter this year."

Katie frowned. "Then as the head judge of the judging committee, I have to agree with Mr. Harper."

"What? Why?"

"The judging agreement you signed specifically says no family members are permitted to compete," Katie said.

"I didn't see that in the agreement," Archie protested.

"Maybe you should have read the fine print," Harold scoffed.

Archie whirled on Harold. "Maybe I should wallop you."

"You're nothing but a bully," Harold taunted.

"Mr. Harper, please." Katie said, holding up her hand. She turned to Archie. "Mr. Kincaid, I'm afraid you have to step down as a judge. There is a five-thousand-dollar prize at stake, and we can't afford an appearance of impropriety."

"You're kidding me, right?" Archie looked at her in disbelief.

"No. I'm quite serious."

Harold laughed, and a smug look crossed his face.

Rather than address his adversary, Archie stalked forward to stand toe to toe with Katie. "Are you accusing me of cheating?"

Katie was taken aback, but she didn't back down. She placed her hands on her hips. "I'm not accusing you of anything, just stating fact. The agreement was clear."

Archie jerked his head at Harold. "He put you up to this, didn't he?"

"Nope, but I sure am enjoying it," Harold drawled.

Archie ignored the barb and turned back to Katie. "What if I refuse to step down as a judge?"

Katie raised her chin. "Then your nephew's sculpture will have to be disqualified."

Archie's brows snapped downward like two angry caterpillars. "If you'd just keep your nose where it belongs instead of favoring Harold, lady, the rest of this judging would go on without a hitch."

Katie's eyes narrowed. "What did you say to me?" Her fist clenched at her side, and Lucy feared her friend would be the one doing the walloping. Lucy was painfully aware that everyone's attention was focused on the pair.

"Just calm down, Katie." Lucy rushed forward to grab hold of her arm.

Lucy felt Katie's muscles tighten. "Like I said,

either you step down or your nephew's sculpture will be eliminated from the competition."

"Let's move on," Lucy urged. "We can report everything to the festival committee and let them toss out his scores."

When neither seemed willing to break the standoff, Lucy tugged on Katie's arm. A group of children, dressed in bathing suits and holding pails and sand shovels, had gathered to stand behind the adults and stare, mouths agape.

Archie had enough sense to look contrite, and he backed up a step. "If those are my options, then I'll step down as judge." He extended his clipboard.

Lucy sprang forward and took the clipboard rather than risk Katie hitting him over the head with it. Together they watched as Archie stormed off the beach.

"You okay?" Lucy asked after they'd moved on.

Katie rubbed her temple. "Yeah. I just lost my temper."

"I don't blame you. Archie acted like a jerk. But Harold was no better in my opinion. He really pushed Archie's buttons. Why do they hate each other?"

"Like I said, they are boardwalk business neighbors. Harold called the township and complained that Archie's using cutthroat business tactics."

"How?"

"They both mostly sell T-shirts, boogie boards, bathing suits, all the other usual beach items. Harold claims Archie has slashed his prices below cost just to put Harold out of business. He claims Archie will turn around and raise his prices after Harold is forced to close his store."

Lucy knew boardwalk business owners had a little over three months—from Memorial Day to Labor Day—to earn their yearly living. The beach town was bursting at its seams with tourists during the season, and there was ample business to sell similar wares. But at the same time, it fed a competitive business nature.

"What can the town do?" Lucy asked.

"Nothing. It's a free economy."

Lucy shook her head. "Both men are stubborn as mules."

Katie let out a slow breath. "I'm just glad it ended before those two came to blows and one ended up dead."

The industrial KitchenAid mixer whirred and mixed the dough to a creamy smoothness. Inside the oven, the first trays of date cookies were almost finished, and they released their delicious smell into the restaurant's kitchen.

The oven timer dinged. "They look perfect," Lucy's mother, Angela Berberian, said.

"I need to make five more trays." Lucy wiped her hands on a clean dishcloth and peered into the oven.

Angela reached for a white apron emblazoned with Kebab Kitchen's name in green letters. "I'll help."

The restaurant would serve cookies and baklava for dessert at the upcoming wine and food tasting event. Their head chef, Azad, would prepare his own savory dishes. Azad was creative, and Lucy couldn't wait to hear what he planned to serve.

The date cookies were a family favorite. Lucy's ten-year-old niece, Niari, was a typical picky tween eater. She wouldn't touch a date, let alone eat one. But the family recipe had fooled her. Niari had bitten into one of the soft cookies, mistakenly believed they were chocolate filled, and loved them. When Lucy had told her that they were stuffed with dates, not chocolate, Niari's eyes had widened like disks and her mouth had formed a perfect *O*, then she'd simply shrugged, and finished her cookie.

"Remove the trays before they overbake," her mother said.

Lucy reached for silicone mittens, pulled the trays out of the oven, and set them on the worktable to cool on racks. They smelled like heaven and her mouth watered at the sight. Each cookie was slightly brown and looked like a half-moon stuffed ravioli.

"Perfect," her mother said.

Lucy beamed. Angela Berberian didn't hand out praise easily. Her mother was the former chef of Kebab Kitchen and was a tyrant in the kitchen. At only five feet tall, she was tiny, but formidable. Anyone who'd ever worked with her knew better than to underestimate her culinary skill or to serve a dish that didn't meet her high standards. Angela wore her hair in her signature sixties beehive and the gold cross necklace she never removed.

Lucy had always believed life had played a cruel trick on her when she'd been born into her family. Her parents had opened Kebab Kitchen thirty years ago, and other than Lucy, every member of her family could cook. Her sister, Emma, could whip up a family meal for her husband, Max, and their daughter, Niari, in little time. Her father, Raffi, grew up knowing how to marinate and grill the perfect shish kebab.

Lucy had been the only one who couldn't boil water or scramble an egg, let alone prepare a tray of baklava. She'd gone to law school instead and had worked at a Philadelphia firm for eight years. But since returning home and taking over management of the restaurant, she'd been determined to learn.

It hadn't been easy. Lucy had spent hours in the kitchen with her mother learning how to make baklava, hummus, grape leaves stuffed with meat and rice, and other savory Mediterranean dishes. Frustrated and often overheated, there were times she wanted to quit, but she'd stuck with it, and she'd surprised everyone, mostly herself.

Her dishes came out not only edible, but good.

Not as good as her mother's or Azad's, but Lucy was more than pleased with her success. Plus, it wasn't as if she was taking over as head chef anytime soon. Lucy liked managing. Nothing was more satisfying than when the kitchen and dining room ran smoothly, and their customers enjoyed their meals.

The timer dinged again, and Lucy took out a second batch of cookies. She'd had to make small batches by herself, but with her mother's help, they could roll, stuff, and bake much faster.

Her mother reached for a chunk of dough covered in plastic wrap. "Did you let this dough rest?" her mother asked.

"Thirty minutes."

"Good. You remembered."

Lucy reached for a rolling pin and joined her

mother at the worktable. Adding a pinch of flour to her work surface so the dough wouldn't stick, Lucy started rolling. Once they rolled out the dough, they cut two-inch rounds with cookie cutters.

As they worked side by side, Lucy's mind turned back to the events of the morning. Angela had been in business in Ocean Crest for years and knew almost everyone in town. Maybe she'd have information on Archie or Harold.

"Hey, Mom, what do you know about Archie Kincaid?" Lucy asked.

"The owner of Seaside Gifts? He came to town about a year ago with his nephew and bought old man John's shop on the boardwalk. Why?" Angela continued cutting the dough with the cookie cutter as she spoke. She worked quickly, and Lucy had often admired her for her efficiency and endurance in the kitchen. Her mother never seemed to tire.

"Archie was a judge of the sand sculpture contest and never told the festival committee that his nephew was one of the sculptors. Archie gave Katie a hard time before he finally withdrew as a judge."

Her mother shrugged a slender shoulder. "I'm not surprised."

"You're not?"

Angela reached for a bowl of pitted and chopped dates that Lucy had prepared. She placed a tablespoon of filling in the center of each cut-out circle of dough. "Archie can be stubborn. His nephew, Neil, is a vagrant, and Archie tries to help the boy."

"Vagrant? What's that supposed to mean?" English was her mother's third language and sometimes she chose the wrong word to convey her meaning.

Angela waved a flour-coated hand. "You know.

Wanderer. Bum. He says he's an artist, but never sells anything. He surfs all day and doesn't work. He needs a haircut and a shave."

Lucy chuckled as she finally got her mother's meaning. She thought negatively of any unshaved male with long hair. Old-school thinking for sure, but Lucy could almost picture Neil Kincaid based on her mother's description. "Mom, *bum* is not a politically correct term."

"Fine. Neil isn't homeless, he's lazy. He could get a job if he wanted. Instead, he spends his days on the beach. He lives with his uncle, Archie, above their store."

"Yes, well. Archie argued with Katie. But Harold Harper instigated it." After adding the filling, Lucy folded the dough to make a half-moon shape.

"It's no secret that the two dislike each other," her mother said.

"How do you know that?"

"Once, they happened to be in the restaurant at the same time. They started shouting across the dining room and drove poor Sally crazy. She threatened to kick them out if they didn't behave."

"Really? I can't picture Sally losing it." Sally was a longtime waitress at Kebab Kitchen. She had an easygoing personality and the locals loved her. As long as Lucy had known her, Sally had never lost her temper.

"Fortunately, both men have never been back to eat at the same time again." Angela set down her spoon and glanced at Lucy's workspace. "Be careful not to stuff the cookies too much."

Lucy immediately scraped some of the date filling back into the bowl. Once each cookie was filled, folded, and sealed, she placed it on a tray. Last, she brushed all the unbaked cookies with egg wash and slid the rack into the oven.

"What smells so good in here?"

Lucy turned to see Azad Zakarian walk in the kitchen. Tall, dark, and lean, the sight of the handsome head chef always made her pulse pound a bit too fast. His hair was wet, making it look almost black, and Lucy knew he'd gone home after the lunch shift to shower and return for the dinner shift. He hadn't yet put on his chef's coat, and he wore a tight white T-shirt that showed off muscled biceps and a lean stomach. She tore her gaze away.

Get a grip, Lucy.

She was his boss, and she needed better self-control if they were to continue to work together.

Not long ago, Azad had left his sous chef job at a fancy Atlantic City restaurant to become head chef of Kebab Kitchen. Her parents no longer worked full-time, and she couldn't have managed the place without him. It hadn't been the smoothest transition. Azad had broken her heart after college, and she'd sworn never to fall for that charming dimple ever again.

But since her return to Ocean Crest, Azad had expressed interest in resuming their romantic relationship.

Trouble.

Lucy was hesitant about any kind of relationship with him outside of the restaurant, but time and his steady pursuit—along with a bout of hormones—was wearing down her resistance.

Lucy cleared her throat. "We're making date cookies and baklava for the festival."

"They look great, too," he said.

Was that a compliment about just the cookies or was there more behind his words?

"What do you have planned for the festival menu?"

"I want samples that people can easily eat without utensils. I'm thinking of small wrapped gyros, bamboo skewers of lamb shish kebab, and grilled vegetable skewers of peppers, tomatoes, and onions. I also plan to make a meat bulgur sausage and falafel."

"Mmm. It all sounds delicious," Lucy said.

Azad flashed a grin, and the dimple in his cheek deepened. She was suddenly overly warm, and it had nothing to do with the heat from the ovens.

"Excuse me. We need more flour," she said. Grabbing the half-empty container, she left Azad with her mother and headed for the storage room. She didn't need more flour, she needed a break.

Shelves of dry items stacked the perimeter of the storage room. A tiny office was tucked away in the corner. She set the flour container on a shelf beside large bags of rice, bulgur, and spices—the essentials of Mediterranean cuisine.

Grabbing a bag of cat food on a far shelf, she headed out the back door to the rear parking lot. She shook the bag and seconds later, a patchy orange and black cat with yellow eyes sauntered from behind the Dumpster to wind around her feet.

"Hi, Gadoo. Where have you been?" She bent down to pet his soft fur and was rewarded with a rumbling purr.

Her mother had named the outdoor cat Gadoo which meant *cat* in Armenian. Not very original, but

Lucy had taken a liking to the feisty feline and took over feeding him twice a day and making sure he always had enough water.

"I have your favorite." She opened the bag of kibbles and poured some into his bowl which she kept outside by the restaurant's back door. Gadoo looked up, blinked, then meowed.

"You want more?"

Another meow, louder this time.

"Spoiled kitty," she said, then added more food to his bowl. "If you keep eating like this, you'll have to watch your feline figure."

He responded with a twitch of his tail, and then began eating.

The back door opened, and Azad stepped out. "Hey. I was wondering where you went off to."

"I wanted to feed Gadoo." Obvious answer since the cat was chowing down at her feet. How long would it take for her to get over this nervousness around him when they were alone?

It didn't help that her parents had always wanted them to be together. "Keep the business in the family, Lucy," her mother had often said.

It had always been enough to make her run for the hills.

But now she was older and wiser. And Azad *had* changed. He was no longer the young, college boy who feared commitment. He'd stuck around and helped her by taking over as head chef.

Azad had put on his chef's coat, and he looked professional in the starched white jacket. Still, he shoved his hands into his pockets and a look of unease crossed his handsome features.

Maybe he was just as nervous as she was.

"Are you free Friday? There's a new French restaurant, Le Gabriel, that I think you'd like," he said. "Your mom is covering in the kitchen and your dad is managing then so it's not a problem."

He'd followed her outside to ask her on a date? "I've heard of Le Gabriel. It's received excellent reviews by the food critic in the *Ocean Crest Town News*."

"Are you free?" Azad's dark gaze met hers, and her heart skipped a beat.

Maybe it was time to take a leap. If a door of opportunity opened, shouldn't she step through it? "Yes," she said. "I'd like that."

Azad's mouth curved in a sensual smile. "Great. This time, I promise nothing will get in our way."

CHAPTER 2

After finishing the cookies, Lucy walked into the dining room to make sure everything was running smoothly for the upcoming dinner shift. Kebab Kitchen was a quaint family restaurant. Tables with pristine white tablecloths, votive candles, and vases of fresh flowers, as well as a handful of similarly appointed maple booths, offered diners a cozy atmosphere. Large bay windows overlooked the glimmering Atlantic Ocean and the pristine stretch of beach. In the distance, diners could see the boardwalk pier with the Ferris wheel and wooden roller coaster.

In the corner of the dining room was a hummus bar—one of the most popular features of the restaurant. The varieties of hummus changed daily, and tonight's flavors were artichoke, black bean, spicy jalapeño, and of course, Angela's famous traditional hummus. There were vegetables for dipping, and fresh pita bread could be ordered from the kitchen. Lucy never got tired of the hummus bar and would often grab a dish and indulge.

Her sister, Emma, and their longtime waitress, Sally, were making sure each table had full salt and pepper shakers and fresh flowers in the vases.

Emma spotted Lucy beside the waitress station and came over. "Hey, Lucy. How'd the sand sculpture judging go?"

Lucy didn't want to go into detail about Katie's confrontation. "You have to stop by the beach on your way home. The sculptures are amazing."

"We plan to," Sally said. "Meanwhile, here comes Butch to tell us tonight's specials."

The swinging kitchen doors opened and a large, African American man carrying a tray of food stepped into the dining room. Butch was another longtime employee and their line cook. He had the broadest shoulders and chest Lucy had ever seen on a man, and he always wore a checkered bandana on his head. He smiled, and his gold tooth glinted beneath the fluorescent lights.

"Hi, Lucy Lou," he called out, using the nickname he'd chosen for her ever since she'd been in kindergarten. "Tonight's appetizers are babá ganoush, and tabbouleh. The entrées are herb meatballs in a tomato sauce, duck with walnuts and rice, and vegetarian moussaka. Do you want to sample?"

Lucy greeted him with a big smile. "You bet." They always sampled the specials in case customers had questions while ordering.

Butch set the tray down on the counter behind the waitress station. Emma fetched three forks and small plates. The women split the entrées and tasted.

The baba ganoush had the perfect amount of tahini, or sesame seed paste, and melted in Lucy's mouth. The tabbouleh was savory and the lemon dressing added just enough tartness. She moved on to sample the main courses. The herb meatballs in tomato sauce were hearty and delicious. The duck was moist and cooked perfectly and served with rice pilaf. The vegetarian moussaka with eggplant and creamy béchamel sauce was heavenly and full of flavor.

Lucy set down her fork. "Oh my gosh. It's all so good."

"I want to keep eating," Emma said.

Butch nodded. "I'll tell Azad."

"Don't. His ego is already too big," Lucy said.

Butch chuckled and carried the tray and their dishes back to the kitchen.

The front door opened, and Emma and Sally stepped from behind the waitress station. "Well, well. Look who just walked in," Emma said.

Sally fanned herself. "What a hottie."

Lucy turned to see a dark-haired man with a bronzed complexion waiting by the hostess stand. Michael Citteroni ran the bicycle shop next door to Kebab Kitchen.

Sally rushed forward to snatch a menu and seat him in one of the maple booths by the window. She lingered a moment, smiling down at her customer, then smoothed her hair as she hurried back. "He asked for you, Lucy."

"Lucky girl. Too bad I'm married," Emma said.

Sally winked. "Don't let Azad see you talking to him."

Lucy rolled her eyes. "Stop. Both of you. Michael is just a friend."

Sally and Emma gave each other looks that said, "Yeah, right."

Lucy ignored them and headed for the table. She slid in the booth across from him and met his gaze. The first time she'd seen him she'd thought his deep blue eyes rivaled a summer sky in Ocean Crest. "Hi, Michael."

"I heard there was an argument while judging the sand sculpture contest. Talk says you tangled with Archie Kincaid."

Nothing in the small town of Ocean Crest stayed private for long. Gossip traveled faster than tzatziki sauce gone bad in the summer heat. It was one of the things that had bothered Lucy when she'd first moved back home. Everyone was in everyone else's business.

"Not me, but Katie. She put him in his place," she said.

"Good for her. Archie can be a royal ass."

"What do you know about him?"

"I hear things at the bicycle shop, especially when my father makes an appearance."

No doubt. Michael's father, Anthony Citteroni, was a bit shady, a mobster depending on who you believed, and according to local gossip he used his many businesses—bike rentals, Laundromats, and trash collection services—to launder money from his illegal activities and connections in Atlantic City.

But Michael was different; he didn't see eye to eye with his father, or his sister who idolized their father. Michael may not have initially wanted to run the bicycle shop, but like Lucy, he'd stepped up to help with the family business.

No wonder he liked riding his Harley-Davidson.

The few times Lucy had ridden with Michael, she'd felt free and, for those brief moments, she'd tossed her worries to the wind. It was an intoxicating experience.

Lucy let out a puff of air. "Don't keep me in suspense. Tell me what you know about Archie."

"He has few friends in town," Michael said. "Archie runs that boardwalk shop like a shark. Just ask the Gray sisters." Everyone in town knew the pair of sweet older sisters who owned Gray's Novelty Shop on the boardwalk.

"Their store is next to Archie's," he continued. "He wanted to buy them out and expand his space. They refused. He knows better than to ask his business neighbor on the other side. The only thing Harold Harper would sell him is a counterfeit dollar."

"You know about their feud?"

"Who doesn't?"

Once again, she was reminded of the Ocean Crest gossip mill. She wondered how many people had already heard about Katie's brawl with Archie today.

Michael opened his menu. "What do you recommend?"

"The baba ganoush appetizer. The duck with walnuts for the main course. Both are amazing."

"Sold." He handed her the menu. "By the way, do you want to go for a ride later this week? I just changed the carburetor on the Harley and it purrs like a dream."

Lucy smiled. "You bet."

Just then, Azad stepped out of the kitchen to get himself a glass of ice water from the waitress station.

He spotted the pair and froze. His brow furrowed and he glared at Michael.

Michael returned the stare.

It was no secret that Azad didn't like Michael, and Michael wasn't a big fan of Azad's.

Just great. She'd had her share of big male egos for one day.

"Looks like your chef wants me out of here," Michael said. "Any chance he'll poison my food?"

She tried not to grimace. "I'd be happy to taste test it for you."

The following morning, Lucy woke to bright sunshine streaming through the open bedroom window, along with a cool breeze. She stretched, and her mouth watered from the scent of freshly brewing coffee.

Thank goodness for Katie.

Lucy had been staying with Katie and Bill, an Ocean Crest beat cop, since she'd returned home. They lived in a rancher two blocks from the beach. The guest room was small, but lovely, and decorated in a beach theme with white wicker furniture and a daybed with a coverlet embroidered with starfish and shells. Watercolors of beach scenes painted by a local artist hung on the pale blue walls.

Lucy dressed in running shorts and a baggy T-shirt that read BEACH HAIR, DON'T CARE. It was a gift from her ten-year-old niece, Niari, after joking one day about how the summer humidity wreaked havoc with Lucy's shoulder-length, curly hair. Lucy had chuckled and wore the shirt with pride. She tied her running shoes and put her hair in a ponytail.

Lucy padded to the kitchen. Bill was already out of the house for his shift at the police station. As soon as Katie spotted her, she handed Lucy a mug of coffee and a chocolate glazed doughnut.

"You spoil me." Lucy sipped her coffee, then took a bite. "Mmm. Are these from Cutie's Cupcakes?"

"Yes. Susan Cutie's doughnuts are better than Krispy Kreme in my opinion."

"Much better. I convinced Susan to offer samples of lemon meringue pie at the food and wine tasting tomorrow."

"Smart girl. I still plan to leave work early Tuesday and can help. Then I'm announcing the winner of the sand sculpture contest and giving away a fat check for five grand."

"I'm dying to know. Who's the winner?"

"I don't even know. Gertrude Shaw and Francesca Stevens were in charge of calculating the scores. The winner's name is top secret and sealed in an envelope," Katie said.

"Are you kidding? Gertrude and Francesca are the town's worst gossips." They were also members of the Ocean Crest town council and had their fingers in everything.

"We know. That's why we gave them the positions on the judging committee. They would have managed to find out the winner's name beforehand anyway. This way, if the name is leaked, everyone will know it's because of them."

"Clever." Lucy placed her coffee cup in the sink. "I'm off for a run."

Her route was always the same. She'd chug to the end of the boardwalk, then run on the sand as she headed back. She wasn't a natural-born runner like Katie, and the three-mile trek had only gotten marginally easier, but it wasn't hard to convince herself to exercise. Being around food all day, especially her mother's specialties as well as her favorite lemon meringue pie from Cutie's Cupcakes, Lucy's jogs had helped keep the weight off and her waist trim.

The Ocean Crest boardwalk was an eclectic mix of shops that drew tourists from New Jersey and neighboring states. She passed two custard stands, a pizza shop, a tattoo parlor, and a self-professed psychic who read palms and tarot cards.

She glanced into the darkened interior of the psychic's small salon and spotted Madame Vega at her table. Dressed in a blue velvet robe with a matching turban, she peeled a card from a stack of tarot cards and placed it on the table before her customers, a pimply-faced teenager and her friend. Madame Vega claimed to descend from Hungarian gypsies and for five dollars she'd read your palm or your cards and predict your future. Angela said Madame Vega was actually from Philadelphia and her grandfather sold water ice at the Phillies' games. Either way, she had been a boardwalk fixture since Lucy was a kid.

Lucy plodded on. It was before eight, and already a throng of early-morning joggers, walkers, and bicycle riders were on the boards. The roller coaster on the pier was still; the rides wouldn't start until noon. At night, the lights from the Ferris wheel would light up the night sky and the screams from the coaster could be heard blocks away.

She passed the popcorn and french fry stand,

breathing in the tantalizing smells, when she heard, *"Watch the tramcar, please!"* blare from speakers behind her. She turned to see Ocean Crest's newest edition—the boardwalk tramcar. Bright yellow and blue, the twenty-seat vehicle offered tired tourists a ride up and down the boardwalk. It stopped at designated spots to pick up and drop off riders—mostly parents, children, babies in strollers, and senior citizens. Two college students, dressed in matching yellow and blue tops and black shorts, worked the tramcar. One stood in the rear to collect the three-dollar fee, and the other drove.

Lucy swerved to the side as the tramcar's speakers annoyingly blared, *"Watch the tramcar, please!"* as it drove by.

Now that she was tired and sweaty, the tramcar looked good to Lucy. She slowly ran past as it stopped ahead to pick up passengers.

Just as she came up to Seaside Gifts and the Sun and Surf Shop, Lucy spotted Archie Kincaid and Harold Harper facing each other, legs braced apart, in combative stances. The business neighbors were going at it again—this time, it seemed, over a rack of clothing.

"I told you that you can't put that in front of my store," Harold protested.

"I'm not. This is *my* storefront," Archie countered.

"Like hell it is. Move that rack or I'll move it myself." Harold's face turned splotchy and red, almost matching his hair.

Seriously? Did they have to argue over inches of space? There was sufficient business during the season for the shops, and in less than a couple hours, the bicycle riders and joggers would leave and the boardwalk would be crawling with tourists looking for beach souvenirs and T-shirts. Lucy rolled her eyes, then spotted a man leaning against the side of Archie's shop. Tall and gaunt, he had shoulder-length, dirty blond hair and looked to be in his early twenties. He had to be Neil, Archie's nephew, the aspiring artist and surfer.

Neil watched the argument with hooded eyes, then pulled a cigarette from the pocket of a ripped and faded T-shirt and lit up. Clearly, he had no intention of getting involved in the bickering.

Lucy couldn't decide if he was lazy or smart.

Next door to Archie's store was Gray's Novelty Shop. Making a quick decision, Lucy darted inside. A large glass tank of hermit crabs with painted shells sat in front of the shop. Inside, were shelves of sand toys, beach towels, and sunscreen. They'd added a large selection of local, handmade jewelry of shells and beads that filled the center of the store and was popular with the tourists.

Edith Gray was arranging bracelets on a display. Edna was stocking the shelves with aloe vera gel.

"Hi, Lucy!" Edna and Edith said in unison. Neither sister had married and the pair were in their seventies. Edna was tall and rail thin with a pointed nose while Edith was short and heavyset with a bulbous, red nose.

"How does your niece like the hermit crabs?" Edna asked.

"Niari loves them." Lucy had purchased two crabs for Niari a few months ago, and they were still alive and crawling.

"The festival is gearing up nicely. Do you know when they'll announce the winner of the sand sculpture contest?" Edith asked.

"Katie said they're scheduled to announce the winner tomorrow beneath the bandstand and hand over the five-thousand-dollar prize."

Edna whistled. "That's a hefty prize. I vote for the mermaid."

"No way," Edith countered. "I say the sculpture of Zeus with his lightning bolt will take home the cash. What do you think, Lucy?"

"I can't say. I was one of the judges," Lucy said.

"Then you're working double duty for the festival. We heard you're in charge of organizing the food and wine tasting," Edna said.

Lucy nodded. "I'll be setting up the tents on the boardwalk tomorrow morning, but the restaurants won't start serving until noon and—"

Raised voices sounded next door, cutting off her response. Lucy's eyebrows drew downward, but the two sisters seemed unfazed.

"What's with your neighbors?" Lucy asked.

Edith removed her reading glasses and they dangled by a chain around her neck. "Oh, posh. Are they bickering again?"

"I jogged past them on the way here. It seems like Archie wants to put a rack of clothes outside his shop, but Harold says it's encroaching on his territory," Lucy said.

Edna clucked her tongue. "They haven't gotten along since day one. Archie lowered his prices on certain items to undercut Harold's business. Harold retaliated by scheduling deliveries for four in the morning. Harold knows Archie and Neil live in an apartment above his store, and the noisy, early deliveries drive them batty."

"They are like children," Edith said.

"Yes, but just like bickering children, they have their redeeming qualities," Edna claimed.

"Such as?" Lucy asked.

"Harold helped us paint our store last year. We couldn't afford to hire a painter and he said he'd do the work for us," Edna said.

"That was nice," Lucy agreed.

"Archie volunteers his time one Saturday every month for a local teen drug program," Edith said.

"Really?" Lucy had trouble envisioning Archie with troubled teens, but what did she know? Maybe Neil had difficulties in the past with drugs, and Archie felt like giving back.

"How about you? Have either of them bothered you?" Michael had mentioned that Archie wanted to expand and buy the Gray sisters' store. She was curious what they thought about their neighbor.

"Heavens, no."

Edith pursed her lips into a worried frown. "Archie had made us an offer, remember?"

"Oh, that. Yes, well he'd wanted to see if we were ready to retire. What I told him was we don't ever plan to retire. We're going to run this shop when we are in our nineties," Edna said.

"How did he take that?" Lucy asked.

"He never troubled us again," Edna said. "As for Archie and Harold's arguing, we stay neutral."

"Like Switzerland!" Edith said.

Maybe Lucy should take the sisters' advice and

stay out of it. But the problem was, Lucy didn't want their petty fighting to ruin the festival. It had already upset Katie and drawn unwanted attention from tourists and locals on the beach.

Stay neutral. Like Switzerland.

The sisters' advice was sound. Too bad Lucy was never good at biting her tongue.

Later that afternoon, Lucy took a quick break to head to the town hall with a take-out container of Greek salad loaded with feta. She knew feta was Katie's favorite and she wanted to surprise her friend with lunch.

The redbrick building was located in the center of town and shared space with the Ocean Crest police station. Lucy knew something was wrong as soon as she opened the front door. Gail Turner, the receptionist, was standing in the hall and wringing her hands. She was in her early fifties, with thin hair the color of coffee grinds that she teased to look fuller. According to Katie, she liked to chatter with the staff.

"Hi, Gail. What's wrong?" Lucy asked.

"Oh, it's just . . . just that there seems to be some trouble today." Gail kept glancing down the short hallway, her plucked brows knitting together.

"What kind of trouble?"

Katie's voice echoed down the short hall. "I'm sorry your application for a mercantile license was denied. But we have to consider the benefits and detriments to the town. The additional traffic is troublesome, and the town is already short on parking spots during the season. Then there are the dangers of more bicycles and pedestrians on the boardwalk."

Then came another voice, male and furious. "I'm not buying any of it."

"I'm sorry you feel that way, but the decision is final," Katie said.

"Well, it's a crappy one."

Lucy recognized the male voice. Archie Kincaid.

Lucy didn't wait. She hurried down the hall, passing other doors, until she came to Katie's office. Sure enough, Archie was hovering over Katie's desk. They were both so engrossed in their argument that neither of them noticed Lucy standing in the doorway.

Katie pushed back her chair and stood. Her face was flushed. "I'm sorry, Mr. Kincaid, but there's nothing I can do."

"I don't believe it. You're holding a grudge because of what happened on the beach during judging of the sand sculpture contest."

"No. The decision was made before the judging."

"Something tells me you were the deciding vote on my license."

Katie placed her hands on her hips. "I'm not regretting my decision. But if you must know, the mayor had a say."

"Then this is prejudice because I'm not a lifetime resident of this small, backward town, isn't it?"

"Absolutely not. The reasons are stated below." Katie jabbed a finger at a paper on her desk. "Traffic concerns and the safety of the residents and tourist alike and—"

"That's bull." He pointed to her. "I know you had something to do with this."

Doors opened and workers stuck their heads into the hallway. Others stepped out of their cubicles to stare.

Katie's professionalism slipped. Lips pursed, she finally lost her temper. "You should leave."

"Or what? You'll shoot me with your husband's gun?"

"Don't tempt me. Out!"

Lucy jumped to the side to avoid colliding with Archie as he stormed past.

Katie's gaze snapped to where Lucy stood in the doorway, and she collapsed in her desk chair. "Hey, Lucy. Sorry you had to witness that."

"What was *that?*"

"Archie's mad because the township won't give him another mercantile license. Is everyone outside gaping?"

"Yes, but no longer. You did give Gail a fright though."

Katie cracked a smile. "Gail's a sensitive gossip."

"What the heck is a 'sensitive gossip?'"

"Gail likes to talk, but she also frightens easily. That's why she works at the town hall and not at the adjacent police station. Both had vacancies when she applied for a job."

Lucy shrugged. "It's a good thing you're not easily intimidated. You stood up to Archie during the judging, and now this."

"He doesn't scare me. I'm married to a cop, and I watch plenty of TV crime shows."

It was true. Katie was obsessed with television murder shows and had the complete set of both

Murder, She Wrote and *Columbo* and watched every spinoff of *CSI* and *Law and Order.* Her knowledge had certainly come in handy, and she'd helped Lucy solve more than one town murder.

Lucy set the take-out container on Katie's desk. "I bought something to cheer you up. Greek salad for lunch."

"Lots of feta?"

"Of course."

Katie opened the take-out lid and peered inside. "You're the best."

Nothing contrasted their different cultural backgrounds as much as food. Lucy grew up eating shish kebab and hummus whereas Katie was raised on meat loaf and apple pie.

Lucy handed her a plastic fork, knife, and napkin. "What do you think Archie will do?"

"Get a lawyer and reapply." Katie speared a piece of salad and feta and stuffed it in her mouth. "Mmm. Your dressing is so good."

"Archie actually talked about you shooting him with Bill's gun," Lucy said.

Katie swallowed and set down her fork. "I was livid. Truth be told, if the gun was on my desk, I just may have done it."

CHAPTER 3

The morning of the food and wine tasting event, Lucy rose extra early and took a fast shower. She had already made a run to Cutie's Cupcakes for blueberry, banana nut, and cranberry muffins and made a pot of coffee when Katie trudged into the kitchen wearing a robe and fuzzy slippers.

"Eager beaver, this morning," she commented, seeing breakfast already on deck.

"I have a ton to do. The tents have to be put up, the Restaurant Supply Depot is delivering refrigerators, freezers, and ovens, and I hired a local electrician, Jose Alvarez, to ensure everything is properly wired."

Katie yawned and rubbed her eyes. "When do you think they'll start serving? I want to be first in line for Azad's specialties."

Lucy handed a mug of coffee and the box of muffins to Katie. She chose a blueberry muffin and slathered it with butter. "By noon, if all goes as planned," Lucy said. "But don't let Azad know that he's first on your list for taste testing. I just told Emma and Sally I thought his ego is too big."

Katie chuckled. "Are you growing to like your head chef a bit too much?"

"He asked me for a date Friday night, dinner at Le Gabriel."

Katie's eyes grew large, and she dropped the muffin on her plate. "Lucky girl! I've been dying for Bill to take me to that fancy French place. It's impossible to get a reservation."

"If you don't tease me about Azad, I promise to bring home a French dessert for you."

"Ugh. It will kill me, but dessert just might be worth it. See you later today beneath the band-stand," Katie said, then headed for the shower.

Lucy took a last bite of a banana nut muffin, then headed for the boardwalk to set up. One thing legal work had taught her was how to organize. Lucy clutched her clipboard and marched onto the boards like a general ready to organize her troops. She had everything mapped out—where each restaurant would be stationed, where each piece of equipment would go, even where she wanted the temporary porta potties—not too close to the food, of course!

She was the first to arrive, but not for long. Jose Alvarez, the electrician she'd hired, rushed to greet her. He was close to Lucy's age, early thirties, and had a full head of dark hair, a swarthy complexion, coffee brown eyes, and a quick smile. He was slim but strong. She'd seen him carry heavy rolls of wire up a ladder during one of her jogs. It was also next to impossible to get a local contractor during the summer months in town, but Jose had a reputation of always showing up promptly and doing good work.

"I'll check all the outlets and the power to make sure the rental equipment doesn't overload," Jose said.

"Thanks. How's Maria feeling?"

Jose beamed. "The baby's due next month."

"Already?"

"She's complaining of low back pain, but otherwise is okay. She said to thank you for the baklava and that she'll send you flan."

"Yum. Tell her I can't wait."

Jose was originally from the Dominican Republic, but his wife, Maria, whom Lucy had met twice at the restaurant, was of Mexican origin. Maria specialized in teaching braille at a school for the blind in an adjacent town. Lucy had enjoyed chatting with Maria about her grandmother's recipes.

Lucy glanced at her clipboard. "The final count is thirty restaurants and vendors."

"It shouldn't be a problem," Jose said. "Oh, and I haven't forgotten about your ceiling fans for Kebab Kitchen. As soon as I finish work at Seaside Gifts, I'll call you to schedule."

"Seaside Gifts? Archie Kincaid's store?"

Jose nodded. "I'm installing a new electrical box for him."

"Is he expanding?" The Gray sisters had turned down Archie's offer, and she knew Harold wouldn't sell him an inch of space. Had Archie decided to move his store to a bigger location?

"There's no room to expand on the boardwalk," Jose said. "Archie's just updating. When he purchased the store, he discovered that the electrical system is not up to code. I've been rewiring everything, and have to change out his electrical box."

Jose reached for his toolbox. "Where do you want everything set up?"

Lucy showed Jose where the restaurant equipment would be located, and he promptly went to work. Each two restaurants would share a small, temporary refrigerator and freezer, while the ovens would have to be shared among four restaurants. The ice cream vendor would have its own freezer.

The morning flew by. The rental tents arrived and were installed, and soon after the rest of the restaurateurs showed up with their food, set up their stations, and were ready to serve. The delicious smells wafted down the boardwalk and made Lucy's mouth water.

At noon, the loudspeaker crackled beneath the bandstand. "The food and wine tasting is starting!"

Waiting tourists and locals rushed to cram each food station. Lucy walked from station to station greeting everyone. Lines quickly formed, and it was soon clear the tasting was a hit.

A hand reached out to grab Lucy's shoulder. "You sure know how to serve killer food!"

A middle-aged man in a Hawaiian shirt with colorful tiki birds grinned at her. The skin on his nose was peeling from sunburn.

A tourist, for sure.

"Thanks," Lucy said. "Have you tried the hot wings from Mac's Irish Pub? He's also serving wine and his own micro beers." She pointed to a tent on the far side of the boardwalk where Mac McCabe, owner of Mac's Irish Pub, had fired up a barbecue. Beside him was a red-and-white check covered table laden with tempting bakery items from Cutie's Cupcakes—a variety of pies, cookies as big as saucers, and specialty cupcakes. Salted caramel, chocolate ganache, carrot cake with cream cheese icing, and lemon drop were just a few of Susan Cutie's flavors.

Lucy walked by each tent to make sure everyone had what they needed. Bubbling trays of baked ziti and hot garlic bread were being served at Guido's table. Lola Stewart, owner of Lola's Coffee Shop, was busy working an espresso machine that hissed and spat clouds of steam as it turned milk into frothy foam. Lola served the best cappuccinos at the Jersey shore. Three different pizzerias from the boardwalk offered different toppings—from meat lovers to vegetarian with arugula, and eggplant to Sicilian.

Lucy wove through the thick crowd and stopped by a smoking grill. The Barbecue King, Ed Simmons, waved a long-handled fork in the air as he made a show of turning over sizzling chicken legs on a grill. His wife stood beside him and ladled spoonfuls of his specialty homemade barbecue sauce into short disposable cups for sampling. Wiping his sweaty brow with his sleeve, Ed bellowed, "Best barbecue in town!" Immediately, his line grew longer.

Next to him was the local bread baker, Eric Scotch, whose table was crammed with loaves of freshly baked bread and jars of flavored olive oil for dipping. Across the way was Nola Devone, owner of the Frozen Cone, who offered homemade ice cream of every flavor from traditional chocolate, vanilla, and strawberry to specialties like pistachio, bubble gum, peanut butter bomb, and birthday cake.

Lucy spotted Azad serving his own specialties from Kebab Kitchen. Handsome and smiling, he served a long line of customers effortlessly. Beside him, Butch helped refill the containers with small wrapped gyros, bamboo skewers of vegetables and lamb, bulgur sausage, and falafel, as fast as they emptied.

"Hey, Lucy. Want a sample?" Azad asked as he held up a skewer of shish kebab.

"You know I do, but I'll wait. Do you need anything?"

"Nope. Everything's good so far."

Of course, it was. Azad was in his element serving his food to clamoring people. He exuded a compelling vitality as he grinned and chatted with each customer, pausing to compliment a baby, and Lucy understood why he'd gone to culinary school. He could easily be one of the stars on the food channel her mother watched. Angela was obsessed with a celebrity chef, Cooking Kurt, but as Lucy watched Azad, she thought Kurt would have some stiff competition if the producers ever spotted Kebab Kitchen's head chef.

Lucy waved to Azad and Butch and continued her tour. A dozen other stations were packed with people sampling food. The Waffle House, the local diner, a seafood joint, and even Holloway's Grocery was present and serving freshly cut fruit.

Lucy's stomach rumbled. How long had it been since she'd had a banana nut muffin this morning? She was suddenly ravenous, and wanted a sample from each tent.

A flash of white from the street caught her eye. The *Ocean Crest Town News* van pulled up to the boardwalk and came to a screeching halt in a no parking zone. The town's sole investigative reporter,

Stan Slade, hopped out and made his way up the ramp to the boardwalk.

On a normal day, Lucy would duck into the nearest shop to avoid Stan. There was no love lost between them. But today was different. The festival committee had paid for an advertisement in the newspaper and they'd requested Stan to cover the wine and food tasting.

"Ms. Berberian," Stan said. "Mind if I snap some pics?" Middle-aged, stocky, and muscular, he wore black-rimmed glasses. For reasons unknown, he'd left a New York City reporting position to come to Ocean Crest and work for the *Town News.*

Lucy motioned to the food stations. "Please do."

A corner of Stan's lips twitched. "Now that's an attitude change for you, isn't it?"

Lucy's checks felt like they would crack from the strain of holding a smile. "What's that supposed to mean?"

"You're only interested in good publicity for yourself."

"You're wrong. I'm only interested in *honest* reporting from you," she countered.

Rather than take offense, he threw his head back and laughed. "Checkmate, Ms. Berberian." He wandered off and started snapping pictures of the milling crowd, as well as getting some of the restaurateurs to pose for him mid-service.

As the day progressed, the lines grew longer and the throng of people grew thicker. The sun shone brightly, reflecting off the ocean, and the air grew humid and hot. By two o'clock, Lucy finally gave in and sampled Guido's baked ziti with garlic bread, Mac's hot wings, Azad's gyros, and a small piece of

Susan Cutie's lemon meringue pie. She washed everything down with a beer from Mac's Irish Pub.

The microphone beneath the bandstand screeched, making Lucy jump. She turned to see Katie walk to the front and take the mic off the stand. A band stood on the stage ready to play at a moment's notice. Lucy recognized them as a local group, and their logo, THE BEACH BUMS was written on the front of their drums in bold, black letters. A large group of people had gathered, including some of the judges of the sand sculpture contest. She spotted Archie in the back with his nephew, Neil.

"I'm pleased to announce this year's winner of the Ocean Crest sand sculpture contest," Katie said. "It was a difficult decision with all the wonderful sculptures, but the winner of the five-thousand-dollar prize goes to Rory Carey for his adorable snowman sculpture!"

Cheers erupted for the winner who approached the front to accept a large cardboard check. Stan Slade snapped pictures while others recorded the event with their iPhones.

Lucy glanced at Neil. A sulky expression crossed his pinched face, and Archie patted his nephew on the back.

Just then, Harold turned to Archie and gave him a smug look. Archie glowered back.

Oh, brother. Those two don't quit.

The band began playing a lively tune. The roller coaster started its first run of the day, and the sound of screaming teenagers added their noise to the music coming from the bandstand.

Lucy waved at Katie, then headed back to the food tents. After one last check that each restaurateur had what they needed, Lucy was exhausted. She'd been on her feet for hours. The Jersey shore sun was blazing hot, and she felt the beginnings of a sunburn on the bridge of her nose and forehead. The smell of smoking grills, food, and coconut-scented sunscreen was overwhelming. She needed a quick break.

"I'll be back in fifteen," she told Jose.

"A cigarette break?" Jose asked as he pulled a pack of cigarettes from his shirt pocket.

"No. I don't smoke. Just a quick walk."

He shrugged and stuffed the pack of cigarettes back in his pocket.

She walked to the stairs leading from the boardwalk to the beach. The music from the bandstand was muted here, and the screams from the roller coaster on the sole pier seemed miles away.

A pleasant ocean breeze cooled her cheeks and teased the wayward strands of hair that had escaped her ponytail. She slipped off her sandals, and the surf sprayed her ankles. Gulls squawked and circled above. She stopped to pick up a pretty shell, then tossed it back into the water. She breathed in the fresh ocean air and felt her stress melt away. The beach always had this effect, calming and soothing, and she couldn't envision herself living anywhere else than in Ocean Crest.

After fifteen minutes, she headed back, but at the last minute she decided she needed a bit more time, and rather than climb the steps to return to the boardwalk, she veered right and walked under it. In a couple of hours, high tide would begin and the ocean would reach under the boardwalk. But for now the sand was cool beneath her feet.

A few yards away, a large shadow appeared ahead on the sand. She stared. What could it be? A stack of boards? A sand dune bush? A large trash bag someone had illegally dumped?

She changed her mind as she crept closer and a shock of white hair came into focus, then an outstretched arm with a Wile E. Coyote tattoo.

It wasn't a trash bag.

Oh, no. It was Archie.

"Mr. Kincaid?" she asked aloud although deep in her gut she knew he wouldn't respond. He'd never speak again. Her gaze lowered to the bullet hole in the center of his chest.

She reached toward him and placed a trembling finger to his neck. She had to be sure.

Nothing. Oh, God.

Archie Kincaid was dead.

CHAPTER 4

Lucy reached for her cell phone and dialed 911. "There's a dead body under the boardwalk." After describing the exact location, she told the responder that the victim didn't have a pulse. As soon as she hung up, she called Katie.

Katie answered on the third ring. "What's up?"

"Katie! Archie Kincaid's been shot and killed!"

"What!?"

"Archie's dead."

"Where are you?"

"Under the boardwalk. A few yards away from the bandstand." Lucy clutched her cell phone. Was that the sound of the ocean over the phone or was she just hearing it from where she stood? "Where are *you?*" she asked Katie.

Lucy heard heavy breathing, as if Katie was running, then Katie said, "I'm on the beach. I'll be right there."

Lucy stepped from under the boardwalk and spotted Katie running toward her from the surf.

Katie puffed as she came to a halt, then took two

steps closer and froze at the sight of Archie. Her hand flew to her mouth. "You called the police?"

"Yes. What are you doing on the beach?"

"I was taking a break. You?"

"Same."

"Oh, God. I wonder who shot him." Katie's eyes grew large. "You think the shooter's lurking around?"

Lucy's gaze darted around. "I wouldn't think so, but you may be right. Let's not take a chance." Together they hurried to the wooden steps leading back to the boardwalk. Lucy clutched the handrail just as Officer Bill Watson, followed by another cop, came tearing down the steps.

"Lucy!" Bill said. "You okay?"

Lucy sighed with relief at the sight of him. Tall and fit, he looked imposing in his officer's uniform. She recognized the young red-haired, freckle-faced officer from her prior visit to the police station weeks ago.

Bill spotted Katie and his jaw dropped. "Katie! Are you—"

"We're both fine, but Archie isn't," Katie said. "Lucy found him."

"Where?" Bill asked.

Before Lucy could describe the spot, another man rushed down the steps. She recognized him immediately. Detective Calvin Clemmons, Ocean Crest's sole investigator. In his late thirties, with straw-colored hair and a bushy mustache, they'd never gotten along. It hadn't helped that she'd interfered in past murder investigations. Any hopes that the detective's opinion of her had improved were dashed when he noticed her, halted, and said, "Lucy Berberian. Why am I not surprised you're involved?"

Lucy frowned. "I found Mr. Kincaid, nothing else."

"Show us where," Clemmons demanded.

Lucy walked the three men to the area and pointed to the spot, but just as she started forward, Bill turned to Lucy and Katie. "Stay back until we decide it's safe."

Together, they watched as Detective Clemmons removed a pair of gloves from his belt, snapped them on, then crouched down to study the body.

Meanwhile, the red-haired officer took pictures of Archie. Number tags were placed on the footprints around the body and photographed as well. It occurred to Lucy that her footprints were mingled with the killer's. Gooseflesh rose on her arms.

"How was he killed?" Katie asked.

"As far as I could tell, he was shot in the chest," Lucy said.

"And no one heard the gunshot?" Katie asked.

It was a good question. How could a man be murdered in the middle of the afternoon on a busy beach under a bustling boardwalk and no one saw or heard anything?

Bill turned away from the scene and came forward, his expression grave as he looked at his wife, but he didn't comment on her appearance. He answered her question instead. "Looks like Archie was shot with a twenty-two-caliber handgun. As far as handguns go, it's small and wouldn't have made much noise. The noise from the crowd, the band, and the roller coaster would have drowned out the sound of the gunfire."

Detective Clemmons, who'd finished inspecting the body, approached. "Who touched him?"

"I did," Lucy said.

"Did either of you find a weapon?"

"No." Lucy hadn't seen a gun lying around, but then again, she hadn't been searching for one. The sight of Archie lying in the sand, eyes unseeing and face ghostly white, had disturbed her too much. "Is there one?"

"We found the casing, but no gun," Bill said.

Katie pressed a hand to her chest. "Who could have killed him in cold blood?"

"That's a good question, isn't it? What were you both doing on the beach?" Clemmons asked.

"I'm in charge of the food and wine tasting, and needed a break. I was walking under the boardwalk when I . . . when I found Mr. Kincaid," Lucy said.

Clemmons looked from Lucy to Katie. "You two were walking together?"

"No," Katie said.

"No? Then what were you doing on the beach, Mrs. Watson?" Clemmons asked.

"I was taking a break, too."

"I see," Clemmons said, his jaw tightening. "You mean to tell me you were both taking a break to walk on the beach? And that neither of you had any idea that the other was doing the same?"

"That's right," Lucy said.

It was true, but the way he made it sound caused Lucy's nerves to tense.

"Did either of you see anything? Hear anything?" the detective asked.

"No," Lucy and Katie said in unison.

"I see. You can both return to the boardwalk until

we finish here. But stay around for questioning," Clemmons directed.

"How long will that be?" Katie asked.

"We need to collect the evidence before high tide washes everything away. Then we'll talk," Clemmons said.

"He's right," Bill said.

High tide. Why didn't she think of that? Already the water had crept closer than when she'd found the body. What if she hadn't decided to go for a walk and had never discovered the body? What if high tide had carried it away?

No one would know. At least, not until the body had washed back ashore. That could take days. Maybe that was the killer's intent?

Katie and Lucy made their way back and trudged up the boardwalk steps.

Lucy let out a held-in breath. "Clemmons thinks I'm a magnet for murder."

"He's stubborn and can hold a grudge," Katie said.

"He thinks we're lying. It was a weird coincidence that we were taking breaks and walking the beach at the same time."

"Not really. Where else could we walk? You've been on your feet for hours. After I handed out the check for the winner, my duties were over," Katie said.

"I guess. But I have a bad feeling about this," Lucy said.

"It may be strange, but it's true," Katie said. "And it's not a crime."

They walked to the railing and looked down at the beach, but couldn't see anything. Archie's body, along with the police who were processing the scene, were under the boardwalk.

A siren sounded and paramedics, followed by the county coroner, arrived. The wheels of a gurney rattled across the boards and the paramedics hurried down to the beach like a pack of rugby players. A short, compact man, with a white jacket that read COUNTY CORONER in big black letters, hurried past.

Stan Slade pressed forward through the crowd. As soon as the reporter spotted Lucy and Katie, he cornered them against the railing. "What happened?"

"We don't know." Lucy's first response was denial. She didn't trust the wily reporter. She suspected anything that came out of her mouth would end up on the front page of the *Town News*.

"You honestly expect me to believe that? You two just came from the beach, and an officer is stationed at the top of the stairs prohibiting anyone from going down."

"How do you know? Have you been watching us?" Lucy asked.

"I was looking for you to ask if there was anything else I should cover for the day. Despite what you are suggesting, I'm not a stalker," Slade said. "Now I'll ask again. What's going on down there?"

"Leave her alone. You'll have to wait for the police to make a statement," Katie said.

Stan glared at them and stalked away to station himself at the railing. His camera was raised, ready at the slightest provocation.

"I know this sounds horrible since a man was just murdered, but I'm afraid this doesn't bode well for the festival," Lucy said.

Katie squeezed her hand. "Shh. We'll talk later. Here comes Clemmons."

Lucy turned to see Detective Clemmons step onto the boardwalk and scan the crowd. He headed straight for them.

Lucy's stomach tightened. Clemmons disliked her family. Her sister, Emma, had dubbed him "Clinging Calvin" in high school, then had promptly cheated on him with his best friend. Definitely bad behavior on Emma's behalf, but who would have thought Clemmons would still hold a grudge all these years later?

Clemmons rubbed his chin with a thumb and forefinger, then pulled a small notepad from his shirt pocket and flipped it open. He reached for a pencil from behind his ear. "Ladies, do either of you know who could have shot Archie?"

"No." Once again they spoke in unison.

The detective's eyes narrowed. "What about you, Ms. Berberian? Aren't you on the festival committee?

"Like I said, I'm in charge of the food and wine tasting," Lucy said. "But I don't see what that has to do with Archie."

As the words left her mouth, her eyes swept the food stations behind the detective's shoulder. She'd been away for much longer than she'd initially thought. Tourists, locals, and even the restaurateurs had abandoned the tents and the food and were leaning on the railing, trying to catch a glimpse at what was happening below on the beach.

"What else?" Clemmons snapped.

Lucy blinked. "Pardon?"

"The sand sculpture contest?" His gaze swiveled

from Lucy to Katie, then back to Lucy. "Weren't *both* of you judges?"

"Yes," Katie said.

"And wasn't there an argument during the judging?" Clemmons asked.

How the heck did he know that? Lucy knew gossip traveled like lightning in Ocean Crest, but she didn't think it reached the police station. Didn't the cops have anything better to do than to talk like magpies around the water cooler or while buying doughnuts at Cutie's Cupcakes?

Katie spoke up. "*I* exchanged words with Mr. Kincaid, not Lucy."

Clemmons shot her a nasty look. "From what I heard, you two became pretty heated. You stripped Archie of his judging position."

"I had no choice," Katie argued. "His nephew had entered as a sand sculptor, and Archie didn't follow the rules."

"I see," he said in a tone that said he didn't believe a word coming from Katie's lips. Lucy grew nervous. She recognized that look in the detective's eyes. She recognized it and didn't like it one bit.

He was treating Katie as a suspect.

"You can't seriously think Katie would harm Archie over a silly argument?" Lucy asked.

"I wouldn't call humiliating Mr. Kincaid by stripping him of his position as a judge in front of his peers a silly argument," Clemmons said.

"You're making it sound worse than it was," Lucy countered.

"Fine. What started it then?" Clemmons asked.

"Archie and Harold were fighting. Katie bravely

stepped in and stopped them from coming to blows," Lucy said.

The detective arched an eyebrow. "Harold Harper?"

At Katie's nod, Clemmons scribbled in his notebook.

"They don't . . . didn't like each other," Lucy corrected. It felt strange speaking of Archie in the past tense.

"How do you know that?" Clemmons asked.

Katie shrugged. "Everyone knew. Just ask around."

He scribbled some more. "I'll look into it. All we know for sure is that someone here put a bullet in him."

"There're more than a hundred people on the boardwalk today. You can't hold them all for questioning," Lucy said.

He glared at her. "No. But the festival is on hold until we know what we're dealing with."

Lucy's pulse pounded as she looked at him with rising dismay. "On hold! But the town depends on it."

"It's out of my hands," Clemmons said.

"You can't be serious! People will know a man died, but not that he was shot. Can't you stay silent? Think of the town. We all depend on the income for our livelihood. If people think a murder happened on the beach, it will cause mass panic and tourists will leave for other shore towns."

Just as the words left her lips, the paramedics, followed by the coroner, began to carry a gurney up the stairs. An ominous black body bag was strapped down.

Silence reigned as everyone gaped.

A series of rapid flashes blinded Lucy. She blinked, focused, and saw Stan Slade with his camera trained on the corpse.

Oh, no.

Even Detective Clemmons had the good sense to grimace. "If we don't release the truth that a murderer is on the loose, then that could have horrible consequences, couldn't it? What if the killer murders again and people learned we didn't tell them? What then?"

Lucy swallowed a lump in her throat. What had she been thinking? Of course, he was right. Everyone had a right to know the truth.

She glanced at the crowd in dismay. Everyone was glued to the railing to watch the spectacle unfold, and the reporter had captured it all.

The summer festival wasn't just on hold—it was doomed.

CHAPTER 5

Late that night, the Ocean Crest mayor called an emergency meeting for the beach festival committee. Lucy had offered Kebab Kitchen as a meeting place, and twenty local business owners and town leaders filed into the dining room. Tables and chairs had been arranged to face the hostess stand, which the mayor would use as a makeshift podium to address the group.

Everyone was talking at once.

Hours earlier, Detective Clemmons had issued an official statement saying Archie Kincaid had been shot and killed under the boardwalk. No suspect had been arrested. Lucy may have argued with Clemmons about releasing the news, but she realized it was the right decision. A murderer was on the loose. People needed to know.

"They're panicking," Katie said to Lucy as they watched the crowd from behind the waitress station and filled pitchers with ice water to deliver to the tables. A low wall separated the waitress station from the dining room and offered privacy. Behind them was the stainless-steel counter with the chef's wheel—now empty. In the corner, a pair of swinging doors led into the kitchen.

"I don't blame them. You can't have a murder without everyone running scared. Plus, there's the festival. It couldn't have happened at a worse time," Lucy said.

Katie leaned on the counter as she peered at the group. "They look and sound like an angry mob that's ready to go out and catch the killer themselves."

"I'm fuming a bit myself," Lucy said.

"Fine. Let's get this over with."

They picked up water pitchers, one in each hand, and delivered them to the tables. Lucy didn't make it past the first table before she was peppered with questions.

"Lucy, do you know who could have killed Archie?"

"The boardwalk was packed. Someone had to see *something.*"

"Archie could be a pain in the butt, but still . . ."

"What about his nephew, Neil?"

Lucy's thoughts spun. Among all this chaos, she'd forgotten there was someone mourning Archie. Neil had been living with his uncle. Where was he now? Was he devastated by the loss?

The barrage of questions continued.

"What's going to happen to the festival? Are the police going to cancel the rest of the activities?"

"No way! We'll all be in a boatload of trouble if they do."

Unnerved by the unwanted attention, Lucy turned to Katie. "Why is everyone asking me?"

Katie set down a pitcher and stepped close. "You solved the last two murders. They think you can help with this one."

Lucy's heart sank with a desperate clunk. "I didn't do it alone, remember? You helped."

"A small detail."

"Hardly."

Lucy scanned the crowd. She knew them all, friends and acquaintances. Guido Morelli of the Hot Cheese Pizzeria sat next to Mac McCabe of Mac's Irish Pub. The two men had hated each other until Guido's daughter and Mac's son had attended the senior prom together last May. Susan Cutie of Cutie's Cupcakes sat next to Lola Stewart who owned the coffee shop. Candace Kent from Pages Bookstore was next to Ben Hawkins, the town barber. Michael nodded in greeting as he caught Lucy's eye.

They were all worried. So was Lucy.

The door opened and the mayor, Thomas Huckerby, stepped inside. He was a good-looking man in his mid-fifties, with brown hair shot through with silver, hazel eyes, and an easy smile. He was also a natural-born politician, and she'd seen him hold two babies and kiss an old woman the same time. The crowd's attention shifted to him.

Thank goodness. Her mind was working overtime, and she needed a moment to get her bearings. She didn't want anyone to depend on her, let alone the residents here, to fix the mess they found themselves in from Archie's murder.

Lucy glanced out the window and saw Gadoo saunter across the parking lot. *Lucky cat.* She was jealous of his freedom tonight. What would it be like to roam the streets without a care in the world except to catch the occasional rodent in the restaurant's parking lot? He certainly didn't have to worry about hunting for his next meal. Between her mother and herself, Gadoo was better fed than most of the people in the room.

"Quiet, everyone," the mayor said as he produced a gavel and rapped it twice on the hostess stand.

"Where'd he get that?" Lucy asked.

Katie shrugged. "You got me. Must keep it stowed in his pocket."

The group quieted down and took their seats like lifelong churchgoers. Lucy and Katie sat in the back. Lucy shifted to the right, then the left to get a better view. Being on the petite side had its disadvantages, especially when it came to seeing the chalkboard in school, watching a Broadway play, or viewing the current speaker.

Katie, who was taller than average, noticed Lucy's angling. "You want to move our chairs up front?"

Lucy shook her head. "No, thanks. Then I'd really be in the hot seat for questions. I can hear just fine."

The mayor cleared his throat. "I called this emergency meeting to update everyone about today's unfortunate events and discuss the beach festival. We are all sad to lose a member of our community, Archie Kincaid. Detective Clemmons will join us shortly to answer questions. Meanwhile, I'll open the floor to concerns that do not involve police business."

"What will happen to the beach festival?" asked Mac McCabe. Tall, with a substantial beer belly, his shaggy, brown hair was tied back with a leather string.

"It will have to be indefinitely postponed," Mayor Huckerby said.

The crowd erupted into chaos.

"Order! Order!" the mayor cried out, banging his gavel.

"It's a done deal anyway. What family would choose to vacation at Ocean Crest and risk their children's safety when there's a murderer on the loose?" asked Lola Stewart. Her steel-gray hair was in its usual bun, and despite prominent cheekbones and sharp chin that gave her an appearance of a no-nonsense schoolmarm, she'd always been friendly. Right now, she looked concerned.

"She's right," Mac said. "There are too many other Jersey shore towns."

"We're all in trouble," Lola said.

"Where were the police on the boardwalk? Maybe we need to hire even more security," said Susan Cutie, who was pretty with shoulder-length blond hair.

Lucy knew the town hired additional temporary police during the summer season. "Rental cops," they were dubbed by the locals. They frequently roamed the boardwalk during the evenings and also handed out tickets to illegally parked cars or to those who were unfortunate enough to end up with expired parking meters.

"It likely wouldn't have made a difference. Archie was shot *under* the boardwalk. Additional police would have been stationed on the boards to monitor the crowd," Katie said.

"Lucy found him. What did you see?" Guido asked. Heavy-set with slicked-back dark hair and a walrus mustache, the pizzeria owner looked at her earnestly.

Lucy stood and opened her mouth to speak when the front door opened and Stan Slade strode inside. Her uneasiness increased tenfold. The reporter of the *Ocean Crest Town News* must have radar. He always showed up at the worst times. Behind large, black-rimmed glasses, his dark gaze sharpened in anticipation of a juicy story. His ominous camera hung around his neck, and he raised it and snapped a picture of Lucy standing and ready to talk.

Just great. She might make the front page alongside Archie's body as it was wheeled onto the boardwalk on a stretcher in the body bag.

"Go on, Lucy," the mayor urged.

"I took a break from the tasting to walk on the beach. I didn't see anything suspicious. I happened to find a body . . . Archie's body. I told the police everything," Lucy said.

"What do you think about hiring additional police presence?" a voice from the crowd asked.

Lucy looked to the mayor hoping he would jump in. She was not a security expert. "I don't know, but I tend to agree with Katie. Security would not have helped in this case. Archie was shot under the board-walk. Police would have little reason to patrol there."

"And you didn't hear a thing?" Stan Slade asked.

"Nothing."

Another flash from his camera. Damn. Would he quote her, too?

Lucy sat. Out of the corner of her eye, she saw the door open again. This time, Detective Clemmons stepped inside. He wasn't much older than Lucy, who was thirty-two, but he appeared a decade older with wrinkles around his eyes and mouth. He wore the same suit she'd seen him in earlier today, and his straw colored hair looked ruffled as if he'd repeatedly run his hand through it.

"Thank you for coming, Detective," the mayor said. He motioned for Clemmons to sit, but the detective ignored him. Rather, he took the mayor's place at the hostess stand.

Clemmons cleared his throat. "First, I want to remind everyone to continue to cooperate with the police during the ongoing investigation of Archie's death."

"You mean murder," Candace said, her blue eyes wide behind tortoiseshell frame glasses.

Clemmons glared at Candace for interrupting. "As I was saying, if you saw anything or have information of interest, I urge you to come forward to the police." He eyed Lucy and his mustache twitched with annoyance.

"What about Archie's store?" Harold Harper asked.

Lucy's gaze turned to Harold. She was reminded again that Harold and Archie had disliked each other. She thought his question was out of left field. Did he really have to ask about the store? A man had been murdered. Is business all he cared about?

"The store has been cleared and can open for business later this week," Clemmons said.

"Who's going to run it?" Harold asked.

"His nephew, Neil."

"I'll be damned," Harold muttered.

"What about the festival?" Lola asked.

"The festival is hereby officially canceled," Detective Clemmons said.

Gasps echoed around the room followed by loud voices. The mayor rapped his gavel. "Order! Order!" It took a full minute before the crowd calmed.

"Mayor Huckerby said the festival had been *postponed.* There's a big difference between postponed and canceled," Lola said.

"What about our livelihoods? We need the business to survive the winter," Guido said.

Clemmons's hands tightened on the edges of the hostess stand. "Right now, my priority is finding the culprit, not the status of the beach festival."

Lucy looked around the room. Archie wasn't particularly liked, but who hated him enough to kill him? Did Harold have that much of a beef with his business neighbor? Or was it someone else? Someone in the room?

She knew them all.

The thought that one of them could be a cold-blooded killer made a sickening pit yawn in her stomach. They were now all her neighbors and friends. She didn't want any of them to suffer.

Lucy marveled at her change of attitude. It had been less than a year since she'd returned home, and she felt fiercely protective of these hard-working people.

"What if the killer is found? Will the festival resume?" Lucy asked.

All heads turned to her.

"Are you volunteering?" Harold asked, his lips twisting in a haughty grin.

"No, she is *not,*" Detective Clemmons snapped. "If you have additional information, you will see me. Otherwise, you will stay out of this, Ms. Berberian. Got it?"

"Of course," Lucy said. His harsh tone was more evidence that the detective distrusted her.

"As soon as the police make an arrest, we can revisit the matter of the beach festival," Clemmons said.

Lola raised her hand. "What's the plan until the killer is found? The reports and news vans will swarm our little town—no offense, Stan."

"None taken," Stan mumbled.

"They'll chase away the tourists that are already here," Lola finished.

"The county prosecutor could get involved," Katie said.

Lucy's stomach tilted at the mention of Marsha Walsh. The wily prosecutor would not be happy to learn that Lucy had found the body. Again. Their past was rocky at best.

"Seems there is nothing we can do about bad press," Ben said. His bushy eyebrows slanted downward in a frown.

Harold cleared his throat. "I want to know one thing. Did anyone ask Archie's girlfriend where she was when he was killed?"

For a pulse-pounding moment, silence engulfed the room.

"Who?" Lola asked.

"Archie's girlfriend. Rita Sides," Harold said.

Had Archie been dating Rita, a beautician at The

Big Tease Salon? Lucy had no idea they were a couple, but then again, she'd been busy managing the restaurant and avoided engaging in gossip. But by the look on everyone's faces, she didn't think they'd known either.

"Isn't it always the spouse or girlfriend who's guilty?" Harold said.

Katie stood. "Don't throw Rita under the bus when she's not here to defend herself. You're just trying to draw attention away from yourself, Harold. It's no secret you and Archie had no love for one another."

Harold glowered at her. "Look who's talking," he snarled. "You all but came to blows with Archie over the sand sculpture contest and ousted him as a judge. I say you're the one who's pointing fingers and trying to draw attention from *yourself.*"

People stared wide-eyed. Everyone loved gossip and these two were giving them fodder to last all year. Plus, Harold had mentioned the fight on the beach. What would happen if they learned Archie had also stormed the town hall with a big chip on his shoulder and had it out with Katie?

"That's enough," Detective Clemmons finally said. "*All* leads will be thoroughly investigated."

Once again, Lucy didn't like the way Clemmons's razorlike gaze traveled from Harold and lingered on Katie.

Stay out of it, be damned.

CHAPTER 6

The next morning, Lucy slipped on a robe and slippers and padded into the kitchen to find Katie reaching for two mugs from the cupboard. Coffee had just finished brewing and there were bagels and cream cheese on the counter.

Lucy yawned. "Where's Bill?"

Katie set the mugs on the counter. "He has the early shift today and left for work."

Lucy poured herself a cup of coffee, added a good dose of cream and two heaping teaspoons of sugar, and put a bagel in the toaster oven. "We never had a chance to talk about last night's meeting." Things had wrapped up late, and they had both gone straight to bed after arriving home. The events of the previous day all seemed to have happened long ago.

Katie filled her mug. "What's there to talk about? Harold acted badly."

Lucy lowered her mug and studied her friend for the first time since walking into the kitchen. Katie had bags under her eyes. Her mouth was as pale as her cheeks. She hadn't slept well, and clearly, she was worried.

"You're right. Harold did act badly. First, he tried to point the finger at Rita Sides. I didn't even know Archie was dating her. Then, when you spoke up on Rita's behalf, he accused you of murdering Archie."

Katie added cream and stirred her mug with a spoon. "That's because he's feeling the pressure. We all are. Officially canceling the festival and having a killer roam free is making everyone tense."

"Are you worried about what Clemmons will think?"

"No."

"Why not?"

Katie shrugged a shoulder. "I got in a small tiff with Archie over his judging eligibility. It's hardly a motive for murder."

Lucy didn't believe her for a second. It wasn't just the judging. Katie had fought with Archie at the town hall over denying him a mercantile license. Katie had to be thinking about that as well.

As for Clemmons, Lucy wasn't certain about anything when it came to him. Katie had once told her that the detective was simple-minded and would go after the easiest lead, even though it may not be the right one. Plus, he had reason to dislike Lucy and her family.

What better way to get to her than through her best friend?

"I hate to bring this up," Lucy said, "but what about what happened at your work? When I showed up with that Greek salad, you and Archie weren't in a good place."

Katie grimaced, then set her mug on the Formica counter. "Bill and Clemmons work together. Clemmons knows better than to go after me without concrete evidence and he doesn't have any. I was doing my job. Even the mayor was adamantly against approving Archie's mercantile license. My disagreement with Archie isn't enough of a motive to shoot a man."

That reassured Lucy a bit. "You're right."

Katie collected her purse and headed for the door. "I have to leave for work. If all goes well, the police will find the guilty person soon."

"Do you have that much faith in Clemmons?" Lucy asked.

"No. I have faith in Bill."

It was the first time Katie didn't ask to start investigating on their own. Lucy couldn't help but think about it. If Detective Clemmons put Katie on the suspect list, then Bill would most likely be dismissed from the case for a conflict of interest. He may already have been. Katie was on the beach the same time as Lucy. Katie had seen the body before the police had arrived. Wasn't that sufficient to create a conflict?

After cleaning the kitchen, Lucy dressed in her running shorts and T-shirt and stepped onto the porch to lock the front door when her cell phone rang.

"Hello?"

"Lucy, it's Bill. Are you free to meet at Lola's Coffee Shop? I need to talk with you."

Lucy's prior unease returned. Bill never called her unless it was important. And didn't Katie say he was working the morning shift? Why meet with her, especially when the police should be busy searching for a murderer?

"Sure. I can meet now. Is something wrong?" Maybe she was making more out of it than she should. Was it Katie and Bill's wedding anniversary, and she'd forgotten? Or even Katie's birthday? Her thoughts chugged along. No, they were married in October, and Katie's birthday was in December.

"I can't talk right now. I'll meet you at the coffee shop in fifteen." Bill hung up.

Lucy stared at her cell phone. What was going on?

She shoved her cell phone into her purse, fished out her keys, and drove to Lola's. The coffee shop was busy this morning and there was a line of customers eagerly waiting for their morning dose of caffeine. Lola Stewart, working behind the counter, reached for a mug at the top of a tower of chunky white mugs. Tucking an errant, gray curl into her bun, she filled the mug with coffee and placed it on the counter along with a poppy-seed muffin from the refrigerated case.

Lucy scanned the coffee shop looking for Bill and spotted him sitting at a wire-backed chair in the corner and reading a newspaper. He looked up from the paper, spotted her, and waved.

He stood and pulled out a chair for her. "Thanks for coming." He was drinking a latte and Lucy inhaled the rich scent. She could use a cappuccino.

She rested her hands on the table. "I'm curious. It's not that I don't enjoy your company, but you've never asked me to meet you for coffee at Lola's before."

"I thought it best if we talked out of the house."

"You mean away from Katie."

His mouth twisted grimly. "Yes."

"You're worried about how Katie looks after Archie's murder, aren't you?"

"I won't lie. There's something you need to know. I haven't seen eye to eye with Calvin Clemmons lately."

That makes two of us, she thought.

"I applied for a position as detective. I learned that Calvin put in less than a shining recommendation for me. Our police chief overrode him and put my name in for the position anyway."

"That wasn't very nice of Clemmons." Bill was an excellent beat cop with a solid reputation in town and with the locals.

"Clemmons feels threatened that I'll take his position," Bill said, answering the question that was on her mind. "He shouldn't be worried. There's room in the budget for two detectives. Especially with the rise in crime."

"I've always believed Clemmons is shortsighted."

"I'm concerned about how he'll treat Katie."

She chewed on her lower lip as she looked at him. "You think he'll consider her a serious suspect?"

"It's possible." He scrubbed a hand down his face. "Katie was on the beach and at the scene of the crime before the police arrived. As a result, I was removed from the case due to a conflict and no longer have access to the files, but I know the way Clemmons works."

"I was worried about a conflict. Katie and I talked about it this morning," Lucy admitted.

"You did?"

Lucy nodded. "I guessed they'd have to replace you with another officer."

"I can't believe I'm asking this, but will you keep your eyes and ears open at the restaurant? You must hear all types of interesting gossip. You can talk with customers without arousing their suspicion."

Lucy had already been thinking about investigating on her own. Katie was her best friend, and she'd do anything to help her. Then there was the beach festival itself. The event was important for the town. How could she sit back and not help?

"I know what you're thinking. You may have gotten lucky in the past, but I don't want you to do anything risky. I'm not pinning a badge to your chest. Just listen and maybe ask your customers a few questions. Nothing else. Report everything you learn to me, okay?"

If this would help both Bill and Katie, she'd do it. "You got it. Just listen and ask a few questions. Nothing else, I promise."

"Where's the rest of the hummus? The hummus bar is missing bins of jalapeño and sweet basil!" Sally said.

"Did you check the walk-in refrigerator?" Emma asked.

Lucy hurried from the waitress station where she'd been checking the fresh brewed iced tea machine to where Sally and Emma stood by the hummus bar. "Azad made them fresh this morning. I saw him."

Emma scratched her head. "Maybe he forgot to make enough?"

"Azad forget? I doubt it." He was a professional chef and took his duties seriously. In that respect, he reminded her a lot of her mother. Angela could be like a female Napoleon—a short and disciplined general—in the kitchen. Everything had to be up to her strict standards and prepared on time.

She hurried to the kitchen to find Azad stirring a large pot. "Hey, Lucy."

"Where's the hummus you made this morning?"

"In the fridge. Why?"

"Sally can't find it and her customers are asking for it."

He shrugged. "I put it on the top shelf. Maybe she just didn't see it."

She shot him a doubtful look. Sally was tall and thin, and if anyone other than Azad could spot the bins, it would be Sally. "You sure?"

He winked at her and sent her stomach in a wild swirl. "Come on. I'll show you." He set his large spoon on the counter, turned the heat down on the pot, and motioned for her to follow.

He opened the door to the walk-in refrigerator and switched on the fluorescent light. A blast of cool air hit her face. The refrigerator was larger than her parents' office, which was tucked in the corner of the storage room. Stainless-steel shelves held everything from meat and seafood to bread pudding. For safety reasons, the door didn't lock, and staff could carry armfuls of items and push open the heavily insulated door with a foot or shoulder and leave.

"The hummus is right here. See?" Azad reached for a bin and the muscles in his arm flexed. Good God. Did his every move have to remind her of his attractiveness?

He took one bin of hummus and handed her the

other. His gaze met hers, and he grinned. "Remember the other time we were locked in here?"

She did. The door had been jammed closed, and he'd held her to ward off the chill. He'd also come close to kissing her. Despite the cold, her skin sizzled from vivid memory.

"Azad, I—"

"Too bad I have something on the stove or I'd ask for a repeat," he said.

"You're incorrigible."

"You haven't forgotten about our date? It's darned hard to get a reservation at Le Gabriel."

She'd wondered about that herself. From what she'd heard, you needed to book a month in advance. Had he thought that far back about asking her to dinner?

"I haven't forgotten. I'm looking forward to dessert even more than the main course," she said.

His eyes darkened, and she realized just what she'd said. Her face heated. The charming, eager affection had set her off balance. "I didn't mean it that way. The French pastry chef is supposed to be superb, and I promised Katie I'd bring home dessert and—"

"Relax. I get it." He handed her the hummus bin he'd been holding. "You better go out there before Emma or Sally come looking for you."

He was always calm and collected. She was certain her face was beet-red by now. Pushing open the refrigerator door, she hurried into the dining room. "Crisis averted," she said as soon as she spotted Sally.

Sally exhaled in relief and took the bins from her and placed them in the hummus bar. "By the way, Katie's here. I sat her at table seven. She's already started with the hummus, and I gave her a basket of pita bread."

"Thanks." Lucy sidled over to Katie's table. Despite the morning caffeine, her friend still had bags under her eyes, and Lucy started to worry.

Katie lowered a piece of pita bread to a small plate and swallowed. "It's my lunch hour. What do you recommend?"

"The dolma—stuffed tomatoes, peppers, and eggplant."

"Sounds delicious."

"You look worried. What's wrong?" Lucy asked.

"Is it that obvious?"

"We've been best friends since first grade. Tell me."

Katie toyed with her napkin, twisting it this way and that. "Detective Clemmons came to the town hall today to ask me more questions."

A warning voice whispered in Lucy's head, but she kept her voice level. "You have nothing to hide. You were right. A small argument over judging a sand sculpture contest is not sufficient motive for murder. Even Clemmons has to acknowledge that."

Katie glanced at her plate. "We both know that's not all."

"Clemmons questioned your coworkers?"

Katie sipped a glass of ice water. "He happened to question the worst person first—Gail Turner."

Lucy knew where this was heading. "She told him about the screaming match I had with Archie over denying his mercantile license. It didn't help that I'd all but told Archie that it wouldn't be a bad idea if I borrowed Bill's gun and shot him."

"Oh, no."

"I tried to explain. The mayor didn't think it was a good idea to give Archie a green light to open another business after Harold complained that Archie had dropped his prices below cost just to put his competition out of business. Archie hadn't been in town that long either, and he thought he needed to wait before opening another store. I agreed. We had no choice but to deny Archie's application."

"Who else did Clemmons interview?" Lucy asked.

"The rest of the staff. Almost everyone was in that day and heard the argument, not just Gail. I didn't expect any of my coworkers to lie for me."

"In my mind, I still don't believe it's enough motive," Lucy said.

"Maybe in yours, but not in the detective's. Bill is worried, too. I could tell when I called him to fill him in."

Bill had already been concerned when he'd met Lucy at the coffee shop this morning. She could just imagine what he was thinking now. First, Clemmons had a reason to dislike Bill for seeking a promotion to detective. Then, Clemmons had learned there was more bad blood between Katie and Archie than a sand sculpture contest gone awry. A mercantile license was serious business.

A nagging in the back of her mind refused to be stilled. She'd promised Bill that she would only listen and ask a few questions. But that was before. The stakes were higher now. "I think it's time we got involved," Lucy said.

"I was hoping you would say that." Katie started rummaging through her purse.

"I have it." Lucy pulled a pen and waitress pad from her back pocket. She always needed one in case she had to quickly fill in for Emma and Sally and take a customer's order. Not that they'd be busy for long. Once the tourists learned there was a murderer crawling the beach, business would come to a screeching halt.

"We need to make a list of suspects," Katie said.

"Harold Harper is the most obvious." Lucy scribbled his name down. "What about Rita Sides? I had no idea Archie was dating anyone."

"I was just as surprised," Katie said. "I saw Rita when I went to The Big Tease Salon for a haircut, but the owner, Beatrice, cut my hair. Rita was tweezing Mrs. Patel's eyebrows."

"We'll have to talk to Rita." Lucy added her name to the list.

Katie picked up her fork, then set it down. "What about Neil Kincaid?"

Lucy looked up and tapped her pen on the table. "Archie's nephew? What motive would he have?"

"Money. Before Bill was removed from the case, I overheard him talking on the phone. Neil gets the boardwalk business, Seaside Gifts. For a twenty-something who hasn't worked a full day in his life, I'd call that motive."

"He was on the boardwalk yesterday. I saw him standing at the back of the bandstand with Archie when you announced the winning sand artist and gave away a five-thousand-dollar check," Lucy said.

"The scores were pretty close. If Archie stayed on as a judge, the winner might have been different.

What if Neil was counting on that cash and he blamed his uncle for his loss?"

Lucy thought back. "Could be. Neil didn't look happy."

Katie pursed her lips. "The question is: Did he look unhappy enough to kill?"

CHAPTER 7

The following afternoon, Gadoo's purring drew Lucy's attention as soon as she stepped outside of Kebab Kitchen's storage room. She shook the bag of cat treats and the orange and black cat's yellow gaze zeroed in on the bag. "Hi, Gadoo. I have your favorite chicken-flavored treats from Holloway's."

The cat meowed in approval as Lucy poured a handful of the chicken-leg-shaped treats in her palm and offered them. Gadoo came close to eat from her hand.

"I've been thinking, Gadoo. How would you like to come live with me when I find my own apartment?"

He answered with a swish of his tail and kept eating.

"Katie won't be happy. Bill either. But it may be time soon. What do you think?"

Gadoo lifted his head and blinked, his yellow eyes sharpening.

"I know. I know. Mom won't be pleased to have

you leave either. You're part of the family, like it or not."

More purring.

She sighed and stood. "All gone. No more treats for today or you'll get fat."

Gadoo didn't like that remark, and he showed it by twitching his tail and sauntering off to disappear behind the Dumpster.

She opened the storage room door, set the treats on the nearest metal shelf, then stepped back outside. Then she started to jog the mile trek to the boardwalk. Each day she jogged it was getting a bit easier, but she doubted she'd ever be a marathon runner. It was in between the lunch and dinner shifts and her father and Azad were working so that Lucy could get a break before the dinner rush.

She ran by Michael's bicycle rental shop. He was outside adjusting the seat of a bicycle for a tween. The parents and older siblings had their own bicycles ready to ride. She passed the Sandpiper Bed and Breakfast. The blinking neon vacancy sign was unusual for this time of year. Had tourists already checked out after hearing about the murder?

Not a good sign.

She trudged up the boardwalk ramp. Madame Vega, at least, was doing a brisk business today with three people waiting in line for her fortune-telling insight. A teenage couple was in line at Cooney Brothers, the custard stand. She approached the Sun and Surf Shop and saw Harold folding sweatshirts on a shelf, but no customers were inside. She slowed down as she came up to Archie's storefront,

Seaside Gifts. It was open, but there was a high school kid manning the register. Where was Neil?

Was he mourning the loss of his uncle? She recalled the Gray sisters saying that Archie had volunteered for a local teen drug program, and Lucy couldn't help but wonder if that's where Neil had ended up as a teenager before his uncle had taken him in.

She kept going until she reached the end of the boardwalk, jogged down the steps to the beach, and kept running. It was harder to run on the sand, and sweat beaded on her brow. Sand sprayed the back of her legs. She was careful to steer clear of the boardwalk. The memory of finding Archie's body under the boards was too fresh. She trudged along. The late-afternoon sun was still hot.

She headed closer to the surf where there was always an ocean breeze. She took a glance at the ocean, and she nearly tripped.

Neil Kincaid was surfing. Dressed in neon yellow board shorts, he rode a wave. He made it to the surf, picked up his board, and walked to where he'd left a towel spread out on the sand.

Lucy headed straight for him. "Hey, Neil!" she called out and waved.

He shook his head, water spraying from his long, shaggy hair in all directions like a wet dog, then looked up. Whiskers covered his chin and cheeks. He looked at her as she approached. "Yeah."

"Hi. I'm Lucy Berberian. We haven't officially met, but I knew your uncle. I'm sorry for your loss."

"Oh, yeah. Thanks." He squinted from the sun, and she was surprised to see he wasn't as young as she'd initially thought. Maybe his late twenties? Not much younger than she was.

He didn't seem overly broken up about his uncle's death. He certainly wasn't very talkative. She needed to engage him and learn more. "I watched you surf. You're pretty good."

His face lit up. "Thanks."

"You ever compete?" she asked.

He snorted in distaste. "Ocean Crest doesn't have great surfing. The competitions are pathetic."

"Oh? Where is it better?"

"California. Hawaii. That's where the true surfers gather for competitions."

Her gaze dropped to his surfboard. "That's a nice board. Is it from your uncle's shop, Seaside Gifts?"

He shook his head. "No way. We don't sell boards like this." Neil rested his hand on the top of the surfboard with pride. "This baby is top of the line. A Firestone."

A Firestone. She didn't know much about surfing, but she'd grown up on the beach and had heard the brand name. Lucy had dated a surfer wannabe in high school. He'd forgotten her birthday, but he could spew out the cost of his dream board. Highly annoying, but the knowledge came in handy now.

A quality Firestone shortboard could cost a little over a thousand bucks.

That was a lot of cash for Neil to put out, even if he had visions of surfing greatness for himself. So how had he afforded it? "You ever use that board to compete in California or Hawaii?" she asked.

"Nah," he said, laughing. "I wish. It costs and arm and a leg just to enter, not to mention the flight, and I'd have to find a place to crash."

"Sounds expensive. Maybe one day," she said.

His eyes filled with a curious deep longing. "Sooner rather than later."

Well, stroke his ego and all kinds of stuff spewed out. "Hey. I was wondering. What's going to happen to Seaside Gifts?"

"I'm taking over." He scratched his scalp and bits of sand fell onto his tanned shoulders.

"Really?" she asked innocently.

"Yeah. Archie willed it to me."

"I just jogged past the store and there was someone at the register," Lucy said.

He shrugged a shoulder, dislodging a clump of sand. "A kid who's helping me out."

Helping him out so he could surf? She knew people mourned the loss of a loved one in different ways. Some cried in private while others were weepy in front of anyone who would lend a comforting shoulder. Others, she supposed, surfed. But she couldn't help but get the feeling that Neil wasn't too broken up about the death of his uncle.

"Well, now that you have the store you may be able to afford to go to Hawaii and compete with the best."

His face brightened. "That's right. Sooner than I'd ever thought."

As Lucy jogged back to Kebab Kitchen she spotted Jose parking his truck in the restaurant's lot. Jose stepped out and opened the two back doors to reveal a packed space full of pliers, screwdrivers, wire strippers, measuring devices, fish tape, and poles.

"Hey, Jose!" she called out as she approached. "Are you here to install the ceiling fans?"

She'd checked the calendar in the small office in the storage room and didn't see anything about Jose coming today. Her father was computer challenged and the calendar was still on paper and not computerized. It was on the list of items she wanted to change as the new manager, but there never seemed to be enough time.

She'd also learned to pick her battles with her father. He may be semi-retired, but Raffi Berberian was still stubborn as ever when he did show up to work in the restaurant. He thought e-mail was evil and couldn't fathom how Lucy read it on her phone. She needed her ten-year-old niece, Niari, to give him smart phone lessons.

Jose took a battered, red toolbox out of the truck. "I'm not ready to install the fans yet. I need to install the electrical boxes first. I also have this for you." Reaching in his truck, he took out a plastic container and handed it to her. "Maria loved the stuffed grape leaves you sent home with me last time. She wanted to give you flan that she'd made today."

Lucy opened the container and her mouth watered. The custard topped with caramel sauce looked and smelled delicious. If she had a spoon, she'd dive right in. "Tell her thank you. How is she?"

"As cranky as ever. She still has lower back pain, but now her legs hurt, too. I massage her back at night."

"I asked my sister, Emma, about it. She used to have back pain when she was pregnant with my niece, Niari. She said moist heat helped a bit."

"I'll pass along the advice." He slipped on a tool belt, and Lucy walked with him to the front door of the restaurant. A thought occurred to her, and she turned to look at him. "Jose, weren't you working on Archie's store the day he was killed?"

His step halted. "I was, but I spent most of my time at the food tasting wiring the rental equipment."

"I remember. I was just wondering if you saw anything strange."

"What do you mean by 'strange'?"

"Did you see anything suspicious or out of the ordinary while you were in Archie's store?"

"No. It was a quick visit. I needed to measure the old electrical box to make sure the new one would fit in the space, then I left."

"Was Archie in the store?" she asked.

"No, only his nephew."

"Neil?"

Jose nodded, then his eyebrows drew downward. "He was talking to a woman. I remember because they seemed to be getting along, and then they started arguing. Their voices carried to the back room where I was working."

"Was this before they announced the winner of the sand sculpture contest?" Lucy asked.

"It was. After everything was wired for the food tasting, I took ten minutes to run into Archie's shop. They must have come downstairs from the apartment above the store after I was already inside. They never even spotted me in the back of the store."

If Neil was arguing with a woman *before* they'd announced the winner of the contest, then she must have left. Lucy recalled seeing Neil with

Archie at the back of the bandstand when Katie announced the winner. A woman wasn't standing with them.

She filed away the information. Lucy wasn't aware Neil had a girlfriend, but then again, she hadn't known that Archie had been dating Rita Sides either.

"Can you describe what she looked like?" Lucy asked.

Jose shook his head. "I was in the back and they were in front of the store. But I do remember that she had an annoying voice."

"An annoying voice?"

"It was very gravelly . . . not pleasant to listen to. I didn't mean to eavesdrop on their conversation, but they were loud and I couldn't help but hear. Something about the cost of a new surfboard. He said he'd pay her back soon."

Lucy had doubted Neil could afford such a pricey board, let alone airplane tickets to California or Hawaii, where the best surfing competitions took place. If his girlfriend had loaned him the cash for the Firestone surfboard and Neil couldn't pay her back, then he needed a way to get the money and fast. As far as Lucy had heard, he'd received the boardwalk store in the will, not a large sum of cash. But the stores were lucrative during the summer.

Either way, money was a great motive for murder.

"Careful when you plate the choreg," Butch cautioned. "They are straight from the oven."

The delicious aroma of freshly baked bread filled the kitchen and spilled into the dining room.

Choreg was a sweet, flaky Armenian bread and best served warm with Muenster cheese.

Emma ripped a piece of paper from her order pad and slipped it into the cook's wheel. "Table four ordered the moussaka appetizer," Emma said. "Table six the lemon chicken soup, and is the pork tenderloin ready?"

"Azad's working on the pork," Butch said as he spun the wheel and checked the additional order. He worked efficiently and soon began plating the next order.

Emma was already busy filling glasses at the soda fountain. Lucy grabbed the finished plates and looked at Sally. "I'll deliver these for Emma. You work on plating the cheese for the choreg."

"Got it," Sally said.

Lucy hurried across the dining room, dodging a customer on his way to the register to pay. When she returned, Emma and Sally were at the waitress station reading a newspaper. Anxiety crossed both their features when Lucy approached.

"What is it?" Lucy asked.

"A customer left this behind," Emma said. "You're going to want to see it."

It was the *Ocean Crest Town News*. Splashed across the front page was a picture of an ominous black body bag strapped onto a stretcher. Paramedics pushed the stretcher, followed by Detective Clemmons and other police officers.

The headline read: SAND SCULPTURE CONTEST TURNS DEADLY. FORMER FESTIVAL JUDGE MURDERED UNDER THE BOARDWALK.

Beneath the grave image of Archie's body was another picture. This time the image was of Lucy standing in the middle of Kebab Kitchen at the emergency festival committee meeting. She was facing the mayor, Tom Huckerby, who stood behind a podium. The committee members were all seated, and serious looking.

The caption beneath the picture read: KEBAB KITCHEN MANAGER FINDS BODY. RESIDENT SLEUTH AT IT AGAIN!

The article went into detail about how Lucy had an uncanny knack for finding bodies and killers. It went on to state how she "vehemently" disagreed with the mayor over hiring additional police to monitor the busy summer season. It suggested she bypass the town detective and take matters into her own hands and solve the murder once again.

Lucy tossed the paper on the counter as her temper flared. "What a liar! I didn't *vehemently* disagree with the mayor. I merely said I didn't think additional police would have prevented Archie from being shot that day."

"He makes you look heartless," Emma protested.

"Not just heartless, but a troublemaking sleuth. I'm already at odds with Detective Clemmons for interfering in past investigations. Now Clemmons has reason to suggest I'm sticking my nose in his business again." She wasn't scared of Clemmons, more like wary of him. But she prayed the county prosecutor didn't read the article. She was already on the woman's bad side, and Marsha Walsh was highly intelligent and *did* frighten her.

"Stan Slade strikes again," Sally muttered.

Emma reached for the paper. "Slade also mentions a fight between Katie and Archie during the judging. Emma read aloud, "'Heated words were exchanged resulting in tossing Mr. Kincaid to the curb like an unwanted mutt.'" Emma *tsked.* "We also heard about it from the customers."

Lucy wondered which customer had blabbed the gossip. "It didn't go down like that. Katie didn't toss Archie out, he violated the rules."

Emma patted Lucy on the back. "Don't sweat it, Lucy. Slade prints what he thinks will sell papers. It's not always a hundred percent accurate."

"I'm not worried about my reputation, but I *am* worried about Katie's. He makes it sound like she shot him."

CHAPTER 8

"All you have to do is go into The Big Tease Salon and ask for Rita," Katie said.

Lucy gave her sidelong look. "We aren't exactly friends. What makes you think she'll talk to me?"

"Offer her sympathy for her loss, then see if you can get her talking. I would do it if I could, but I'm on my lunch break and have to get back soon," Katie said.

"I thought you didn't work Fridays in the summer."

"I don't, but I'm covering for a coworker who's on vacation this month."

Just great. It was the day after Lucy had spoken with Neil, and she'd met Katie outside the salon. They'd driven there separately, and Lucy's Toyota Corolla was parked next to Katie's Jeep. One of them had to speak with Rita Sides and find out what she knew about Archie's death.

It was Lucy's lucky day.

She eyed the bright red awning of the salon. The Big Tease Salon was in the center of town across from Ben's Barbershop, Cutie's Cupcakes, and the town park. Lucy made a mental note to stop by the bakery after leaving the salon for a slice of her favorite lemon meringue pie. If she had to get a haircut or manicure in order to talk with Rita, she'd deserve the pie and the calories.

"Okay. I'll do it. If Rita knows something, I'll try to wheedle it out of her," Lucy said.

Lucy knew deep in her bones if she left it up to Detective Calvin Clemmons, he may not get Rita to admit to anything. Bill had wanted Lucy to ask around and see what she could learn. At his request, she hadn't shared that conversation with Katie, and she was feeling guilty about it. She'd never kept anything from her best friend.

"We have nothing to lose. Plus, you might also get a new hairdo or polished nails out of it," Katie said.

"You know how I feel about salon stuff." Lucy wasn't high maintenance and rarely got a manicure. Spending time in the kitchen with her mother had convinced her to keep her nails short and unpolished—the same way her mother claimed aspiring chefs did. Lucy was far from an aspiring chef, but she knew better than to show up for a cooking lesson with long, painted nails. She still remembered Angela's laser-eyed look of disapproval when she'd arrived in the kitchen with bubble-gum pink nails from her last manicure. She'd been looking into a murder then, too.

"You sound like you're marching to your doom. It's a salon, Lucy, not a gynecologist visit."

"Easy for you to say. Every time I step inside, Beatrice Tretola wants to give me a keratin treatment to straighten my hair. I looked into it. It has enough formaldehyde to preserve the frogs in the jars from back in high school!"

"Don't be a drama queen. You can always tell her just to blow-dry it straight."

Lucy didn't have time for a two-hour-long beauty appointment. And why bother?

Her curly hair would frizz as soon as she stepped outside in the Jersey shore humidity or when she walked into the hot kitchen. Plus, she couldn't ask questions with a noisy hair dryer buzzing in her ear.

"And if she insists on the keratin?" Lucy asked.

"You'd look nice with straight hair for three months. Completely different, but nice. It might be worth the smelly treatment if you can get info out of Rita."

"It's unfair. Your hair is naturally poker straight."

Katie grinned. "Our differences make us a good team. Good luck."

The bell above the door of The Big Tease Salon chimed as Lucy stepped inside. Ladies sat in black vinyl chairs getting their hair cut and styled while others, at manicure tables, soaked their fingers in bowls of pink suds or were having their nails filed and trimmed with ominous-looking instruments.

Beatrice Tretola, the owner, was busy wrapping a woman's hair with dozens of small pieces of tinfoil. The woman looked like she could pick up radio signals. Beatrice reached for what looked like a paintbrush and started to dab bleach on the tinfoil sheets when she spotted Lucy.

"Hi, Lucy! How's the restaurant business going?"

Beatrice, who preferred to dress in a Bohemian style, wore a flowing green dress with bright yellow flowers, chunky jewelry, and gladiator sandals. She was chewing a wad of pink bubble gum as she worked.

"Managing Kebab Kitchen is a lot of work, but I like it," Lucy said.

"I plan on stopping by soon," Beatrice said. "Does that hot chef of yours come out to ask if the customers like his food?"

Lucy cracked a smile. "Azad's been known to leave the kitchen from time to time."

"Woohoo! A man who can cook and who looks like he does is a woman's dream come true," Beatrice said, fanning herself.

"I'll be sure to tell him you were asking," Lucy said. "Meanwhile, I'll bring over a tray of baklava."

"The ladies will love it."

There was a chorus of yays from the other hairdressers.

"Forget the cook," Billy Jean, another stylist said, as she teased the hair of a middle-aged brunette with a comb and sprayed each section with a good amount of Aqua Net. "I saw you with that bad boy motorcycle man. You were riding on the back of his Harley-Davidson."

Beatrice popped a bubble. "I'll be damned. What have you been up to, Lucy?"

"Michael and I are just friends," Lucy was quick to add. How had the topic of conversation veered from Kebab Kitchen and baklava to men?

"First, she hires the chef, then she rides with the biker? She must be a man-killer!" cried the radio signal lady in the chair.

Lucy didn't want to be called a killer of anything, let alone men. "Now, that's not true at all and—"

"Maybe it's the hair." Hands on her hips, Billy Jean studied Lucy with a critical stylist's eye.

Beatrice set down a sheet of tinfoil and eyed Lucy with renewed interest. "You may be right, and we're going at it all wrong. Instead of a keratin straightening treatment, we should be providing perms for our customers."

"I want hair like hers," the lady in the chair chimed in.

"You may have started a new trend," Beatrice said.

Lucy wasn't sure about that, but just as she opened her mouth to answer, she spotted Rita Sides walk in from the back room.

Rita sauntered more than walked in four-inch-high heels. Her blond hair was styled in loose waves to her shoulders and her makeup was heavily applied. A black tank top and skintight jeans combined with stilettos made her look six feet tall. Rita headed straight for her customer, a lady who worked at Pages Bookstore.

"Now why are you here, Lucy? A haircut?" Beatrice asked.

"No." Lucy's gaze darted to where Rita Sides stood in the corner of the salon. Rita studied her customer, then dabbed what looked like wax across the woman's eyebrows with a thin Popsicle stick. With a quick jerk of her wrist, Rita ripped it off.

Eeow! Lucy inwardly cringed.

Maybe a manicure wouldn't be so bad after all. Lucy needed information, and if suffering through another cuticle cutting and nail filing session was the only way to get it, then she'd gladly sit through it.

When Rita applied wax to her customer's other eyebrow, Lucy thought fast. "I'd like Rita to do my nails," she blurted out.

"Rita doesn't do manicures, honey." Beatrice popped a bubble. "Lin will be happy to do your nails. Didn't she do them a while back?" Beatrice eyed Lucy's short, unpolished nails and her brow furrowed. "You shouldn't wait that long between manicures. Your nails are a mess."

If Rita didn't do nails, then she must cut hair. Lucy was resigned to some kind of salon treatment. Maybe she could get away with a two-inch trim. Rita quickly finished with her customer, and the woman's pencil-thin brows looked like they had been drawn on.

"Can Rita give me a haircut, then?" Lucy asked.

"No. Rita specializes in waxing. Eyebrows, upper lips, underarms, legs, bikinis. She even offers Brazilians if you want."

No way! Lucy was the first to admit that she didn't have a high tolerance for pain.

"She can shape your eyebrows to look just like Ms. Smith's over there," Beatrice said.

A hair straightening treatment was sounding better and better. Lucy glanced to where the thin eyebrow lady sat. Rita had disappeared.

"Where'd Rita go?" Lucy asked.

"Out back for a smoke break. She wasn't as successful as I was when it came to kicking the habit." Beatrice popped another bubble. "If it wasn't for constant gum chewing, I'd be out there smoking with her."

"Can I take a seat and wait for Rita to come back?" Lucy asked.

"Sure thing." Beatrice went back to work on her customer.

Lucy made a show of walking to the rear of the salon, but instead of sitting in one of the black vinyl chairs, she ducked behind a curtain that separated the front of the salon from the back room. Bottles of shampoo, conditioners, hair dye, and others lined the walls. Manicure equipment was stacked neatly on a counter. A sink was full of dirty mixing bowls.

The smell of strong dyes and hair products mingled with the odor of cigarette smoke. Rita hadn't made it outside. The rear door leading to the alley outside was cracked open, and Rita was leaning on the doorjamb and puffing on a cigarette. It was hot and humid out and she probably didn't want to melt her makeup or sweat in her tight jeans in order to smoke.

"Hi, Rita."

Rita started, then turned at the intrusion. "Lucy? You're not supposed to be back here."

"Sorry. I was looking for the ladies' room."

"You passed it on the way back here." Rita watched her warily. "Hey, promise you won't tell Beatrice that I'm smoking inside."

"I promise. Now that we happen to be alone, I want to express my sympathies. I heard you were dating Archie. I'm sorry for your loss."

Rita's eyes sharpened. "Where'd you hear that?"

She was clearly taken aback that Lucy knew. Why? There had been more than twenty people at the festival committee meeting when Harold had blurted out the news that Archie and Rita had been an item.

"Harold Harper mentioned it," Lucy admitted.

Annoyance flashed across Rita's face. "Harold's a jerk. Archie wanted to keep it quiet."

Is that why Rita was working only days after her boyfriend's death? "Well, I'm sorry for your loss."

"Thanks." Rita puffed her cigarette and a flicker of sadness crossed her face, but then she exhaled and the melancholy expression vanished.

Lucy coughed and waved the cloud of smoke away with her hand. "The truth is, I'm surprised you're at work. Beatrice should give you some time off."

"She didn't know. Besides, it's better if I'm with people rather than alone at home." She lowered her cigarette. "Why do you care anyway? It's not like we're friends."

Lucy needed to find out what Rita knew, and she wasn't leaving until she learned something. "I still feel bad for you. Plus, I'm on the festival committee and have to look into a few things. Do you know who could have wanted to harm Archie?"

"It's no secret Archie didn't get along with Harold."

That wasn't anything new.

"I know what people say about Archie. That he was a mean businessman who didn't get along with his neighbors, but it wasn't the *real* Archie. We were going to get engaged, and we even went ring shopping at Marion's Jewelers," Rita said.

Lucy looked at her in surprise. The couple had been serious enough to shop for an engagement ring? "I'm really sorry for—"

"The man I knew was kind and giving. He took in his nephew, Neil, and gave him a job in his store.

As far as I'm concerned, Neil didn't deserve it," Rita said.

They were getting somewhere now. Lucy just had to push a little. "What do you mean? I met Neil once. He seems like a nice young man." A far stretch to describe the wannabe surfer, but would it work on Rita?

Rita snorted. "He's a lazy bum."

Rita sounded like Lucy's mother when she'd first described Neil. "Do you think Neil hurt his uncle?"

"I'm not saying that."

"Where were you during the food and wine tasting?"

Rita ground out her cigarette in the sink. "Wait a minute. Why are you asking me all these questions?"

"I told you. I'm on the festival committee and—"

"Bull. You're not a cop. That slimy investigator already asked me a boatload of questions."

In hindsight, Lucy shouldn't be surprised. Detective Clemmons had been at the festival committee meeting when Harold had blurted out that Rita had been dating Archie. Any detective worth his salt would have followed up on the lead. A part of her was relieved Clemmons had done his job.

"For your information, I was on the boardwalk at the tasting that day and never left the boards. Others saw me. Ask around and you'll see. But I would never harm Archie. We were getting engaged." Rita's lips thinned, and she placed her hands on her hips. "Festival committee, my butt. What's it all to you?"

"I'm just trying to help, is all." Lucy knew when it was time to make a hasty exit. "Thanks for the chat, Rita. If I need a wax, I'll be sure to ask for you.

Meanwhile, I won't say a word to Beatrice about your smoking inside."

Rita's scowl eased. "Thanks."

Lucy hurried back through the curtain and returned to the main part of the salon.

"No wax today?" Beatrice called out as Lucy hurried past.

"I just remembered I have to pick up some items from Holloway's for the restaurant. Our supplier was short. I'll be sure to return with a tray of baklava," Lucy said as she waved on her way out of the salon.

Once Lucy was in her car, she looked back at the salon to see Rita staring out the bay window at her.

CHAPTER 9

"What do you think?" Lucy asked, as she held up a pink blouse and a black skirt on hangers. Katie was in Lucy's bedroom helping her pick out an outfit for her date night with Azad. Lucy was nervous about their night out, but at the same time, excitement thrummed through her veins.

Katie folded her arms across her chest and eyed the clothing. "I like it. Not too dressy, but nice enough for an upscale French restaurant like Le Gabriel. Let me see your shoes."

Lucy held up a pair of black ballet flats.

"You're kidding, right? Azad is a little over six feet tall. You're only—"

"Petite. Not short." At Katie's *What's the difference?* expression, Lucy relented. "Fine. I'll wear heels. Not everyone can be nice and tall like you. Now how should I style my hair?"

"Leave it down and I'll style it back. I'm envious of your curls. My hair won't hold a curl with a screaming hot curling iron and an entire can of Aqua Net."

"Stop. You sound like Beatrice today."

"Tell me what happened at the salon," Katie said.

Lucy summarized her conversation with Rita as she stowed the ballet flats in a shoe box and returned them to her closet. "Clemmons questioned Rita. I only hope she doesn't mention my visit to him today."

"She won't. If she did tell him, he'd ask her more questions, and I don't think Rita wants that to happen."

"I hope you're right. Clemmons would love an excuse to charge me with interfering with an ongoing murder investigation. He may even call Marsha Walsh. It's not like I've had a rosy relationship with either of them."

Prosecutor Walsh had visited Lucy at the restaurant and questioned her in the past. Lucy didn't want her to come around again unless it was to bring the prosecutor's family to eat.

"Rita only named Harold. We already have him as a possible suspect. She doesn't like Neil, but she didn't go so far as to accuse him of murder," Lucy said.

"Did she tell you why Archie wanted to keep their relationship off the grid?" Katie asked.

"No, but I'm not surprised. The Ocean Crest gossip mill is always in high gear." Lucy left out how Beatrice Tretola asked about her "hot chef" and the other salon ladies had seen her riding with Michael on his Harley.

"You better watch out that Stan Slade doesn't follow you tonight and sneak a picture of you and Azad at Le Gabriel," Katie said.

Lucy rolled her eyes. "I wouldn't put it past him,

except a murder in town is big news. Stan has bigger fish to fry."

Katie opened a nightstand drawer and pulled out a notepad and pencil and started writing. "We need to confirm Rita's alibi at the food tasting. Someone must have seen her."

Lucy removed the blouse and skirt from the hangers and spread them on the bed. "It doesn't matter if a dozen people saw her that day. She could have slipped away, lured Archie under the boardwalk, and shot him. Rita had opportunity and is still a suspect."

Kate slipped the pencil behind her ear. "Opportunity, yes. But what's her motive?"

Lucy clutched the black skirt in her fist. "Wait a minute. We never asked the most obvious question. Why was Archie under the boardwalk in the first place?"

Katie blinked. "Good question."

"Maybe he took a walk, just like we did, and was robbed," Lucy said.

Katie shook her head. "The police never mentioned a robbery. Bill said that Archie still had his wallet with all his cash and credit cards. If Rita hadn't lured him under the boardwalk, then why was he there?"

"That's the million-dollar question."

Le Gabriel was located twenty minutes outside of Ocean Crest. Azad had arrived at exactly seven to pick up Lucy. He looked amazing in a navy sports jacket, which highlighted the breadth of his shoulders, a white button-down shirt with a striped tie, and gray slacks. His dark hair was tapered neatly to his collar.

"You look beautiful, Lucy." His dark eyes were warm and she felt her insides jitter.

Lucy gazed out the window as they drove in his pickup truck. It was a pleasant evening and the sun was a low glowing ball in the ocean, the sky an amazing mix of pinks and blues. The sand dunes that protected the beach danced beneath a breeze, and seagulls circled above. The beach was empty, except for a lone couple walking hand in hand in the distance.

"I've been looking forward to this evening," Azad said.

She stole a glimpse at the clear-cut lines of his profile. His long, tapered fingers gripped the leather-covered steering wheel, and she knew they could wield a chef's knife with efficient skill and could be tender when they touched her cheek. "Me, too."

It was true. She had looked forward to their date. She was reminded of her girlhood crush—only it had changed, along with the both of them.

Azad pulled into a parking lot, and Lucy's attention was diverted. The French restaurant was a lovely building of white stucco that overlooked the Atlantic Ocean.

Azad stepped out and came around to open the truck door for Lucy, then offered his hand. She placed her hand into his larger one and accepted his aid. There was no graceful way to get out of a truck in a tight skirt and high heels.

He escorted her inside, gave the maître d' his name, and once their reservations were confirmed, they were escorted to a table set with fine china, silver, and glass, overlooking the glistening ocean.

"Wow. How did you get this table?" Lucy asked.

"I made the reservation four months ago."

Four months!

That was soon after she'd first arrived at Ocean Crest. She'd suspected he'd made reservations in advance, but she had no idea it had been *that* far in advance. She hadn't even known she was going to stay in town or that she'd end up managing Kebab Kitchen. She'd been wary of Azad then and couldn't be in the same room with him and not have a fight-or-flight response.

He must have read her thoughts.

"Wishful thinking on my part," he said with a grin.

How could she be mad when his lips curled in that sexy grin?

A waiter approached, and Azad ordered a bottle of wine and appetizers. She wasn't a wine connoisseur but she could read the price on the menu. Two hundred bucks! She looked up and caught his eye.

"It's a special occasion. I know we didn't get off on the best foot when you came home, but I think working together has been successful. We should properly celebrate."

If you didn't count the times her libido went into overdrive when they were alone in the kitchen, then yes, their working relationship had been a success. "Yes," she agreed. "It has worked out well. I couldn't manage Kebab Kitchen without such a great chef. Plus, I wouldn't want to work with my mom on a daily basis."

His eyes took on a mischievous glint. "Angela can be a bit tough."

"A bit? It's like working with a tyrant." They laughed just as appetizers were delivered. Escargot served in their shells with a delicate butter sauce flavored with shallots, garlic, and parsley; lemon-infused poached baby artichokes; and French onion soup. The artichokes were tender, the soup divine, but it was the escargot that danced with flavor on her tongue.

Lucy used small tongs to grip a shell and a long, thin snail fork to extract the escargot. She dipped one in extra butter sauce and popped it into her mouth. "Oh my gosh. The escargot is so good. Any chance you can incorporate snails into Mediterranean cuisine?" she asked.

Azad raised his own fork. "I'll definitely look into it."

A thought came to her and she rested her fork on her plate. Azad had worked on and off in town for years, and he knew a lot of people.

"Azad, did you know Archie Kincaid?"

"Sure. I stopped by his store a couple of times for beach clothes. He also ate at Kebab Kitchen a few times. Once, he gave Sally a hard time."

"My mom told me. Archie and Harold exchanged words."

"I was about to leave the kitchen and step into the dining room to help poor Sally out, but Butch went out instead. At the sight of him, those two cut it out."

Lucy chuckled. "Butch can look scary." Butch had a chest the size of a small armoire and hands that looked like meat pounders. With his checked bandana and gold tooth, he was downright intimidating. The funny thing was that Butch was the kindest and most mild-mannered man she knew.

"It's a shame what happened to Archie," Azad said.

"You didn't happen to see anything suspicious that day?"

"No. I was swamped serving food."

Lucy recalled the eager tourists and locals alike in line for Azad's mini shish kebab skewers, gyros, sausages, and falafel.

"Your date cookies were a hit," he said.

"Thanks." She knew her cookies weren't the big draw, but Azad was being kind. He *had* changed. Gone was the college boy who thought about parties and beer as much as his girlfriend and his classes. He was a thirty-five-year-old man who was serious about his career as a chef and his future.

A future with her.

It was all so overwhelming. She liked Azad. A lot. But she was just figuring out what she wanted in life.

The main course arrived. Veal ragout for Azad and duck breast for Lucy. She tasted hers, then his. Both were delicious. The veal was hearty and flavorful and the duck breast, which had a tendency to be dry after cooking, was succulent and moist. Dessert was next. Cream puffs with chocolate sauce, lemon-ricotta soufflé, and butterscotch crème brûlée.

"The pastry chef is renowned here," Azad said.

Lucy agreed, and her eyelids fluttered close as the crème brûlée melted on her tongue. *Heaven.* "You think we can hire him?"

"It's a her, and no. We couldn't afford her. Besides, we're a Mediterranean restaurant, remember?"

"I can dream, can't I?" She savored another spoonful.

Leveling his gaze on her, he said, "I like to watch you eat."

She blinked and lowered her spoon. "You do?"

"You eat with abandon."

She felt her cheeks grow warm. Was she unladylike? She swallowed and wondered if she did something wrong. She didn't think so. Not from the way he was looking at her. His gaze looked . . . intense . . . heated.

Wow. What was she supposed to say to that? "I can't help it. I like food."

"I don't want you to help it. It's a turn-on."

Double wow. All she had to do was eat—not hard for her—and he grew attracted. She grinned. "We should definitely do this more often."

His look intensified. The moment was broken when the attentive waiter returned to refill their water glasses.

"I promised Katie I'd bring home dessert," she said. "Katie's a chocoholic so I'll go with the cream puffs with chocolate sauce."

Azad cleared his throat. "No problem." He ordered extra cream puffs, and soon Lucy was handed a little take-out box with the Le Gabriel label. She could envision Katie's joy when she gave it to her.

"Let's take a walk. The restaurant has nice grounds," Azad said.

They left the restaurant and followed a lit path to the restaurant's expansive grounds overlooking the ocean. The sun had gone down and the moon was full. A gleaming, white gazebo shone beneath the moonlight. Lucy had heard that the restaurant catered onsite wedding receptions. The food was fabulous and the view was lovely. Brides would clamor to have their special day here, and fathers would spend a fortune to accommodate their daughters. She envisioned a happy bride and groom having their pictures taken inside the gazebo.

Azad took her hand as they walked. The humidity had ebbed and a cool breeze felt wonderful on her cheeks. The sounds of the ocean waves echoed through the night.

They reached the gazebo. She leaned against the railing, and stole a glimpse at him through lowered lashes. Half his features were illuminated by moonlight, the other half in darkness.

"I'm sorry about the beach festival being canceled," he said.

"Me, too. I was hoping Detective Clemmons would put it on hold, not cancel it outright."

He shrugged as if there wasn't much difference. He was most likely right. The result would be the same. The town had already begun to suffer economically, and if they never found the murderer, it could even harm next year's season.

"Do you know anyone who would have wanted Archie dead?" she asked.

Azad joined her at the railing and looked down at her. "No. Why all the questions? You aren't thinking about solving the murder yourself, are you?"

She immediately shook her head. "No. Why would you think that?"

"I know you, Lucy. Better than most. I recognize the gleam in your eye," he said.

Her spine straightened. "What gleam?"

"That little light in your eyes when you are up to something."

She blinked.

"You also have a 'tell' when you're lying. A muscle ticks by your left eye," he said, stepping close.

Her heart fluttered wildly in her breast. She was reminded of when he'd pointed out her "tell" in the past. She'd known him for more than half her life, and his instincts could be troublesome when she wanted to keep something hidden.

She raised her chin a notch. "I don't know what you're talking about."

"Just because you figured out the last two crimes in Ocean Crest doesn't mean you should do it again. You gave me gray hairs after your narrow escape in a killer's car. Remember that?"

How could she forget that nail-biting event?

"Promise you won't get involved. Stay safe. I don't want to lose you after I just found you again."

His fervent words, combined with his intense look, caused shivers to travel down her spine.

"Are you cold?" He took off his jacket and put it around her. Immediately, his heat enveloped her and the pleasant scent of his cologne teased her senses.

"Lucy?"

"Hmm."

"I want to kiss you."

She felt her face flush. *I want to kiss you, too.*

Rather than speak, she stood on tiptoe and met him halfway. His large hand cradled her face and held it gently as his lips caressed hers once, twice, driving her a bit mad. She clutched his shirt and gave a little tug. Thankfully, he got the message. Gathering her into his arms, he pulled her close and deepened the kiss. Sizzling silk met cotton, and she kissed him back, lingering, savoring every moment. She melted against him, and her knees grew weak.

The take-out box dropped to the floor with a small thud. Lucy didn't bother to look down to see if Katie's dessert was safe. Cream puffs were the last thing on her mind.

He pulled back and looked in her eyes. "Wow," he said, his voice husky. "That's even better than I remembered."

Beneath his transfixed gaze, her heart pounded. "Yes, it was."

CHAPTER 10

Azad held Lucy's hand as they drove back. The move felt comfortable and right, and she entwined her fingers with his. Tonight had changed things between them. The romantic atmosphere of Le Gabriel, the sumptuous food, the moonlit gazebo . . . the kiss. It was a memory she would relive for a long time.

Soon the WELCOME TO OCEAN CREST sign came into view, and they came to the first of three stoplights in town.

"Katie will be upset." Once they had separated from their kiss, Lucy had looked down in dismay to see cream puffs scattered on the deck of the gazebo.

She pushed aside any regrets. The kiss had been worth it. She'd make it up to Katie another way.

Azad squeezed her hand. "I'll stop at Cutie's Cupcakes first thing tomorrow morning and get her a pie and a dozen doughnuts."

"That's very thoughtful of you, but I should be the one to take her to Cutie's. I'll also be sure to deliver lunch Monday morning, too."

Sirens sounded outside, battering the amicable

atmosphere in the truck. Frowning, Lucy lowered her window and stirred uneasily in her seat. "Those sirens sound really close."

"Can you tell which direction they are coming from?" Azad asked.

Lucy released Azad's hand to lean out the window. "Oh, no! I see blue and red police lights headed in the direction of Kebab Kitchen."

The stoplight turned green, and Azad pressed the pedal to the metal. The truck sped down Ocean Avenue.

"No," he said as they got closer. "It's past the restaurant."

Relief flood through her as they passed Kebab Kitchen's striped awning. There were no police cars or ambulances anywhere near the building. She swore she saw Gadoo's glowing eyes as he sprinted across the parking lot toward the fence that separated the restaurant from Michael's bicycle rental shop.

Azad drove past one of the ramps leading to the boardwalk, and Lucy spied three cop cars parked between the buildings. "Oh, no. That's where the Gray sisters' shop is located."

Azad pulled the truck over and killed the engine. "Let's go see."

Lucy didn't wait for him to open the door, but hopped down herself. "Next time I'm not listening to Katie and wearing my flats," she grumbled as she hurried as fast as she could in her high heels.

"You agree to a next date, then?"

She stole a glance at him. "I suppose I do."

A corner of Azad's lips curled in a grin.

Under any other circumstances, she would have

analyzed his reaction, but there was no time as they rushed up the boardwalk ramp.

They both came to a halt as soon as they reached the boards. It wasn't the Gray sisters' shop.

It was Seaside Gifts—Archie's store.

A police barricade had been set up to keep curious onlookers away. It was late, after the shops had closed, and thankfully there were only a few boardwalk strollers watching as the police processed the scene. The Gray sisters huddled together outside their own shop, their expressions grim. Harold stood outside his own store.

Lucy approached the elderly spinsters. Edna was twisting her hands, and Edith's arms were folded tightly across her chest.

"A travesty. We haven't had a burglary in over ten years," Edna said.

"It's been that long?" Azad asked.

Edith clucked her tongue. "Michelle Palmer's herb and vitamin shop was robbed back then. But that was because the thief thought she sold cannabis."

Lucy held in a chuckle. Michelle Palmer was a bona fide hippie from the sixties who'd most likely had marijuana growing in her backyard.

"Who called the police tonight?" Azad asked.

"We did," Edna said. "We noticed something off. The rolling security gate was open by about two feet. Enough for someone to slip beneath."

"Not just someone. A burglar," Edith chimed in.

Lucy knew the shops did not have doors they could lock at the end of each business day. Instead they had rolling security gates that were lowered in the evenings and raised each morning.

"Do they know what was taken?" Azad asked.

Both sisters looked at each other, then shook their heads. "No clue."

"Where's Neil?" Lucy asked.

Edith pointed to the far end of the shop. "Standing with Detective Clemmons."

Lucy's gaze followed to where they pointed to see both Neil and Clemmons. Neil wore a white tank top and basketball shorts. His hair was disheveled, and some of the long locks stuck out in different directions. She couldn't tell if he'd just woken up or if he had returned from an outing with friends.

Neil was gesturing with his hands as Clemmons scribbled on the small notebook he carried in his shirt pocket. Lucy inwardly cringed. She'd been on the other end of the detective's interrogation more than once with Clemmons jotting down her answers to his questions.

"Excuse me a moment." Lucy slipped past the police barricade and approached the rolling security gate, which had been raised a little more than half way now to allow police to enter and leave. No one noticed her. Clemmons was occupied with Neil, and the other officers were inside the shop. Lucy stared at the gate. Something fluttered in the ocean breeze and caught her eye. She inched closer to study it.

What on earth was that?

A piece of red fabric that had snagged on the bottom of the gate.

"What is it?" Azad asked, causing her to jump.

She hadn't realized he'd followed her. "I'm not sure, but it looks like a piece of clothing—possibly a shirt."

Just then, Officer Bill Watson stepped out from the store.

"Bill!" Lucy called out.

Bill approached, his brow furrowed. "Katie said you were both going out tonight. What are you two doing here?"

"We were on our way home when Lucy heard the sirens. What happened here?" Azad asked.

"Someone broke in," Bill said.

Lucy frowned. "We can see that. Do you know who or what was taken?"

"We don't know who and it doesn't look like anything was taken. The thief used a small jack to pry open the rolling security gate just enough for him to slip beneath the gate and enter the store. Thanks to the Gray sisters' vigilance, the prowler was interrupted. But he fled before we could catch him."

Lucy spotted a cop taking pictures of what looked like a small jack that could be found in the trunk of a car to fix a flat tire. The thief must have left it behind in his flight to escape the police. They'd dust it for fingerprints, but if the criminal had used gloves, they would be out of luck.

"Did anyone get a look at the burglar?" Azad asked.

"Unfortunately, no," Bill said.

"He may have left something behind." Lucy pointed out the red fabric speared on the end of the security gate.

Bill stepped close to take a look and scratched his head. "I'll be dammed. You're right."

"It could be a piece of the burglar's shirt or pants. Maybe the burglar snagged himself on the gate as he hurried to get away. Based on the thick cotton, I'd say it was from a sweatshirt or sweatpants," Lucy said.

"I'll bag it and send it for processing. Good eye, Lucy." Bill left to fetch an evidence bag.

Azad and Lucy backed up to allow the police to work. "How'd you see that small scrap?" Azad asked.

Lucy shrugged. "I just did."

Azad looked at her with renewed interest. "You should have been a cop, not a restaurant manager. You seem to have better instincts than all of them."

CHAPTER 11

The following morning, Lucy woke early and showed up for her cooking lesson. She knew better than to keep her mother waiting. Angela was used to waking up at the crack of dawn to work in the kitchen. Lucy had mistakenly thought her mother would have given up the early-morning work ritual once she was partly retired.

She'd proven Lucy wrong.

They needed to prepare baklava and kufta this morning. Lucy had already learned how to prepare baklava and the flaky buttered pastry with walnuts, cinnamon, and a simple sugar syrup was one of her favorites. She had yet to prepare kufta, but she knew the basic ingredients were ground meat and bulgur mixed together in what looked like a large meatball. The kufta could be served in a broth soup or by itself in a savory tomato sauce.

"Be careful when you unroll the phyllo dough. I don't want any tears," Angela said.

Yes, sir, Lucy almost bit out then caught her tongue. No sense teasing her mother. When it came to stamina in the kitchen, her mother was in a league of her own.

Lucy would never be able to compete. The woman could prepare fifteen trays of baklava in one morning without breaking a sweat. Lucy's record was eight and that was with aching feet and a sore back from bending over the worktable to butter the endless sheets of phyllo dough.

But Lucy didn't mind. She was smart enough to acknowledge that when it came to Mediterranean cooking, she could never find a better teacher. Angela meant well and truly wanted Lucy to learn. Cooking was a way to connect with each other—a mother and daughter bonding session—and Lucy had come to appreciate their time together.

As Lucy spread the delicate phyllo sheets, each the thickness of a sheet of newspaper, her thoughts turned back to last night. Her date with Azad had gone well, better than she'd ever expected. Her mind relived the moment they'd kissed. The chemistry was still there—only stronger now that they were older and more experienced. It would take a long time to forget how warm and sweet his lips had been, how her knees had weakened like wet noodles when he'd deepened the kiss, and how muscular his chest had felt when she'd snuggled against him.

How would she look at him in the kitchen today and not think about that kiss?

"Lucy!"

"Yes."

"Are you paying any attention to what I've said? You need to chop the walnuts in the food processor."

"Sorry, Mom. I'm on it."

Her mother eyed her with suspicious intensity that made the hair of Lucy's nape stand on end. It was the same look she'd given Lucy and Emma as teenagers when they tried to slip a ten-dollar bill from their mother's purse.

"What's wrong with you? Why are you distracted?" Angela asked.

"I'm not."

"Hmm. I know my daughter and your mind is elsewhere."

Uh-oh. That she'd gone on a romantic dinner date with Azad at a fancy French restaurant was *not* something she wanted to confess to her mother. Her matchmaking mama would run out and reserve the church for their wedding. Lucy's mind scrambled with an excuse for her distraction.

"I was thinking about the break-in at Archie's shop last night," Lucy said.

Angela's buttered pastry brush clattered on the worktable. "There was a robbery?"

"The Gray sisters noticed something amiss and called the police. The thief fled. Fortunately, nothing was taken."

Angela crossed herself. "First a murder, now a burglary. What's going? Ocean Crest has always been a friendly and safe town."

Lucy didn't have the heart to bring up the past crime since she'd returned home and kept quiet.

"Do you think Archie's murder and the break-in of his shop are related?" her mother asked.

Most likely. "I'm not sure." Lucy hadn't given it much thought, but it made sense. Archie had been murdered, then days later, his store had been broken into. It was too much of a coincidence to be overlooked.

Her mother patted her hand. "I'm just grateful

you're safe and with me now. No more sleuthing for you or putting yourself in danger."

Lucy swallowed the sudden lump in her throat. "You don't have to worry about me, Mom."

Angela nodded, satisfied with Lucy's answer. "All right. How about I turn on the TV while we work? Cooking Kurt's show comes on soon."

Lucy knew that her mother liked to watch the hot celebrity chef while she worked. Angela claimed it was because of his recipes, but when Kurt flexed his muscles while taking out a heavy roasting pan from the oven, she'd caught her mother's admiring gaze.

At that moment, her father, Raffi, stepped in the kitchen, took one look at the television, and frowned. "Why do you watch that nonsense?"

"It's not nonsense. It's cooking." Her mother's chin rose an inch.

Her father's brow wrinkled.

Oh, no.

Her parents quarreled about a lot of things, but Cooking Kurt was a big bone of contention between them. When the celebrity chef hosted a book signing a few weeks ago at Pages Bookstore, Lucy had taken her mother. Raffi had refused.

Based on the stubborn looks on both of her parents' faces right now, Lucy needed to step in fast.

"Hey, Dad. What did you want to tell us?"

He scratched his chin. "Katie's here. Should I tell her you're busy?"

He knew Angela took their cooking lessons seriously, but Katie was family. Plus, it was Saturday and she didn't work weekends. "No. Please, tell her to come into the kitchen. She can help."

Her mother's face brightened. "Good idea."

Raffi left through the swinging kitchen doors and seconds later, Katie walked into the kitchen. "Hi, Mrs. Berberian," she said cheerfully.

"Hello, Katie. Do you want to help? We're almost finished with the baklava, and we need to move on to the kufta. I'll be sure to send you home with some dinner."

"Sure. Bill will be thrilled tonight." Katie washed her hands, then slipped on an apron.

"I'll fetch some extra bulgur," Angela said, marching toward the storage room.

As soon as Angela was out of sight, Katie whispered, "Bill told me there was a break-in at Archie's store. I can't believe I missed all the fun last night," Katie said.

"You were asleep when Azad dropped me off. I didn't want to wake you."

"That's what Bill said when I asked him about it this morning." Katie eyed the ingredients on the worktable. "Tell me what to do while we talk."

"Mix the meat with the bulgur, then make a small pocket with your thumb, fill it with a teaspoon of pan-fried onions and seasoned ground beef, then roll it closed. It should be the size of a large meatball when you're done."

Katie eyed the ingredients on the prep table. "I had this before in a chicken broth soup. It was delicious. The first time I saw it, I thought it was matzo ball soup."

"It looks like it, but it's meat instead of matzo meal."

Katie began hand rolling the mixture into a

meatball. Angela returned to the kitchen with an extra bag of fine bulgur.

A familiar jingle sounded from a television mounted in the corner of the kitchen. Katie glanced up at the screen. "Look, Mrs. Berberian. It's Cooking Kurt." Katie had accompanied them to the chef's book signing at Pages Bookstore.

"I try never to miss a new episode," Angela said.

"I think he's even better looking in person. What do you think?" Katie asked.

"He is, isn't he?" Angela said wistfully. Then, in the space of a heartbeat, her expression changed to look serious and she cleared her throat. "I use his cookbook."

"I bet it's helpful." A corner of Katie's lip curled in a smile.

Angela looked flushed. "If you two don't mind, I have work to do in the office."

"Sure, Mom. We got it from here," Lucy said.

As soon as Angela left the kitchen, Lucy chuckled. "There's a small TV in the office."

"Do they still argue about it?" Katie asked.

"They do. I keep telling my dad it's harmless fun on my mom's part, but he gets jealous."

Katie rolled her eyes. "Parents."

They continued to roll the kuftas. It was slow work, but with each attempt they improved at filling and rolling perfectly sized meatballs.

"My mom brought up a good point about the burglary," Lucy said. "Do you think Archie's murder and the break-in at his shop are connected?"

"Bill always says that coincidences aren't always coincidences." Katie set down a lopsided meatball, and looked at Lucy. "My gut tells me they're connected, too. But you said nothing was taken."

"The thief was interrupted. He snagged his clothes on the rolling security gate and left a piece of fabric behind."

"Bill had said you noticed it. Red and black are the colors of Ocean Crest's high school. Probably every household in town has a red hoodie or sweatpants," Katie said.

"Another dead end?"

Lucy's mind turned over what they knew so far. Rita admitted to attending the food and wine tasting. But despite opportunity, what was her motive? According to Rita, Archie was a great guy and he intended to propose. He even took her to Marion's Jewelers to look for an engagement ring. It didn't make sense for Rita to want Archie dead.

Harold disliked Archie. He was at the boardwalk and his rivalry with his business neighbor was notorious in town. He had opportunity and motive.

Neil had motive: money. He'd inherited Seaside Gifts. She'd seen his Firestone surfboard, and according to Jose, Neil owed a girlfriend money for the pricey board. Neil had also been at the food festival. Lucy saw him with Archie at the back of the bandstand when Katie had announced the winner of the sand sculpture contest. Had he somehow lured his uncle under the boardwalk and shot him?

"If the police found the gun it would help," Katie said.

"If I was the killer, I would have tossed it off the boardwalk pier," Lucy said.

"Me, too," Katie said.

They continued to roll the meat mixture, lost in thought.

"Hey, Lucy."

"Hmm."

"I never asked you about your date with Azad."

Lucy glanced around to be certain her parents weren't within earshot. "It was good."

"Just good?" Katie leaned close and whispered, "Spill it."

"It was romantic and the food was fantastic." She wouldn't forget the escargot or the veal ragout or duck anytime soon.

"Where's my dessert?" Katie asked.

Lucy felt her face grow red. "Ah . . . well . . . I had the waiter wrap perfect cream puffs, but I accidentally dropped the container."

Katie shot her an incredulous look. "Dropped it? How?"

"We strolled around and one thing led to another and well . . . I dropped it." Lucy's heart pounded like a drum.

"You *kissed* Azad." Katie's blue eyes lit with excitement. "If you dropped my dessert it had to be a good kiss."

It had been. Not just good, but amazing.

"Who kissed Azad?" a male voice asked.

Lucy and Katie jumped apart at the sight of Raffi standing in the doorway. Lucy felt lightheaded at the sight of her dad's curious expression.

Oh, crap.

Katie looked wide-eyed and guilty. "Hi, Mr. Berberian. I'm helping Lucy cook."

"I'm grateful, but I heard you say something."

His olive-black eyes met Lucy's, and he gave her a big smile. "Are you and Azad dating? I'm pleased. Your mother and I have always wanted him for you."

Lucy raised a hand. "Just stop, Dad. I'm not having this discussion with you."

Raffi ignored her. "Fine. I'll go fetch your mother. You can tell her all about it."

"Don't you dare!"

He shook a finger at her. "Don't forget that you need Azad as the head chef. You can be very stubborn, Lucy."

Lucy's temper flared. "Just like you, Dad."

He had the nerve to look shocked. "What are you talking about? I'm not stubborn."

"Ha! Then why are you so against computerizing the inventory?" Lucy seized the moment to change the topic from Azad to the restaurant.

"That's different. My method has worked just fine for thirty years. Why change it?"

"Because we can save countless hours each month counting the storage room shelves, the walk-in refrigerator and freezer. Inventory could be a breeze."

"It doesn't take that long," he said.

"It does," she argued. "I prefer not to stay late every Saturday night."

Raffi nodded once. "Of course not. I should have suspected. You want to go out with Azad."

"Dad!" Lucy almost ran her hand through her hair in exasperation, then remembered she'd been cooking. "Why are you here?"

"I almost forgot. The electrician, Jose, is here to finish installing the electrical boxes." He gave her a knowing look. "Just so you realize, I didn't protest your idea of the new fans."

He *had,* but her father had selective memory.

"Oh, and by the way, I obtained a copy of Mr. Alvarez's electrician's license and insurance for our records just in case our insurance company asks for documentation. Everything looks good," Raffi said.

Lucy experienced a feeling of unease that had nothing to do with her parents learning of her date with Azad or her battle to update the restaurant with her father. She hadn't bothered to check Jose's license or insurance. She eyed her father with renewed interest. Raffi had handled the paperwork, bills, invoices, and inventory for years. He'd been teaching her, but she realized there was a lot more to learn about how to run a restaurant properly. If she was going to take her job as a manager seriously, and she wanted to, then she needed to master basic Mediterranean cooking from her mother and business from her father.

"Thanks, Dad. Where's Jose?"

"Outside with his truck. He'll be in soon. I'll leave you ladies to your work," Raffi said as he left the kitchen.

Once they were alone, Katie turned to Lucy. "Didn't you say Jose had been working in Archie's shop the day of the tasting? Maybe he'll know how Neil is handling the break-in."

They washed their hands and took off their aprons just as Jose, carrying his toolbox, was entering the storage room. "Hi, ladies."

"Hi, Jose. Thanks again for the flan. It was delicious."

"I have more in the truck for you from Maria."

"That's kind. I'll share it with Katie."

"She owes me dessert," Katie chimed in.

"I'll have freshly baked baklava for Maria," Lucy said.

"She's eating for two these days, so she'd love that," Jose said. "It's going to take me a couple of hours to finish installing the electrical boxes. I'll be ready to put in the ceiling fans next week."

"Thanks, Jose. Are you still working at Archie's shop now that Neil is running it?" Lucy asked.

Jose shifted his toolbox from one hand to the other. "I finished my work there, but I haven't submitted my bill yet. I feel bad doing it after what happened to Archie."

If he'd completed his work, then chances are he wouldn't know much about the burglary or Neil's reaction. But still, it couldn't hurt to ask. "We heard about the burglary. Do you know how Neil is handling it? I mean first he lost his uncle, and now the shop he inherited has been burglarized."

"I can't say. But I know Neil lives above the shop. He must have been worried to learn about a break-in," Jose said.

"We still can't believe it. There hasn't been a burglary in town in a long time," Katie said.

The room was silent as they all contemplated that fact. Then Lucy eyed Jose. "The burglar opened the rolling security gates with a small jack just far enough for him to slide through. How could someone do that?"

"The rolling security gates are manual, not electrical."

"He's right," Katie said. "I've walked the boardwalk at night when shopkeepers lower their security gates."

Jose nodded. "A few stores have motorized doors that I've serviced. But most don't. Archie's was manual. A crank and chain hoist assists someone to raise and lower the gates from inside the store. Owners can then leave their stores from a back storage room door."

"Could someone just physically lift the gates?"

Jose chuckled. "Those gates weigh a ton. You'd need a small lift."

"Like a car jack?"

"I guess that would do it." He scratched his head. "But I also think the rolling, manual gates lock at the bottom from the inside. I don't know how the burglar got past the lock even to use a jack to raise the gate."

What little Lucy knew of Neil, she wouldn't be surprised if he'd forgotten to lock it. "Thanks, Jose."

He waved on his way to the dining room with his supplies.

Katie twirled her ponytail. "Neil doesn't strike me as responsible. He probably lowered the gate, but must have forgotten to lock it."

"That's what I originally thought. But maybe we're looking at this all wrong. Maybe Neil purposefully left the gate unlocked?"

"That doesn't make sense. Why stage a break-in when you already live there and can take anything you want at any time?" Katie nibbled her bottom lip. "Unless Neil is worried he's under suspicion for murder by Clemmons. Maybe he staged the burglary to draw attention away from himself?"

"It's possible." Another answer occurred to Lucy. "But there's another scenario to consider. Neil's in debt. What if he wanted to claim something valuable was stolen in order to file an insurance claim? He could have unlocked the gate and cranked it open a few feet in order to fake a robbery. Only, he had to ditch his efforts and take off when the Gray sisters called the police."

"What's so valuable that he'd fake a theft?" Katie asked.

"His pricey surfboard. Or the engagement ring Archie was planning to give Rita."

"Maybe his inheritance isn't enough to cover his surfing dreams," Katie said. "After all, if Neil murdered his uncle, what's one more crime?"

CHAPTER 12

"You don't have to do this," Katie said as she parked her Jeep outside of Cutie's Cupcakes later that day.

"Of course, I do! I owe you for dropping your dessert," Lucy said.

"The kiss was worth it though, wasn't it?" Katie asked, a teasing note in her voice.

Lucy ignored her friend's prodding for details. She was still processing her reaction to Azad's kiss and what it meant to their relationship—in and out of the kitchen.

"What about you? Will you get a slice of lemon meringue pie?" Katie asked.

Lucy stepped out of the Jeep and shut the door. "Not today. I already have another of Maria Alvarez's flans waiting for me at the restaurant."

Lucy opened the door to the bakery, and they stepped inside. The aroma of freshly baked cookies wafted to her and made her mouth water. Susan was placing cookies the size of small saucers from a tray into a display case. A tall, refrigerated case displayed a variety of pies—apple, blueberry, cherry, and Lucy's favorite lemon meringue.

"Hi, ladies," Susan said brightly. "What can I get you today?"

Susan Cutie was in her early thirties with blond hair, blue eyes, and a quick smile. Lucy couldn't understand how she was still single and didn't weigh at least two hundred pounds from baking tempting desserts all day.

"Hi, Sue. I owe Katie dessert. What's your most decadent cupcake?" Lucy asked as she approached the glass case showcasing an entire shelf of cupcakes.

"That's easy. Double chocolate brownie chunk. Definitely decadent if you are a chocolate lover."

"It's too chocolatey," Katie said.

Lucy shot Katie an incredulous look. "Is that even possible?"

"How about salted double caramel?" Susan offered.

Katie's eyes widened like a kid's on Christmas morning. "I'll take it."

Susan turned to Lucy. "What about you? A slice of lemon meringue?"

Both friends knew her so well. It wasn't just Maria's flan that held Lucy back today. She'd indulged at the French restaurant last night, and she needed to watch her calorie intake today. "Next time."

Susan boxed the cupcake and handed it to Katie. Lucy dug into her purse and paid.

"Come back soon for that pie, Lucy," Susan said as she headed to the back room of the bakery.

Lucy waved just as the shop's bells chimed.

"Look what the cat dragged in," Katie whispered beneath her breath.

Lucy turned to see Rita Sides step inside the bakery. She couldn't imagine skinny Rita had a sweet tooth. Her skintight jeans looked to be a size zero. Her highlighted hair was in a high ponytail and her bangs were teased and spiked up with hair gel. Her pencil-thin brows arched into triangles as soon as she spotted them. Did she wax them herself?

"Hi, Lucy."

"Hi, Rita. Funny seeing you here. Sometimes I forget how small Ocean Crest is," Lucy said.

"Actually, I was looking for you."

"Me?" Lucy asked, surprised. They hadn't exactly parted on amicable terms when she'd left the hair salon.

"I went to Kebab Kitchen and your father said you were headed to the bakery with your friend," Rita said.

"That would be me," Katie said.

Rita's gaze flicked to Katie. "I know who you are. Beatrice cuts your hair. You've never seen me for a brow wax. You should make an appointment."

An anxious look crossed Katie's face, and she touched her eyebrow. "Why? Is something wrong with my brows?"

"Your eyebrows are fine, Katie." Lucy looked at Rita. "What did you want to see me about, Rita?"

Susan returned from the back room carrying a plain iced cake. She stopped short when she spotted Rita. "Sorry, I didn't know I had another customer. What can I help you with?"

"I'll take a doughnut. Chocolate glazed. It's Beatrice's favorite at the salon," Rita said.

Susan set the cake on the counter by pastry bags full of colorful icing. She took the doughnut out of the case, placed it in a bag, and handed it to Rita who slid a dollar bill across the counter.

"Tell Beatrice I said hello," Susan said.

Rita waved and headed out the door.

Lucy and Katie were hot on her heels.

"Rita, wait! Why were you looking for me?" Lucy asked.

Rita swung around. "You asked me if I knew anyone who could have wanted to hurt my Archie."

"That's right," Lucy said.

"I thought of someone. Anthony Citteroni."

"Anthony Citteroni? Michael's dad?"

"Yes," Rita said.

Mr. Citteroni had mobster connections in Atlantic City, a few shore towns north of Ocean Crest. He owned numerous businesses in town, and it was rumored that he used them to launder money.

And his son, Michael, was her good friend.

"I don't get the connection," Lucy said. "Why would Anthony Citteroni want to harm Archie? Archie owned a boardwalk T-shirt and novelty shop. Mr. Citteroni owns a lot of businesses, but he's not in retail."

Rita shifted on her high heels. "Archie had only been in Ocean Crest for about a year. He was doing well and wanted to expand. He always commented about all the tourists who rode rental bicycles, tricycles, and surreys up and down the boardwalk every morning. Only one shop rents to all of them. Archie often said, 'Why should

Mr. Citteroni's bicycle rental shop get all of the profits?'"

"Are you saying that Archie wanted to capitalize on the market and open his own bicycle rental shop?" Lucy asked.

"That's right. Archie said he'd have Neil run it. But when Mr. Citteroni found out, he wasn't happy," Rita said.

"You think Mr. Citteroni shot Archie to stop him from opening a competing business?" Katie asked.

Rita looked from Lucy to Katie to back to Lucy. "That mobster is one scary dude. He should be a top suspect."

After Rita glided away on her stilettos, they sat in Katie's Jeep. Lucy held the salted caramel cupcake on her lap.

"What do you think about what Rita said?" Lucy asked.

"It makes sense. You've always been nervous around Anthony Citteroni."

He could definitely be "one scary dude" as Rita had described him. "I like him just fine as long as I don't cross him. He is friendly with my parents as business neighbors. But Mr. Citteroni rarely visits the bicycle shop. Michael runs it."

"Your motorcycle-riding buddy?"

"Hey, Michael's fun and a good friend. And riding his Harley can be addictive."

Katie clamped her lips tight and shook her head. "You couldn't pay me to get on one of those motorcycles."

"That's what I used to say. You never know until you try it."

"I bet it helps that he's really good-looking. He could grace the cover of *GQ*."

"I suppose." Lucy wasn't blind to Michael's looks, but there was more to their friendship.

"How does Azad like him?" Katie asked.

Lucy let out a puff of air. "Oh, brother. Don't ask. Now let's get back to the topic at hand. How far do you think Mr. Citteroni would go to prevent another person from opening a competing business?"

"I'm not sure. You think he'd murder Archie over it? Or would he have one his goons take care of the problem?" Katie asked.

The question hammered at her. She'd had a run-in with one of his "employees" not long ago, and it had been a frightening experience she didn't want to repeat. Lucy's mind worked almost as fast as Katie sped down Ocean Avenue. Her friend tended to drive a bit too fast.

"Hey, don't take me back to Kebab Kitchen. Stop next door," Lucy instructed.

"The bike shop?"

"Yes. It's time to talk with Michael to see what he knows about his father."

Katie dropped Lucy off outside Citteroni's bicycle rental shop. Lucy reached for the Jeep's door handle. "The garage light is on. Michael's inside."

"Give me a call when you get back to tell me what you learn," Katie said.

Lucy waved as Katie drove away. The Jeep's tires squealed as Katie took off down the street. Lucy shook her head. She'd never get used to her friend's driving.

Lucy made her way up the driveway to the shop. A shiny black-and-chrome Harley-Davidson was parked in the middle of the driveway, and a black helmet hung from one of the oversized handlebars.

The garage was crammed with bicycles, tricycles, and four- and six-person surreys. A variety of bicycle parts and tires were mounted on the walls. A dark-haired man was squatting down by a bicycle, his back to her, as he replaced a flat tire.

"Hi, Michael."

Michael turned at the sound of her voice and grinned. "Hey, Lucy." He stood, his long, lean frame gracefully unwinding. "You want a ride?"

Her heart thumped in her chest. She did. After her first hesitant motorcycle ride where she'd clung to him like a vine out of fear, she'd cracked open an eye and learned something about herself. She loved it. She'd been hooked on motorcycle rides ever since. She eyed him. The company wasn't too shabby either.

"Yes, I would, but later. That's not why I stopped by."

His lips parted in a dazzling display of striking white teeth and Lucy was reminded of Katie's reference to Michael gracing the glossy cover of a men's magazine. His piercing blue eyes, the color of a cloudless sky, had always captured her attention.

He wiped his greasy hands on a rag and tossed it on a nearby bicycle. "By the serious look on your face, I take it something's bothering you."

She wrinkled her nose. "Is it that obvious?"

"Not to everyone, but I know you by now. What's up?"

"It has to do with your father."

Was it her imagination or did he stiffen slightly? "It always does," he drawled.

She knew there was no lost love between father and son. Mr. Citteroni had often been at odds with his son. It was Michael's sister, Teresa, who was most like their father and who wanted to take over his businesses—legal and illegal.

"Sorry," Lucy said. "I didn't mean to upset you. I just want to ask you about your father's dealings with Archie Kincaid."

"His dealings? I didn't think he had any."

"I just spoke with Archie's girlfriend, Rita. She claims Archie wanted to open a bicycle rental shop."

Michael reached for the handlebars of the bicycle with the newly repaired tire and pushed it to join a row of others. "Hmm. How about we go for a motorcycle ride and I'll tell you everything I know."

"Now?"

He cocked his head toward the Harley in the driveway. "I was going to ride right after I finished with this tire. Is that a yes?"

How bad did she want to know? Bad enough to agree to ride in the middle of the day? She wasn't dressed for it and still wore her work uniform of a white button-down shirt and black slacks.

She needed to learn about Mr. Citteroni's dealings with Archie. If riding with Michael was the way to get answers, then she'd just have to hop on the motorcycle. "Let's go."

Michael grinned. "I'll get an extra helmet."

He disappeared in the bowels of the garage and

emerged with a helmet in hand, one with a skull and crossbones painted on the sides. She placed it on her head, and he helped her snap it beneath her chin. He sat on the Harley and she climbed behind him and held on to his sides.

The bike roared to life. Her heartbeat pounded in her ears as he drove onto the main road. Cool air rushed by her cheeks and ruffled her shirt. She breathed in the fresh ocean air as they sped past buildings. Riding with Michael never lost its appeal. It was thrilling . . . exhilarating. They usually rode at night, and the headlights of the passing cars and the lights of the brilliant Ferris wheel combined into a brilliant kaleidoscope of color against a dark, velvet sky.

It was a different experience in the day. It was just as adrenaline-fueled and exciting, but different. She could see the drivers' faces as they passed cars, the pedestrians walking to the beach, and even the blue line of the ocean between buildings. Michael turned onto the Garden State Parkway and headed south toward Cape May. This wasn't their usual route and she wondered where he was headed. She had forgotten to ask. Several miles later, he exited the parkway and slowed the bike.

"Where are you going?"

"It's a surprise."

A surprise? She wanted to ask questions about his father, not tour another South Jersey beach. Then he turned down a rural road, and her pulse leaped at the sight of a tall white tower with a red ball on top. "It's the lighthouse!"

He stopped the motorcycle, parked, and lowered the kickstand. She stepped off the bike first, then

Michael followed. He helped her remove her helmet and hung it on one of the Harley's wide handlebars, his own on the other.

"When was the last time you were here?" he asked.

She gazed up at the Cape May lighthouse. A deep-seated memory returned of when Azad had brought her here when they were both in high school. It was the first time they'd kissed—awkward, but eager—nothing like their recent sizzling kiss beneath a moonlight gazebo. "It's been a long time. Why here?"

"It's a nice, cloudless day. I thought it would be fun. We can also talk."

She couldn't deny the appeal. As Michael paid the entrance fee, Lucy read the sign. "It says the lighthouse was built in 1859, and is still used today by the U.S. Coast Guard to operate the light as an active aid to navigation. It has one hundred and ninety-nine steps."

Michael winked. "We better get started then."

Together they began to climb the tower's cast-iron spiral staircase. It was warm inside, and the temperature increased as they climbed higher. She was hot and winded by the time they reached the top.

Lucy puffed. "I need to jog more."

Sweat beaded on Michael's brow. "It's hot as Hades inside, but not for long." They stepped through a red door to the viewing deck and she gasped.

"Look at the view. Isn't the climb worth it?" Michael asked.

It was. They could see for miles from the top—a stunning view of ocean and white crested waves.

A brisk sea breeze cooled her heated skin. In the distance, a ship sailed along. Seagulls cried out, and a crane, searching for its next meal, skimmed the surface of the water. She could also spot the Delaware Bay to the south, Cape May and the Wildwoods to the east, and Cape May Court House to the north.

"It's beautiful."

For long minutes they stared at the sea in silence, until he spoke. "We're the only people up here. Ask me what you want to know."

Her fingers curled around the railing. The vastness of the ocean view had been calming, and she didn't want to taint it with questions about his father. She sighed. But that was the entire point of riding with Michael today, wasn't it?

"Did your father know about Archie's plans to open a bicycle shop?" she asked.

"He did."

"How did he take the news?"

"I don't know. All I can say is that my dad doesn't deal well with two things: rejection and competition. He's had the sole bicycle rental shop in town for as long as I can remember."

"Me, too. Do you think he acted upon Archie's news?"

The wind blew a lock of dark hair across his brow and gave him a youthful appearance. "You mean do I think he used strong-arm tactics to eliminate the possibility of future competition?"

"Yes." She would have phrased it differently, but nonetheless, the question hung between them like a heavy cloud.

"Do you want me to ask him what he did about it?" Michael asked.

"Would you?"

"Sure. But if he wants to talk to you himself, I think I should be around just in case."

Just in case? Michael made his parent sound even more ominous. Anthony Citteroni may have no reason to wish her harm and may even like her, but the man made her heart thud and not in a good way. She'd had limited experiences with the mobster in the past, and the thought of another encounter, even with Michael present, was enough to make her jittery.

Still, she needed to know the truth. "Thank you, Michael."

Once again, they stood looking out at the view in silence. Lucy was thinking about what she'd learned. She could only assume Michael was deep in thought as well.

"Ready to go down?" he asked.

The climb down was easier than their way up. Once their helmets were secure and Lucy was sitting behind Michael on the Harley, she spoke up. "It was lovely. I'm glad you brought me here."

"You didn't exactly learn everything you wanted to know," he said.

"No, but I know I will. Our dads can be frighteningly similar."

He laughed, his voice a bit gruff. "You mean overbearing and manipulative?"

"You said it." They may have come from different ethnic backgrounds, but Lucy had always felt a kinship with Michael. "Hey, I have to get back to work. I told them I'd only be gone for a couple of hours."

"I don't want to get you in trouble. I know all about family obligations."

She nudged his elbow. "I know you do. That's why you're such a good friend."

They rode back and she savored the wind on her hot cheeks. He pulled into the back parking lot of Kebab Kitchen rather than the bicycle shop next door.

Lucy climbed off the motorcycle and Michael attached her helmet to a saddlebag on the side of the bike.

"I'll talk to my dad and get back to you," he said.

She gave him a quick hug and a peck on the cheek. "Thanks for today."

The Harley started with a rumble, and he drove away. Lucy turned to head back, then stopped short at the sight of Azad leaning against the side of the building. His arms were folded across his chest.

"What the heck was that?" Azad asked.

"What?" Alarm slithered along her spine. She knew Azad didn't like Michael, nor did Michael appreciate Azad.

Both men could be a bit maddening.

Azad pointed to the fence separating Kebab Kitchen's parking lot from the bicycle shop. "Why are you riding a motorcycle with *him?*"

She could still hear the Harley-Davidson purring next door. "Michael's a friend."

"That didn't look like a friendly hug or kiss."

"Well, you're wrong. It was, not that it's any of your business," she added.

Azad's lips thinned. "After last night, it is my business."

His tone got her back up. She knew Azad was

referring to their date at Le Gabriel. If he thought that gave him a right to decide whom she chose as friends, then he was sorely mistaken. "You're acting ridiculous."

"I'm being ridiculous? What if it was the other way around? How would you feel?"

"I'd hope I would understand and not act jealous."

He straightened from the wall, tall and angry. "Okay. Where did you go?"

Oh, no. She couldn't admit they went to the Cape May lighthouse. It was sure to bring up memories of their teenage years and their first kiss and sound like a romantic date. Her mind reeled. She also knew she couldn't confess that she'd sought information about Archie's murder from Michael, and that she planned to follow up on that information once she received it. Azad had already said she'd given him gray hairs from her last involvement in a murder, and she'd promised she was staying out of the current one.

What am I supposed to do?

"Well, where did you go?" he asked again.

"We just rode around town."

Azad pushed away from the wall. "You're not being truthful. Remember, you have a tell." He tapped his left eye.

Damn. Did he have to know her that well? She clenched her fist to stop her hand from touching her own eye. The fact that he knew she was withholding the entire truth, made everything seem much worse.

She shook her head. "It doesn't matter where we rode."

"It does to me. You need to make a choice, Lucy."

"A choice?"

"Me or him."

"Are you serious?" she sputtered, bristling with indignation.

His jaw set like granite. "Yes."

Her temper rose in response to his demand. He wasn't seriously acting this medieval, was he? They'd recently crossed a threshold, been on *one* date, shared *one* kiss—even if it was heated. She was entitled to have friends and Michael was one of her close confidants. If Azad thought he could make her choose, he had a lot to learn about her.

"Fine. I choose *friends.*" Head held high, she swept past him into the restaurant.

CHAPTER 13

"I just can't believe Azad's nerve. Make a choice!" Lucy said as she stormed into Katie's kitchen the following morning. Lucy had filled her friend in about her motorcycle ride with Michael and her request to meet with Mr. Citteroni, and then her fight with Azad.

"Maybe you were too hard on Azad," Katie said as she made a beeline for the coffeepot. Lucy had risen early and made a pastry run to Cutie's Cupcakes for coffee rolls before making a pot of coffee. She needed caffeine to make sense of yesterday's events.

Katie reached for the bakery box, but Lucy beat her to it and snapped the lid closed. "What do you mean I was too hard on him? He told me to pick. As if!" Lucy's outrage returned in a rush.

"He did see you get off Michael's motorcycle, then hug him and kiss his cheek," Katie pointed out.

"So?"

Katie lunged for the pastry box again, but Lucy

was faster and pushed it out of reach. "Don't hold out on the pastries!" Katie cried.

"Fine." Lucy opened the box and slid it across the counter.

Katie licked her lips as she selected a large coffee roll drizzled with white icing. "Azad really likes you. Maybe if you explained that you were with Michael in order to ask him questions about his father regarding Archie's death, he'd understand."

Lucy shook her head. "Azad would pitch a fit. He doesn't want me to investigate. If I told him the truth, he'd worry. Besides, that doesn't excuse his medieval behavior regarding my friendship with Michael."

"Okay. I get it. But you can lure him with honey, Lucy. I've seen you do it before with others," Katie pointed out.

"That's different. They never worked for me, and I never kissed them."

"You're in a pickle."

"I guess I am." Lucy bit into the coffee roll she'd taken from the box and savored the sugary sweetness, before sipping her hot coffee.

"What are you going to do?"

Lucy sighed and ran a hand through her hair. "I don't know. I already made a mess of things with Azad. It's going to be awkward at the restaurant this morning."

"Think about other things. Like who really killed Archie?" Katie asked.

"I'm thinking about Rita. She said they went shopping for engagement rings at Marion's Jewelers."

"You think she's lying?" Katie asked.

"I don't think so, but we should confirm it. Maybe

Marion heard something when they were in her store," Lucy said. She needed to focus on the investigation, instead of on Azad.

"Good idea. Marion's opens at nine-thirty. I'll drive."

Two cups of coffee later and one more roll, Katie and Lucy arrived outside the jewelers. Marion Hunt's store was located in a shopping strip next to Magic's Pharmacy.

Marion was in the shop arranging gold and silver necklaces on black velvet displays behind a glass case. Tall and heavy-set, she had dyed auburn hair and an abundance of freckles and, unsurprising given her profession, always wore pretty jewelry.

Lucy's eyes were drawn to the beautiful pieces on display throughout the store. On top of the counter sat tall plastic cases, which could be spun to view earrings in individual boxes. An entire glass case was dedicated to engagement rings, their diamonds gleaming beneath the store's fluorescent lights.

"Hello, ladies. May I help you find anything in particular?" Marion asked, her charm bracelets jangling as she approached.

Katie pressed her hands on the glass, fascinated by the diamond rings on display. "They're beautiful."

"The four C's. Carat, cut, color, and clarity. I can go over everything if you wish," Marion said.

"No, thanks. We were wondering if you remembered Rita Sides and Archie Kincaid shopping here." Lucy said.

Marion *tsked*. "Rita and Archie? How tragic. I still can't believe he's gone."

Katie looked up. "It is sad. Rita told us that they had shopped for engagement rings."

"They did more than shop. After they left, Archie returned the next day and purchased a ring," Marion said.

Katie's gaze returned to the glittering diamonds behind the glass case. "Was it one of these?"

Marion shook her head. "Not exactly."

"What do you mean?" Lucy asked.

"I don't mean to gossip about the dead, but it isn't as if Rita doesn't know."

"Know what?" Katie and Lucy asked in unison.

Marion reached for a set of keys behind the counter and unlocked the glass case to remove one of the engagement rings, a lovely pear-shaped diamond with a gold band.

Katie's eyes widened. "Wow! That's a big rock."

"One and a half carats," Marion confirmed.

"That must have cost an arm and a leg," Lucy said.

"It sure does. Archie wanted this setting, but not the diamond that went with it," Marion said.

"You mean he special-ordered one?" Katie asked.

"In a sense. He wanted the setting, but with a cubic zirconia stone."

Lucy and Katie looked at her in surprise.

"Archie wanted a fake stone? Did Rita know?" Lucy asked.

Marion's lips thinned. "Not at first. She came back a week later without Archie, and she asked about returning the ring."

"A week later?" Lucy asked.

"They must have split," Marion said. "It happens more than you'd like to think. Rita wanted cash for her ring. When I told her how much the ring was worth, she didn't believe me," Marion said.

"She must have been shocked," Katie said.

"And angry," Lucy added.

Marion nodded. "Both. I refunded her what Archie had paid, and she stormed out of here."

"Thanks, Marion. You've been a big help," Katie said.

Once they were outside, Lucy whistled. "That's a bait and switch."

"Maybe Archie didn't have the money to buy Rita the diamond she wanted," Katie said.

"If he didn't have the cash, then how could he afford to open a second business—a bicycle rental shop to compete with Mr. Citteroni's store?" Lucy asked.

Katie paused, then leveled her gaze. Maybe all his money was tied up with his business dealings. Either way, it sounds like Rita was mad enough to kill."

Lucy's sneakers pounded on the boardwalk as she jogged. Seagulls squawked and circled above, hoping for a child to miss a trash can with an unfinished hot dog or ice cream cone. It was Monday morning, and she'd risen early and decided to get a bit of exercise and some fresh air before heading back to the restaurant.

Things with Azad were on her mind. She'd managed to avoid him at work yesterday by staying out of the kitchen. She'd had a mountain of paperwork—ordering and payroll—to finish and she'd stayed all day in the tiny office. But she couldn't hide forever. Katie's advice came back to her mind.

"You can lure him with honey," Katie had said.

Lucy's lips thinned. She wanted to hit him over the head with the honey jar. His possessive words didn't jibe with this century. How dare he tell her who she can be friends with? Her temper spiked, and she sped up her pace.

Tourists and locals were out and about, some walking and others riding bicycles—their own or those rented from Michael's bicycle shop. She was glad to see them. It was bad enough that the end-of-summer festival had been canceled after Archie's murder. But not every tourist had fled Ocean Crest. Granted, it wasn't as busy as it should be for this time of year, but at least it wasn't empty. Lucy moved over when she heard the all-too-familiar speakers blare, *"Watch the tramcar, please!"* The tramcar moved past, half-full of parents, excited children, and crying toddlers.

She jogged by Gray's Novelty Shop to see Edith Gray putting out a display of sand pails and shovels. Lucy waved in greeting. Neil's shop was open as well, and a family with two young kids were shopping for T-shirts. She spied several customers in Harold's shop next door.

By the time she made it halfway down the boardwalk, the morning sun had grown stronger and the temperature had risen. Sweat beaded on her brow and her stomach grumbled, reminding her that she hadn't eaten breakfast, but had only had a cup of coffee. She'd stop by El Paso, the burrito shop at the end of the boardwalk for a breakfast burrito.

Lucy was lost in thought and didn't see the raised board. She tripped and turned her ankle. "Ouch!"

Pain seared up her leg. She hobbled to the metal rail and rubbed her throbbing ankle. After several minutes, the pain ebbed, but was still there. Thank goodness, it wasn't a bad twist. She had experienced a sprained ankle in middle school, and couldn't put weight on it for a month. She couldn't manage a restaurant if she had to hobble through the place with crutches or a boot.

Still, she could use some ice. The closest business was Madame Vega's fortune-telling salon. Making a snap decision, Lucy slowly walked inside, careful not to put too much weight on her ankle.

"Welcome!" Madame Vega said. She was dressed in her customary blue velvet robe with a matching turban and sat behind a round table draped in a scarlet tablecloth. Deep crow's feet lined her eyes.

The medium had been around as long as Lucy could remember. Lucy had a memory of riding on her father's shoulders when she was five and glancing inside Madame Vega's psychic salon. Her crystal ball and cards had captured Lucy's imagination as well as her trepidation. If nothing, else, Madame Vega put on a good show.

"I'm sorry to bother you, but I rolled my ankle. Do you have any ice?"

Madame Vega rose, and opened a small refrigerator in the back of the room. Lucy glimpsed a six-pack of beer. She returned and handed Lucy a zip-lock bag full of ice.

"Thanks," Lucy said as she applied the ice to her ankle.

"Your fortune?"

Lucy couldn't be rude. Not after Madame Vega had helped her. Heck, what harm could it do? Lucy unzipped a pocket in her running shorts and pulled out a twenty-dollar bill. She pursed her lips in thought. She needed ten for her breakfast burrito. "How about ten?"

"Good enough for the cards." Madame Vega slipped the twenty into a pocket of her robe, then gave Lucy change.

"You won't read my palm?"

"No. The spirits sent you to me to have your cards read."

"I thought they sent me here because I tripped and needed ice."

Madame Vega pursed her lips as if she was in deep thought. "No. You are troubled."

Did the woman really think Lucy would buy her act? She rubbed the ice on her ankle. It was starting to feel numb, but thankfully the pain was subsiding. She could sit here for a bit longer and play along.

Madame Vega picked up a stack of cards, turned them upside down, and spread them in a U-shape across the scarlet tablecloth. "Run your hands cross the cards. Put all your hopes, feelings, and desires into the cards."

A smile curved Lucy's lips as she touched the cards. "Okay, all my hopes and feelings."

"No. Not just your hopes and feelings, your desires as well. I traveled with my ancestors as a child, Hungarian gypsies, and we believe the cards will answer your desires as well. What is your question?"

Her question? She wasn't sure she had one. She hadn't walked in here with a question in mind.

"Put the cards back in order and hand them to me," she instructed.

Lucy complied, and her skin tingled as the woman pulled three cards and set them before her.

Madame Vega touched a sapphire in her turban. Judging by the size of the gem, it had to be fake. "The three-card spread signifies your past, present, and future."

Lucy's gaze dropped to the cards, and she felt a sudden trickle of anxiety. *It's normal,* she told herself. Who wouldn't want to have their cards read even if they didn't believe it?

"Now what is your question?" Madame Vega asked again.

"My question?"

"What's bothering you?"

Lucy pondered the thought. What wasn't bothering her at the moment? Her fight with Azad was on her mind. In all fairness, maybe she hadn't handled him that well. In hindsight, it really was ridiculous. For years, her love life had been as dry as dirt and now she had two men in her life. Both were tall, dark-haired, and good-looking. But only one made her heart race. The other was a friend.

Then there was the big question. Who had shot Archie? The end-of-summer festival had been killed along with Archie. Everyone in Ocean Crest would suffer the effects—all the businesses and her friends. The very reputation of the small beach town could be destroyed if they didn't find the murderer. Worse, would Detective Clemmons keep Katie on the suspect list?

"Is it a love question?" Madame Vega said, drawing Lucy from her musings.

"Partly. I also . . . ah . . . need to find someone."

"Someone from your past?"

"You could say that." Archie's murderer may have been just that—someone she knew.

Madame Vega nodded. "Let us ask the cards."

"The present card." Madame Vega flipped over the middle card. "The High Priestess."

Lucy stared at a colorful picture of a veiled woman sitting on her throne. "What does it mean?"

"There is much more to your situation than meets the eye."

Tell me something I don't know.

"Someone is hiding information from you. You seek the facts, but you are being blocked and do not have them all. Secrets surround you. You must use your talents to seek the truth."

The hair on the back of Lucy's neck rose. This fortune sounded surprisingly true. Someone was hiding—a murderer. But what talents did she have to unearth him or her? She may have lucked out in the past, but she felt completely out of her element when it came to finding Archie's killer. She wasn't even close.

"What about the other cards?" Lucy was suddenly anxious to hear them all. Maybe there was some truth to this tarot stuff after all.

Madame Vega tapped the right card. "This is the card of the future and represents the direction things are going." She flipped it over to reveal a young man holding a single golden cup with a tiny fish emerging from the cup. "The Page of Cups. News fills your heart with joy and bliss. You have reached a new level in love, but you are still unsure."

"Unsure? How?"

"The future is tricky. A new love can turn into heaven or hell."

This was sounding more and more frighteningly close to reality. Her uncertainty in her relationship with Azad could ruin their working relationship. Everything was at risk.

"The card of past," Madame Vega continued, then flipped over the third card to reveal a young apprentice and two others working in a cathedral. "The Three of Pentacles. Your talents are put to good use, but only because people have helped you along the way. They will continue to do so."

Lucy thought of Katie. Without her best friend, she wouldn't have been able to solve any murders and she knew without a doubt that Archie's killer would go free. Katie's obsession with crime shows had turned out to be helpful. Bill was Lucy's newest ally. Others had helped her along the way by supporting her return home and teaching her the business—her parents, Emma and Sally, Michael, and yes, Azad.

She owed them all.

Maybe this tarot card reading was a good thing and something she should do more often. She was starting to believe that Madame Vega really knew her stuff. Lucy glanced at her through lowered lashes and a thought occurred to her.

The woman was a boardwalk fixture. Lucy couldn't recall a time that she'd jogged or walked by and Madame Vega wasn't here. Had the medium seen something the day Archie was killed?

Lucy pressed her palms on the table. "May I ask

you something? Were you here the day Archie was shot?"

Madame Vega's hands stilled, and she set the deck of tarot cards down. For a brief instant, her brown eyes sharpened. "I was."

"Did you happen to see anything suspicious?"

"No. I was busy that day with customers and never left here. I realize now that must have been your question. Remember what the cards said."

Lucy nodded. "Someone is hiding something. I have a chance at love. People will help me along the way."

Madame Vega's lips pursed. "It is never that simple."

It never was.

"Thanks for the ice. My ankle feels better." She wouldn't jog back, but she could put weight on it and walk.

"Come back soon for another reading," the medium said.

"I will." She was surprised that she meant it.

Lucy stepped outside and blinked, her eyes adjusting from the darkness of Madame Vega's salon to the bright morning sunlight. She took a few steps when her cell phone rang, and she pulled it from her pocket.

"Hello?"

"Lucy, it's Michael. My dad can meet you tomorrow night at seven. Are you free?"

Her pulse picked up. Mr. Citteroni was giving her a face-to-face meeting? "Yes."

"Great. I'll pick you up. No motorcycle. We're going to an Italian restaurant. Dress nice."

* * *

Dinner service was pleasantly busy. Two-thirds of the customers were locals, not tourists, but Lucy was still happy to seat each one. Lucy knew tonight's specials had something to do with it. Grilled chicken and beef shish kebab were always popular, and Azad and Butch were in the kitchen putting out dish after dish.

Another benefit of a busy service was that Lucy didn't have to try to avoid Azad. She was busy in the dining room talking with customers and helping Emma and Sally serve the dishes as soon as they came out so that they were hot.

She was in the kitchen and refilling the large coffee urns when she spotted Azad heading into the storage room. Her thoughts returned to her tarot card session with Madame Vega.

The future is tricky. A new love can turn into heaven or hell.

Heaven or hell. She didn't like the latter. Her past with Azad wasn't something she could easily forget. He'd broken her heart after college. Since coming home, she'd given him a second chance. Had she made a mistake or was she letting the past dictate her future?

Then there was Katie's advice. *Lure him with honey.*

Maybe she should be the better person. In hindsight, her impromptu motorcycle ride with Michael and their quick embrace and a peck on the cheek could have looked bad from Azad's point of view.

She also knew Azad wanted her to stay out of any murder business, but she could share some of the truth without fully lying to him. If it would explain her motivation, then it could also put Azad's mind at ease regarding Michael.

Taking a deep breath, she headed for the storage room to find Azad lifting a heavy bag of bulgur from one of the metal shelves.

"Hey, Azad," she said.

He turned at the sound her voice. "Lucy."

She took a deep breath. "I know you're busy, but I want to clear the air between us. I wasn't exactly nice the other night and—"

He lowered the bag of bulgur back onto the shelf and came close. "You were right. You have every right to have friends. If you say you and that bike guy are friends, then I should trust you."

"Really?"

"Yeah."

The words came easier. "Well, we are just friends. I rode with him to ask if his dad knew anything about Archie."

Azad's eyebrows drew downward. "Archie Kincaid? You're not trying to solve another murder, are you?"

She forced aside any trepidation and looked into his eyes. "It's not what you think. Bill asked me to ask around. He's worried Detective Clemmons is treating Katie as a suspect." It was stretching the truth a bit. Bill had asked her to keep her eyes and ears open at the restaurant. Lucy and Katie may be going a bit further, but they planned on staying safe and informing Bill of what they learned.

Azad was standing close, his coffee eyes staring down at her with an intensity. "Bill asked?"

What was it about him that made her feel like a breathless eighteen-year-old girl?

"That's right. That's why I went to see Michael."

"That's it? You're not meddling in the murder more than that, are you?"

"No," she stammered. "I'm not meddling in the murder. Asking a few questions doesn't count as fully investigating."

His expression eased. "Thanks for telling me, Lucy. I had fun with you the other night. How about we do it again soon?"

Her heart gave an anxious little jolt. "I'd like that."

"Azad!" a booming masculine voice shouted from the kitchen.

Lucy jumped.

Azad rolled his eyes. "Butch needs bulgur," he said, then picked up the heavy bag.

"I better let you get back to work then." She turned to leave when his voice stopped her.

"And, Lucy?"

"Yes?"

His irresistible grin made her pulse leap. "I'm glad you're staying out of it."

She waited until he was gone, before taking a deep breath and smoothing her hair. A trickle of guilt pierced her chest, but she pushed it aside. She wasn't exactly "staying out of it," but she was doing her best to stay safe. If a dinner with Michael and Mr. Citteroni could lead to some answers that she could share with Bill, then it was worth the risk.

One thing was clear—she felt better and made a mental note to go back to Madame Vega's soon. The cards had helped with her love life, but would they help solve the murder?

CHAPTER 14

"Are you sure about this?' Katie asked as she rocked on the wicker rocking chair in Lucy's bedroom.

"I'm sure," Lucy said. "I won't be alone with Mr. Citteroni. Michael's coming with me."

"Still. I have the feeling you're walking into the lion's den."

"You're not helping my nerves. Now, how do I look?" Lucy smoothed the skirt of her blue dress. She wore ballet flats from her closet and had refused the killer heels Katie had offered. Her ankle was a still a bit tender from when she'd tripped on the boardwalk, and the flats were comfortable. Besides, Michael may be over six feet, but Mr. Citteroni was short. No need to tower over the man.

Katie stood and picked a piece of lint from Lucy's skirt. "You look beautiful. Michael's going to gape."

They headed into the living room, and Katie pulled aside the curtains overlooking the driveway. "Michael's here. No motorcycle, but a respectable mid-sized, two-door sedan."

Lucy took one last look in the hallway mirror on

her way to the door. She'd used a large-barrel curling iron, and her hair fell in loose curls and brushed her shoulders. She'd let Katie apply her makeup and she had to admit that the effect was pretty and very different from her everyday appearance at the restaurant.

Michael's eyes widened when she opened the door. "Wow! You look great, Lucy."

"Thanks. So do you." He looked handsome in a dark shirt and jacket with tailored pants. She'd only ever seen him in faded jeans and a leather motorcycle jacket.

They headed outside, and Lucy glimpsed back to see Katie smiling in the window. Her friend reminded Lucy of her mother when Lucy had left the house as a teenager with a date.

Michael opened the car door for her and then walked around to the driver's seat. Soon, they were driving down Ocean Avenue. "My dad was curious when I told him you were asking about Archie."

"Curious in a good way?"

"You can never tell with him. But the fact that he asked for you to join us for dinner tonight tells me that he has information for you."

"He couldn't just pass it along through you?"

Michael's smile turned into a chuckle. "You don't know my dad. That would ruin all the fun."

Fun? She didn't want to be Mr. Citteroni's entertainment for the evening, but she did want to hear his side of the story. Had Archie and Mr. Citteroni exchanged words over Archie's plans to open another bicycle rental shop? And how had that conversation turned out?

"We're here," Michael said, interrupting her thoughts.

Lucy looked out the window to see a quaint red-brick building with a yellow awning. Blooms of vinca, marigolds, and geraniums added pops of color to the landscaping. The red sign read NONNA IN CUCINA.

"Grandmother in the Kitchen," Lucy translated. "What a great name for an Italian restaurant."

"You'll love the food, too." He put the car in park and turned to look at her. "Ready?"

"Let's not keep your father waiting."

He escorted her inside and after giving his name to a hostess, who looked like a grandmother dressed in a long black dress with gray hair pulled back into a bun, they were led to the back of the restaurant where a lone man sat at a table. A bottle of wine rested in a wine holder with ice.

Mr. Citteroni stood when he spotted them. "It's good to see you again, Ms. Berberian," he said in a deep voice. Stocky and short, he had a square face, thick eyebrows, black eyes, and thinning, dark hair. Before she could respond, he raised her fingers and pressed a kiss to the back of her hand. His mustache tickled her skin, and she experienced a moment of trepidation.

"Thank you for inviting me," she said.

"We haven't had a chance to speak since Michael's birthday party a while back, remember?"

How could she forget? Mr. Citteroni had invited her to Michael's surprise birthday party at a Victorian mansion in Cape May. The evening had turned disturbing when he'd introduced her to one of his associates, a man Lucy and Katie had previously followed.

But that was long ago. She was now here at his invitation.

"Please sit," Mr. Citteroni said. "I took the liberty of ordering appetizers. I hope you like mussels and calamari. They are a specialty here."

Lucy's mood buoyed at the mention of the food. She was famished. "I like both."

A waiter approached to fill their wineglasses and set a large bowl of mussels on the table. The first mussel easily came out of its shell, and Lucy popped it into her mouth. The spicy sauce combined with the tender muscle was delicious. The calamari were fantastic as well.

She glanced at the menu and everything looked tempting. She was torn between fettuccini with Bolognese sauce and veal scaloppini. She settled on the fettuccini. The waiter returned and took their orders and refilled their wineglasses.

"Michael tells me you want to know about my dealings with Archie Kincaid."

Lucy sipped her wine. "Did you have dealings?"

He wiped his mouth with his napkin. "I have dealings with many people, in Ocean Crest and outside of town."

No doubt. He was legendary. She'd always feared him as a kid. Heck, with the Godfather vibe, he still intimidated her. "Michael said you knew that Archie wanted to open a bicycle rental shop in town. How did you find out?"

"Archie told me."

"He did?"

"We were waiting in the township office. I needed

to pay my real estate taxes; he claimed he was applying for a mercantile license. That's when Archie told me of his business intentions."

Lucy looked at him in surprise. She was expecting Mr. Citteroni to admit that he'd learned the truth through one of his many associates, not from Archie himself. "How did that make you feel?" Lucy asked.

"You mean was I angry enough to have him killed?"

Lucy swallowed a sudden lump in her throat. If anything, Mr. Citteroni was forthright. "Did you?"

He shook his head. "No. But I admit that I wasn't pleased. I've had the only bicycle rental shop in town for years. I wasn't about to let anyone encroach on my territory."

"How could you have stopped him?" Lucy asked.

His mouth spread into a thin-lipped smile. "I have my ways. It turns out I didn't need to use any of them."

That was true. Someone had put a bullet in Archie for him. Mr. Citteroni no longer had to worry about a second bicycle shop opening in town.

The food arrived, and Lucy picked up her fork and took a bite. The Bolognese meat sauce was hearty and flavorful and the fettuccini was cooked perfectly. The dish was topped with freshly grated Parmesan cheese and everything blended together in a forkful of heaven.

"You still have questions?" Mr. Citteroni asked.

Yes, she did. A lot of them. "What did you think of Archie?"

"Arrogance in a man is good, but only if he has the power to back it. Archie Kincaid did not."

Mr. Citteroni hadn't liked him. And from her own experiences with Archie, she tended to agree with him. Archie had been arrogant to a fault.

Maybe it was the wine talking, but Lucy decided to be even more forthright. "Do you know who could have killed him?"

Mr. Citteroni lowered his wine, his dark eyes assessing her. "Politics, like business, can be dirty."

Her brow furrowed in confusion. "What exactly are you saying?"

"Ocean Crest will have an election for a new mayor next spring."

She knew their current mayor, Thomas Huckerby, was retiring from politics. What did that have to do with Archie?

"I know Mayor Huckerby had denied Archie's license to open another business. Did you have anything to do with the mayor's decision?" Lucy asked.

"You mean did I influence the mayor? I already told you I have many ways. It would not have been beyond me, but no, I did not influence the mayor," Mr. Citteroni said.

She tilted her head to the side and regarded him. "Then what does politics have to do with Archie's murder? I'm not following."

"Ben Hawkins, the town barber, threw his hat in for election. He is running unopposed," Michael added.

Lucy had heard this, but she didn't stay on top of local politics. Both Ben and Mayor Huckerby had been at the emergency festival committee meeting. "What does this have to do with the shooting?" The answer struck her just as she finished asking the question. She looked from Michael to Mr. Citteroni. "Did Archie have some dirt on Ben? Something that would hurt his chances for election for mayor?"

Her question was cut short when the waiter arrived with dessert. A plate of tiramisu was placed before her along with cappuccino with a sugar stick for stirring. Despite her desire to reach for her spoon, she held still and kept eye contact with Mr. Citteroni.

"I have many acquaintances. I asked a few of them the same question before agreeing to meet you," Mr. Citteroni said.

She held her breath. "And what did they say?"

He picked up his spoon, ate a bite of tiramisu, then took his time to answer. "You followed one of my men once. I think you should follow Mr. Hawkins."

Lucy froze. She'd suspected he'd learned about her and Katie's surveillance of his henchman months ago, but he'd never *directly* said anything to her. Anxiety kicked in her gut.

Was that one of the reasons he'd asked her to meet for dinner? So he could tell her he knew she'd meddled in his business in the past *and* give her critical information about Archie's murder?

"Like I said, Ms. Berberian, politics is a dirty business," Mr. Citteroni said, then continued to eat his dessert.

It was clear that he was finished speaking. Michael had once said his father enjoyed toying with people like a puppeteer playing with a marionette's strings. Lucy certainly felt like a marionette at the moment. But she was grateful. Mr. Citteroni had shared important information with her.

She glanced at Michael and he shrugged a shoulder. She knew, without a doubt, that her friendship with Michael had aided her with his father.

Her mind spun as she ate her tiramisu and contemplated Mr. Citteroni's mysterious words. Was Ben a gambler in Atlantic City? Did he have a criminal rap sheet? He wasn't married so he couldn't be cheating on a spouse.

The question was: What dirt had Archie had on the future mayor of Ocean Crest?

Stan Slade was the last person Lucy wanted to run into on her way to town hall to see Katie during her lunch hour. A hot pizza box in her arms, Lucy was bringing Katie lunch and planned to summarize her dinner conversation with Mr. Citteroni last night.

"Ms. Berberian, what are you doing here?"

Lucy glanced at the pizza box as if the answer was obvious. "I'm delivering lunch for a friend."

Stan sneered at her. "I thought you worked in a Mediterranean restaurant." He was stocky and muscular. Dressed in a shirt and tie, he didn't look like he had much of a neck, his head resting directly on his shoulders.

"I've been craving pizza, and Guido Morelli makes the best," Lucy said.

He eyed her though his black-rimmed glasses. "Any chance you'll give me a quick interview about the boardwalk shooting?"

Lucy blinked. "I have nothing to say."

"Sure you do. You found the body, and my readers want to read all about it."

"No."

She'd rather get a flu shot than give him an interview. Knowing Stan, he'd twist her words and take something out of context.

"You were quick to call me for publicity for your wine and food tasting. But when things go south, you're not willing to talk?" he said.

"That's right."

"Is that pizza for your friend Katie?" he asked.

"None of your business."

He drew his lips in a tight smile. "Really? Last I heard, Mrs. Watson was a person of interest."

She glowered at him. "Where do you get your information? I thought reporters had to confirm their facts."

Stan lowered his voice a notch. "You can put me off as long as you like, but I'm not leaving town anytime soon."

Footsteps on the tile drew their attention. They turned to see Katie step into the vestibule.

"Hey, Lucy. We can eat on the bench outside and . . ." Katie stopped short at the sight of Stan standing behind Lucy. "Oh, I didn't realize you weren't alone."

"It's okay. Mr. Slade has town hall business. I just happened to run into him here."

Stan glanced from Katie back to Lucy. "I'm here to see the tax assessor. It's part of my research about an upcoming tax assessment in town. The only thing more important to my readers than taxes is murder."

Katie's brow knit, but she didn't rise to the bait.

"The tax assessor is in his office. You can head on back."

Katie took Lucy's arm and ushered her outside. "What was that about?"

"Stan's getting antsy about an interview. He actually mentioned that you were a person of interest."

"Damn!"

"Either way, we have to be careful around him," Lucy said.

They headed for a single bench that rested beneath a tall sycamore tree in front of the building. Lucy set the pizza box down on the bench, and they sat. "It's a margarita pizza from Guido's pizzeria."

"Smells great."

Katie opened the pizza box and inhaled the scent of fresh mozzarella, basil, and tomato sauce. Lucy had brought paper plates and napkins and they helped themselves.

"I'm glad I went to meet Mr. Citteroni. But I was also happy that Michael was there. His father still makes me nervous," Lucy said.

"I take it he told you something useful."

"He did." After quickly summarizing her conversation with Mr. Citteroni the prior evening, Lucy took a bite of pizza. She chewed slowly, then swallowed. "Mr. Citteroni also said Ben is running for town mayor."

"That's right. Thomas Huckerby is stepping down," Katie said.

"Mr. Citteroni suggested that Archie had something that could harm Ben's chances of election."

Katie whistled through her teeth. "Ben's running unopposed, but that could change. If Archie had dirt on Ben, it's motive for murder. I wouldn't put it past Archie to stoop low enough to use blackmail. Did Mr. Citteroni say what Archie had on Ben?"

"No." Lucy's lips drew in as she thought. "He told me to spy on Ben."

"Spy? How?"

"We can always set up a stakeout and follow him."

"Are you crazy?" Katie glared at her.

Even though Katie loved watching crime and detective shows, she was hesitant to act like a detective herself.

"Why? We did it before, we have experience," Lucy said.

"One time does not make us experts," Katie argued. "Plus, we barely escaped unscathed, remember?"

It would be a long time before Lucy forgot their narrow escape in a dark back alley. "You're right. We'll have to think of a way."

"When? Archie's funeral is tomorrow," Katie pointed out.

"Let me think about—"

Lucy's thought was cut off by the scrape of footsteps on the walkway. She looked up to see Harold Harper barrel toward them. Sunlight glinted off his reddish hair, and his goatee was untrimmed. He was dressed in an untucked, collarless shirt, tan cargo shorts, and sandals.

"Why am I not surprised to see you two together again, ladies?" Harold said.

"I work here," Katie said.

His gaze turned to Lucy. "Her, too?"

"No," Lucy said.

Harold shrugged. "I'm here to renew my dog license."

"I handle that," Katie said.

"I didn't know you had a dog," Lucy said.

"A ten-year-old bulldog." Harold whipped out his wallet to show her a picture of a solid, barrel-bodied bulldog lounging on a couch. "That's Axel."

The dog looked like the owner. Or the owner looked like the dog. It was uncanny.

Harold snapped his wallet closed and shoved it into his back pocket. "I never thanked you for ousting Archie at the sand sculpture contest, Mrs. Watson."

Lucy and Katie both stared at him in surprise. Archie was dead and he showed no remorse. He'd been the one to point his finger at Rita at the emergency beach festival committee meeting, and when Katie had stuck up for the beautician, Harold had been quick to point the finger at Katie.

And now he was thanking her?

Katie sat straight. "I find it disconcerting the way you talk about Archie."

"Why?" Harold asked.

"Because he's dead," Lucy said.

"There was no love lost between us. I wasn't the only one Archie rubbed the wrong way. If you ask me, the shooter did us all a favor."

CHAPTER 15

Thursday rolled around, and Lucy and Katie contemplated not attending Archie's funeral, but at the last minute they decided to go and pay their respects. Most of the town would attend the Catholic church on the corner of Ocean Avenue and Shell Street that morning, and Lucy felt like they should join them.

The streets around the church were packed with cars, and a black hearse was parked directly in front of the church. A bright, orange flag imprinted with FUNERAL was attached to the rear-view window and waved in a slight ocean breeze.

The last funeral Lucy had attended was for her grandmother. It had been in the dead of winter, and she'd stood shivering at the gravesite as the casket had been lowered into the snow-covered ground. She'd cried and had come down with a cold the next day. It was a miserable experience.

She'd hated funerals ever since.

A closed casket, surrounded by arrangements

of fresh flowers, was in the front of the church. Lucy and Katie sat closer to the back of the church and listened to the organ music as more and more people shuffled inside and filled the pews. Lucy wasn't surprised to see that the church quickly filled. Ocean Crest was a close-knit town and when one of their own passed, many mourners would show up and pay their respects. Even though Archie had only been an Ocean Crest resident for a little over a year, he was a boardwalk businessman and considered a local.

Lucy spotted Mayor Huckerby in the front pew. Directly behind him was Ben Hawkins. Ben tapped him on the shoulder and Thomas turned and they exchanged words.

Interesting.

She wondered what kind of relationship the current mayor and the man running for his political position shared.

Rita Sides was also in the front row. Dressed in a form-fitting black dress, her blond hair contrasted with her dark outfit. She sat with Beatrice Tretola and several others ladies from The Big Tease Salon.

Beatrice passed Rita a tissue and Rita blew her nose. She wasn't sporting an engagement ring, and once again, Lucy wondered at Rita's reaction when she'd learned the diamond Archie had given her was not real, but a fake, cubic zirconia stone. Still, Rita appeared pretty broken up about Archie's death, and a lump rose in Lucy's throat.

"I really hate funerals," Lucy whispered to Katie. "They remind me of my grandmother's."

Katie reached into her purse and pulled out a

travel pack of tissues. "I brought these just in case. I don't like them either. My nana died before I married Bill, and I cried like a baby."

A rustle behind them drew their attention to the door. Neil entered the church with a woman on his arm. He must have borrowed a suit because the jacket and pants were too big for his tall, lanky frame, but he'd shaved and smoothed his long hair and tied it in a ponytail. He looked somewhat presentable.

But it was the woman he was escorting that captured Lucy's interest. Dressed in a tight-fitting black pants suit and stilettos, her mahogany hair was styled in an elegant chiffon. She was older, probably in her late fifties, but her makeup was expertly applied. She sported a large diamond and sparkly, matching band. As they walked by, her perfume wafted to Lucy. A crisp citrus scent that probably cost over a hundred dollars an ounce.

"Who's that?" Katie asked.

"I've never seen her before. Maybe she's Neil's mother."

They watched as Neil escorted the woman to the front pew. Rita shot her a questioning look, then turned to whisper in Beatrice's ear. Beatrice shrugged, and Lucy suspected they were just as clueless as to the woman's identity.

"Look who else is here," Katie said, pointing to the left side of the sanctuary.

Detective Clemmons sat with three other Ocean Crest officers. As if he knew they were talking about him, Clemmons turned and caught Lucy's gaze. His lips curled in what could only be described as a smirk, and he turned away.

"Clemmons really doesn't like me," Lucy said.

"Don't worry about him. Bill says that he doesn't like anyone. But he's not the one I was pointing to. Harold is here."

"Harold? Where?" Lucy spotted him sitting two rows behind the police officers. His reddish hair and square chin were unmistakable. "I can't believe he's here. He hated Archie."

"Maybe he's here for show. And if Harold did kill Archie, then he'd draw attention to himself by *not* coming to the funeral."

Lucy wasn't sure, but her thoughts were interrupted when the organist began playing and a black-robed priest took to the podium. Everyone obediently stood and joined in a prayer and hymn.

"Receive the Lord's blessing. May the Lord bless you and watch over you."

Lucy's gaze was drawn to the closed coffin, then back to the mourners. The priest continued speaking, but the words were a distant murmur as her gaze kept returning to the coffin.

Questions arose in her mind. Was the murderer in the church? Could he or she be hiding in plain view? Chances were the killer was someone they all knew—someone who had a strong enough motive to want Archie dead.

Sunlight streamed through the stained-glass windows. The church's air-conditioning struggled to keep up with the packed room, and mourners fanned themselves with funeral programs about Archie's life.

Her thoughts continued to churn as the priest droned on and on.

Everything changed when Neil stood and went

to the podium. He tapped the mic, causing a burst of static. Once again, she thought his borrowed suit and ponytail were a big improvement over his normal beach attire and mussed, shoulder-length hair.

Neil cleared his throat. "My uncle was a great man. He helped me and volunteered at the local teenage drug shelter."

Lucy wondered if that was where he'd found Neil. So far, his speech wasn't half bad.

"Even though he's gone, he still took care of me and left me his shop. I'll always be grateful." Neil turned to look at the woman he'd escorted into the church. "But I'm not the only one who is feeling his loss. He also left behind my aunt, his wife."

His wife? Silence descended in the sanctuary.

"What's he talking about?" Lucy whispered.

Katie shrugged. "No clue."

"My aunt would like to say a few words," Neil said.

Everyone watched, riveted, as the polished, dark-haired woman climbed the steps to the podium. She reached up to lower the microphone and a glint of sunlight from the overhead stained-glass window reflected off her bloodred painted nails. "I'm Kristin Kincaid, Archie's wife."

A loud gasp sounded from the front row. Beatrice and the salon ladies began to vigorously fan Rita with their programs.

Did Rita know about Kristin? Judging from her waxy complexion, it didn't look like it. Or was Rita putting on her own show?

Kristin cleared her throat. "Many of you expect me to say Archie was a good husband. He wasn't. We had our difficulties, just like many married couples. But the saying 'opposites attract' is true, and we were drawn together from the first moment we met. He was also supportive. I took a job as an editor in New York City for a fashion magazine, and he encouraged my decision, even though he knew we would be apart for long periods of time. Sadly, I never had the opportunity to visit my husband in Ocean Crest . . . until today. He understood my ambitions just as I understood his. He made the effort to visit me once a month for years. He was loyal."

Loyal? Did Kristin know about Archie's mistress sitting a few feet away in the front pew?

"Archie also looked after my nephew, Neil." Kristin looked at Neil and he nodded.

"I just have one more thing to say," Kristin continued. "To whoever shot my husband"—her laserlike gaze roved the pews—"what goes around comes around." She ended her speech with that remark and stepped down from the podium.

Silence reigned once again. Lucy's thoughts raced as she grasped the meaning behind Kristin's words.

Organ music resumed, ending the awkwardness, as the funeral came to a close. One by one, mourners shuffled out of the church. A reception had been set up in the church hall, and most people would head straight there.

"That was unexpected," Katie said.

"More like shocking."

Katie chuckled. "You're right. No one in town knew Archie was married. Most of all, Rita."

"I want to talk to Rita," Lucy said.

"Now?"

"This may be the perfect time," Lucy whispered.

"She's emotional, and she might say something she wouldn't otherwise. It doesn't look like she knew Archie had a wife, but she could be acting. Maybe Archie had promised Rita he'd divorce Kristin but lied. It's motive for murder."

Katie rubbed her chin with a forefinger. "You're right. Maybe that's why Archie purchased a fake diamond in the engagement ring. He wanted to pacify Rita, but had no intention of leaving Kristin."

Together, they watched as Neil escorted Kristin out of the church. They hung back and waited until Beatrice and the salon ladies, with Rita nestled between them, headed out.

"Rita!" Lucy called out.

Beatrice turned. "Hi, Lucy. Rita's not feeling that well. I'm afraid we're going to have to miss the reception and take her home."

"I just wanted to ask her a question," Lucy said.

"Come by the salon, hon," Beatrice said as she ushered Rita out of the church and into the parking lot.

"Did you see Rita's face?" Katie said. "She's pale as a ghost. I don't think she's acting."

Lucy craned to see outside the church. Beatrice opened a car door, and Rita slid inside. "What if she knew Archie was married, but she never met Kristin? It could still be a shock to see her face-to-face."

"But how can we find out?"

"I need to make another trip to the salon," Lucy said.

"A manicure?"

"I wish it was that easy. Rita does waxing."

Katie smirked. "Better you than me."

* * *

The air-conditioning in the church hall was working better than in the sanctuary. The guests breathed an audible sigh of relief as soon as they stepped inside. Everyone in town wanted to meet Kristin. Lucy and Katie watched as people waited in line to expresses their condolences and speak with Archie's widow. Gossip was valued in Ocean Crest and the funeral did not disappoint.

Two ladies from the town council, Gertrude Shaw and Francesca Stevens, were standing in line and whispering behind hands as they shifted from side to side to get a better look at Archie's wife. Both women were notorious gossips.

"Kristin doesn't seem like Archie's type," Katie said.

"You mean she's too sophisticated? She said she works for a New York fashion magazine. It explains the clothes, hair, and makeup," Lucy said. "Maybe what she said about opposites attracting is true. I know couples like this. The heart wants what it wants."

"Maybe, but Bill always says spouses are usually at the top of the suspect list. It's the same in all the TV crime shows," Katie murmured.

Katie was on a kick of *Hawaii Five-O* episodes and *Matlock* reruns. Katie had liked detective shows for as far back as Lucy could recall, and Lucy had suspected it was one of the reasons her friend had been attracted to Bill in high school after he'd announced he was attending the police academy.

"Kristin couldn't have killed Archie. She said today was the first time she'd visited Ocean Crest. Archie had traveled to see her in New York, not the other way around," Lucy said.

"Detective Clemmons should interview her to verify her story and to see if she knows anything," Katie said.

Lucy scanned the crowd. Detective Clemmons was at the end of the buffet line, adding food to his heaping plate. "Could he be less interested in solving the case?" Lucy asked.

"He can't question Kristin here with all these people present. Plus, it's her husband's funeral. Clemmons should interview Kristin later."

"We can only hope," Lucy said. But she didn't have much faith in the town's sole investigator.

"There's no sense standing in line now. Let's get some food, then come back when the line to meet Kristin dies down," Katie suggested.

The funeral was catered by a seafood restaurant just outside of town, the Crab House, which had a reputation for fresh seafood. They headed for the buffet table and filled their plates with herb-stuffed oysters, mini crab quiche, and berry tarts for dessert. Unlike most buffet food that was underseasoned and plain, the crab quiche was tasty, the oysters expertly prepared, and the tart was surprisingly flavorful.

The line for Kristin was still long, so they headed for the bar and ordered glasses of Chardonnay.

"That was a surprise," a man said to Lucy's right.

"All that time and I didn't know Archie was married," a second male voice added.

Lucy recognized the voices and turned to see Mayor Huckerby, speaking with Ben.

Lucy stepped forward and caught the mayor's eye. "Well, hello there, Lucy. Hello, Katie," Huckerby said.

"Hi, Mayor. Mr. Hawkins," Lucy said.

"The buffet is good, but it's not as tasty as Kebab Kitchen's shish kebab," the mayor said, then winked.

Lucy smiled. The mayor's charm was one of the reasons he'd been elected. Even her parents liked him, and Angela and Raffi could spot a phony person a mile away.

"I hear Mr. Hawkins is running for your position. No hard feelings between you two?" Lucy asked.

"None. I want to retire and fish." The mayor slapped Ben on the back. "Ben's a hardworking businessman, and a lifelong resident of Ocean Crest. He's a perfect replacement for mayor."

"I'll have to work hard to fill his shoes," Ben said.

"Who will run our barber shop?" Katie asked.

"The shop will stay open. I plan to hire help and fill in as much as I can," Ben said.

"I'm sorry to bring this up, but can you reconsider resuming the festival? We feel it should still go on," Katie said.

"With a murderer on the loose?" Huckerby said. "As mayor I must take our townsfolk's safety and that of our visitors into consideration and listen to our detective's recommendations. I'm sorry, but the festival is on hold."

"I agree with the mayor as well," Ben said.

Lucy's gaze shifted to Ben's. He was in his early forties, with a lightly pockmarked face, bushy eyebrows, and thinning brown hair.

Mr. Citteroni's words came back to her regarding the barber. *Politics is a dirty business.*

Was Ben corrupt? He didn't seem to have a rivalry with the current mayor. Rather, they appeared to be amicable, even good friends.

So what could Archie have had on the barber?

"We were just on our way to meet Mrs. Kincaid and express our condolences," Lucy said.

"You better get in line before she tires and leaves," Huckerby said.

After finishing their food, Lucy and Katie set their plates down and stood in line. Lucy watched Kristin as she met person after person and accepted condolences. The widow wasn't crying. Not a smudge marred her expertly applied makeup. Still, she could be in shock. Funerals were difficult and Kristin was surrounded by strangers. It wasn't a far stretch to believe she'd grieve in private.

At last it was their turn, and Lucy and Katie approached Kristin. "I'm Lucy Berberian and this is Katie Watson. We knew your husband. We're sorry for your loss, Mrs. Kincaid."

Kristin's handshake was weak. "Thank you. I miss Archie very much."

"To be honest, we didn't know he was married. I don't think anyone in town knew," Katie said.

"Archie was a quiet man."

Quiet? Lucy's mind turned back to the sand sculpture contest. Archie had nearly gotten into fisticuffs with Harold and then Katie.

"Funny, but we don't remember him that way," Lucy said. She struggled with how best to describe him without insulting his widow. "He was very . . . very animated."

"Oh? Well, you didn't know him as well as I did." A haughty look crossed Kristin's face.

Lucy's opinion changed. *Definitely not grieving.*

"How long were you married?" Katie asked.

"Three years."

"And you were in New York the entire time?" Lucy asked.

"Yes. Like I said at the funeral, we saw each other one weekend a month. Archie always traveled to see me."

"When was the last weekend you saw him?" Lucy asked.

"A full month ago."

"You weren't in Ocean Crest the weekend of the festival?" Lucy asked, hoping to get her to admit to something.

"No. Today is the first time I've ever set foot in this little ocean town." Annoyance streaked across her face. "Why all the questions? There's an Ocean Crest detective right over there." Her gaze darted to where Clemmons stood and continued to stuff his face with food. "If anyone is going to ask me so many questions, I'd expect it to be him. Now if you will excuse me, there are other people here who want to express their condolences."

It was clear they'd been dismissed. Lucy waited until they were out of earshot before whistling through her teeth. "She's a nasty one."

"We probably shouldn't judge her too harshly. We rubbed her the wrong way by asking her all those questions. Besides, if her story checks out and she wasn't in town when Archie was shot, then she couldn't have killed him," Katie said.

Another dead end.

Lucy's gaze shifted to Ben. He was talking with the mayor and laughing. Why had Mr. Citteroni warned her about him? The mobster never did anything without a purpose. What was she missing?

They needed to find out. If Archie had been

blackmailing Ben with something . . . something that could ruin his political aspirations, then it could be motive for murder.

Neil crossed the room to stand beside Kristin.

"They look friendly," Katie said. "He must have known about her. He lived with Archie."

"I wonder if Neil is unhappy with Kristin back in the picture."

"What do you mean?"

"He's the new owner of Seaside Gifts. Don't you think the business should go to Kristin as Archie's wife?" Lucy asked.

"The business has to be worth a good chunk of change," Katie said.

"But it's not liquid cash." Lucy knew this first-hand. Kebab Kitchen was worth a sizeable amount of money when you added up the real estate, the building, and the equipment, but none of it was liquid, and her parents lived modestly and within their means.

"Excuse me. I need to go to the ladies' room," Lucy said.

"Go ahead. I see Francesca Stevens. She loves to gossip, so maybe I'll learn something about Kristin," Katie said.

Lucy made a right out of the church hall and headed down a long corridor. The church hall had gone through numerous additions and was a maze of corridors. She thought the ladies' room was one direction, but when she'd walked for a while and didn't see a sign, she realized she'd made a wrong turn. Just as she was about to backtrack, she heard a male voice farther down the hall.

"I told you not to call me today."

Was that Ben's voice? Lucy crept father down the dim hall until she came to the end, then risked a peek around the corner.

It was Ben. He clutched his cell phone and paced back and forth. A row of closed doors, marked with brass nameplates, lined the hall. One of the brass nameplates read SUNDAY SCHOOL.

"I'm not avoiding you. I promise. How about you come see me tonight at the barbershop?" Ben said, wiping his brow with a handkerchief as he paced back and forth.

He was clearly nervous. Lucy wished she knew who was on the other end of the line.

"Tonight. I promise. We can talk then," Ben said.

Lucy jumped at the sound of a door opening behind her. She swung around to see a man pushing a catering cart loaded with cut pies and pastries toward the church hall. He never looked in her direction.

She turned back in time to see Ben shove his cell phone in his pocket and head her way.

Crap.

She'd never make it back to the church hall in time. Making a snap decision, she turned the corner and ran smack into Ben.

"Oh! Hi, Ben. I'm sorry. I'm looking for the ladies' room. You don't happen to know if it's this way?" Lucy asked, as she quickly masked her nervousness.

Ben's brows drew downward. "It's at the opposite end of the hall."

"Thanks!" she said, then waved and hurried in the direction he'd pointed. She felt his gaze boring into her back as she slipped into the ladies' room. Heart pounding, she gazed into the mirror and prayed he didn't suspect she'd eavesdropped on his conversation.

Once she was back among the throng of people, she immediately sought out Katie. Her friend was helping herself to a mini cheesecake from the dessert tray.

"What are you doing tonight?" Lucy asked.

"Nothing. Why?" Katie asked.

"We need to set up a stakeout outside the barber-shop."

CHAPTER 16

Ben's barbershop was located in a small shopping strip next to Cutie's Cupcakes. Katie had parked her Jeep down the street. It was late and the sun had gone down. Close to closing time, the spiraling red and white barber pole shone brightly in the darkness. The windows of the Jeep were rolled down and a warm breeze blew the hair at Lucy's nape and carried a hint of the ocean.

"Looks like he has one last customer inside," Katie said.

"Hope he's done soon." Lucy reached for a coffee in the Jeep's cup holder. They had hit Lola's Coffee Shop for two large cups before heading over for their stakeout of Ben's shop.

Inside, Ben set down a pair of clippers, brushed loose hair from the neck of a seated customer with a bristled brush, then whipped a cape off the man. The customer stood and headed for the counter to pay.

"You sure Ben is expecting someone tonight?" Katie asked.

"That's what he said when I overheard his conversation. And from the tone of his voice, he seemed uptight about it," Lucy said.

The customer left the shop, and Lucy and Katie continued to drink coffee and watch the front door.

"What if he changes his mind and leaves to meet the mystery person?" Katie asked.

"If he does, we'll know it. His car is parked out front."

They waited for another forty-five minutes until they were out of coffee. Katie yawned. "What's he doing inside?"

"Maybe he's cleaning up." Lucy never left Kebab Kitchen right after the last customer departed. Tables needed to be set for the following day, the dishwasher had to be run, and the kitchen had to be swept and wiped down. She didn't think it would take as long for a barbershop.

So what was Ben doing inside?

As they watched, Ben sat in one of the black chairs and began to check his cell phone.

"This could take all night," Katie said.

"Wait! Who's that?"

Lucy's eyes were drawn to a black car that drew up to the corner of the shopping strip and parked. The door opened and a pretty woman dressed in a Catholic school uniform stepped out. She was in her mid-twenties, with long brown hair, and lots of makeup. Her pleated blue and green plaid skirt was ridiculously short and she wore a short, collared white top that revealed her pierced belly button. Combined with the tall blue socks and black-and-white saddle shoes, she looked like a centerfold model.

"Check out her getup," Katie drawled. "She's a teenage boy's dream come true."

"She's headed for Ben's shop. Duck so she doesn't spot us."

They slouched in their seats and watched as she approached the barbershop. She didn't enter the front of the shop as Lucy had anticipated, but walked down the side alley of the building toward the back.

"Where's she going?" Katie asked.

"I'm not sure, but let's follow her," Lucy said.

Katie grasped Lucy's arm before she could open the Jeep's door. "Are you sure about this?" Her voice was full of anxiety. "Remember what happened the last time we followed a person down a dark alley?"

They'd also hidden behind a Dumpster and barely made it to Lucy's car before being caught by Mr. Citteroni's henchman. Lucy pushed aside her trepidation. "I remember that we overheard helpful information that night."

At Katie's hesitation, Lucy pressed. "Come on. I don't want to lose her."

Katie sighed, then opened the door and trailed behind. They crept down the side of the brick building, careful not to make a sound. A back-security light cast an eerie glow on the trash and recycle cans. An old fishing boat that had been covered with a faded, green tarp sat on cinderblocks in the corner.

The woman stood on the back porch and rapped

on the back door. The door opened and Ben stepped onto the porch to join her.

"Did anyone see you?" Ben asked, his voice tense.

"Don't worry. There's no one around at night in this town, Benny."

Benny?

Lucy moved closer. She couldn't hear the pair as clearly as she wanted, and she didn't want to miss any of their conversation. She eyed the old boat and motioned to Katie.

Katie shook her head.

Lucy tugged her hand. Katie bit her lip, then nodded in agreement.

They crept closer, careful to stay in the dark shadows of the alley, then sprinted the remaining distance and pasted their backs to the old boat. Lucy feared the pair could hear her pounding heart. She lifted the tarp, stepped on a cinderblock, and slipped inside the boat. Katie was quick to follow.

The seats had been removed, so Lucy and Katie landed on the bottom of the boat. Despite the tarp, there was an inch of old rainwater inside.

"It stinks in here," Katie whispered.

Lucy pressed a finger to her lips, then lifted the edge of the tarp to peek outside. From here, they could see and hear everything.

"It's risky, baby," Ben said.

"I needed to see you, Benny," the woman said, then sidled up to him.

"God, it's been too long, Vanessa." Ben pulled her into his arms and kissed her. She rose on her tiptoes in the saddle shoes and kissed him back.

"Ugh," Katie mumbled.

Ben lifted his head to gaze down at his girlfriend. "I don't want you to work at the Pussy Cat anymore."

The Pussy Cat? Lucy had heard of it—a strip club out of town. She used to see billboards on the Atlantic City Expressway advertising the place, but she hadn't seen them in a long time and assumed the club had closed.

Vanessa pouted. "You know I'll quit as soon as you give me a ring."

"I can't do that yet. Not until after the election."

"You're embarrassed of me."

Ben shook his head. "No, baby. It's just that Ocean Crest is a small, family-friendly town. I don't know how the residents would take to us."

"You mean because I'm a stripper."

"Well, yes."

Vanessa's face hardened, and she pulled out of Ben's embrace. "Archie is dead. You don't have to worry about those pictures anymore."

Ben's mouth dipped in a frown. "Archie may be dead. But pictures of our lap dance and more are still out there."

Vanessa planted her hands on her hips. "That bastard blackmailed you when he was alive. Don't let him blackmail you from the grave. Find those pictures."

"I tried once and failed. I don't know if I can do it again and—"

"You have no choice." Her expression softened, and she stepped close to rub against him. "Don't you want to officially tie the knot?"

"You know I do," Ben whined.

"Then do it for us, Benny. Finish the job."

* * *

"This will calm our nerves," Katie said as she handed Lucy a glass of merlot.

Lucy accepted the glass and took a sip. Only after they'd returned to Katie's house had they been able to breathe a sigh of relief. Their clothes had been dirty and wet from hiding in the old boat, and they'd both changed into yoga pants and T-shirts.

"Mr. Citteroni was right. Politics is a dirty business. Archie had been blackmailing Ben with pictures of him with a stripper," Lucy said as she sat on a sofa.

Katie refilled her wineglass. "It looks like Ben and Vanessa are having a fling."

"Not just a fling, but a serious relationship. They were talking about getting engaged."

"A political candidate and a stripper. That will go over like hotcakes in Ocean Crest," Katie said.

Lucy sipped her wine. "Archie knew just how bad it would look. Ben's political aspirations for mayor would be ruined."

"How did Archie get the pictures of the two of them?" Katie asked.

"Sounds like Ben met Vanessa at the Pussy Cat. Archie could have taken the pictures anywhere. At the club. In the car. Snooping outside Ben's barbershop or even his house," Lucy said.

"Ben said he'd tried to get the pictures back and failed. Maybe Archie was blackmailing him for cash, and Ben lured him under the boardwalk and shot him," Katie said.

"Or maybe Archie wasn't blackmailing Ben for cash, but something else."

"Like what?"

"Mr. Citteroni confirmed that Archie wanted a mercantile license to open a bicycle shop. You said Mayor Huckerby was opposed to the idea, and Archie's license was denied. But Ben is running unopposed for mayor. Once he was elected, he could help Archie get whatever business license he wanted," Lucy said.

"Archie would have the future mayor in his back pocket. It's brilliant," Katie said.

As Lucy sipped her wine another thought occurred to her. "Something else is bothering me. Ben told Vanessa that he'd tried to get the pictures back. What if Ben was the one who tried to break into Archie's shop?"

"You think Ben was the burglar who was interrupted when the Gray sisters called the police?" Katie asked.

"It's a likely scenario. Ben had a strong motive to get those pictures," Lucy said.

"If so, then he never found them. Bill said nothing was taken or disturbed. The burglar fled as soon as he heard the police sirens," Katie said.

"That means the pictures could still be there. We need to search Archie's store and find them," Lucy said.

Katie lowered her wineglass. "You're not thinking what I think you're thinking, are you?"

"We have to find a way to sneak into Seaside Gifts," Lucy said.

"You're kidding."

"We have nothing to lose."

"Only getting arrested," Katie said.

"We'll be careful. More careful than Ben. If we find those pictures, we can give them to Bill. It will help clear *your* name."

CHAPTER 17

Early the next day, Lucy visited The Big Tease Salon. It was Friday, and Katie was still covering for a coworker. They'd decided to hold off on their plans with Seaside Gifts until Katie's lunch hour.

Beatrice Tretola was counting money at the register when Lucy walked into the salon.

"Hi, Lucy! What can I do for you today? A trim? A manicure? Or a pedicure?"

"No, thanks. I'm here for Rita's services. Is she here today?" Lucy wasn't sure she'd return to work so soon after Archie's funeral, but Lucy was rewarded when Beatrice nodded.

"Rita's out back for a smoke break. She's been smoking more than working since yesterday's funeral, but I'm not complaining. Turns out they had a thing for each other, and the ladies here never knew. Myself included." Beatrice lowered her voice. "Of course, none of us knew he was married. Rita didn't know either, poor thing."

Did Rita know or not? Lucy hoped to learn the answer to that question today.

"I'll fetch Rita." Beatrice strode off and parted the curtains to the back room. Soon after, Beatrice reappeared through the curtains, followed by Rita.

Rita wore a tight red dress, black tights, and high-heeled boots. Her blond hair was pulled back tightly from her face in a ponytail. The hairstyle emphasized her high cheekbones and sharp chin. Except for missing a whip, she looked like a dominatrix, not a grieving woman. Lucy wasn't sure she wanted her anywhere near her with a pot of hot wax.

Lucy swallowed. "Hi, Rita."

"Beatrice says you asked for me."

"I did. I'd like to have my eyebrows thinned a bit." A very small bit. Lucy didn't have bushy brows. She actually liked her God-given eyebrows.

Sacrifices for the greater good. Or, in this case, for information.

"Take a seat over there." Rita pointed to one of the shiny black seats.

That wouldn't do. She needed to speak with Rita in private. "Ah, isn't there a back room?"

"That's only for customers who want a leg, underarm, or bikini wax."

Good grief. An eyebrow wax was painful enough. Did she have to endure more to get Rita alone?

"Let's start with the eyebrows and see how it goes," Lucy said. "I may want to have my lower leg waxed."

"Fine. Follow me."

Rita's boot heels tapped on the linoleum floor as she walked to the back of the salon. Lucy passed ladies with rollers sitting beneath hair dryers and reading fashion magazines. Rita led her through the back curtain, but instead of heading into the room with all the supplies, they turned right and stopped at a closed door. Rita pulled a key from her pocket, unlocked the door, and ushered Lucy inside.

It was a small room with a table covered with similar paper that a doctor's office used. The room was painted a buttercup yellow, and what looked like a Crock-Pot sat on a counter. Rita lit an aroma therapy candle and the scent of jasmine soon filled the room.

"Sit on the table."

The paper crinkled beneath Lucy as she sat. Rita set to work mixing the contents of the pot with a wooden Popsicle stick—the same kind that the doctor stuck in your mouth, held down your tongue, and swabbed your throat with and nearly choked you to death.

"I saw you at Archie's funeral. Again, I'm so sorry for your loss," Lucy said.

"It was a bad day."

"We were all shocked to learn about Kristin."

Rita halted mixing and her face paled a shade, then she went back to stirring the wax with increasing rigor. It reminded Lucy of a cauldron of witch's brew.

"I tried to talk to you as you left the funeral, but you didn't look so good. Was it the funeral or the unexpected appearance of Archie's wife?" Lucy asked.

Rita swung around. "Are you here to ask me questions or to get your eyebrows waxed?"

She didn't wait for an answer and approached with the Popsicle stick. Before Lucy could respond, she smeared the wax on a portion of her right eyebrow.

Rip!

"Ouch!"

"Don't be a baby. It looks much better." She grabbed a hand mirror and thrust it at Lucy. "See."

Lucy looked in the mirror. Her right eyebrow was definitely thinner. It also no longer matched her left one.

Damn. She had to go through it again.

"After we're done with your eyebrows, I can wax your lower legs. The hair only has to be as long as a grain of rice."

"It's not. I shaved yesterday."

"Too bad. Stop shaving and come see me in two weeks."

No way.

Lucy shifted on the bench and the paper crinkled beneath her. "I know you dated Archie. Did you know he was married?"

Rita planted her hands on her hips. "You're really here to question me, aren't you? No wonder you asked to come back here instead of having me wax your eyebrows out front."

"I'm not here to judge you."

"Oh?"

Lucy scrambled with a plausible excuse. "I'm on the festival committee, remember?"

"There is no festival. It's been canceled because Archie was shot."

Rita was quick to catch on. Lucy decided to just go for it and confront her with what she knew. "I know the engagement ring Archie gave you had a fake diamond."

Rita's face fell. "How do you know that?"

"I visited the jeweler. She let it slip."

"Fine. I'll tell you, but not because of your fake excuse of a festival committee. When we started dating, I didn't know Archie was married. He never said a word, and he didn't wear a wedding band. Neil never said anything either, the jerk."

"But you found out?" Lucy asked.

"I overheard Archie talking to someone on his cell phone. He called her his 'bunny,' which is the same thing he used to call me. I took his cell when he wasn't looking, searched the call history, and called Kristin. That's when I learned he was married."

"That must have been awkward."

"Oh, I never actually spoke with Kristin, but with her secretary. I asked when was the best time to deliver flowers, and the secretary said his wife would be working in the office all week and would love them. I would have confronted her face-to-face, but she didn't travel to Ocean Crest to see Archie. He visited her in the city."

Kristin had said as much during the funeral. Archie traveling had a twofold purpose: he'd visit his wife, and Rita would never know he was married.

"Did you confront Archie?" Lucy asked.

"I did. He admitted he was married, but he said he never loved Kristin the way he loved me."

What a cheesy line. Did Rita buy it? If a man lied to Lucy about his marital status, she would be furious.

"Did you—"

"Take him back? No. I kicked him to the curb."

"You must have been furious," Lucy said.

"You mean was I mad enough to kill him?"

"Were you?"

"Yes, at first. But then I calmed down. I deserve a man who is honest, not someone living a double life."

A double life.

It was an accurate way to describe him. There was a lot more to Archie Kincaid than they'd thought. Even more than Katie had suspected. He had a wife, but kept a girlfriend. No one in town had known he'd been married. Archie wanted to expand his business and open a bike shop, and rather than take the current mayor's no for an answer, he'd targeted the upcoming Ocean Crest mayor and blackmailed him with pictures with a stripper.

What else was Archie hiding?

"You're right. You do deserve a better man."

Rita let out a sigh. "I can't let you leave here looking lopsided. Hold on." She dipped a new stick in the wax pot and came at Lucy. This time, Lucy flinched.

"Don't do that. Your brows won't be symmetrical if you scrunch your face."

Lucy forced herself to relax as Rita applied the wax. Lucy gripped the edge of the table in anticipation of the pain.

Rip!

Lucy rubbed her eyebrow. "People voluntarily get their legs waxed?"

"Yup. Their legs, their underarms, their backs.

You name it. You haven't lived until you've had a Brazilian wax."

God, no.

Rita handed her the mirror again. Lucy grudgingly admitted that her eyebrows looked nice.

"I didn't go overboard, just cleaned them up a bit," Rita said.

"Thanks. I was worried you'd take it out on me for asking personal questions."

Rita tossed the Popsicle stick in the trash and turned to look at Lucy. "I didn't kill Archie. You believe me, don't you?"

Either Rita was a spectacular actress, or she truly was innocent. She wouldn't be the first woman who'd been bamboozled by a cheating man.

"Why is it important to you that I believe you?" Lucy asked.

"You solved two murders before. I figure your track record is better than that detective's."

"Are you sure about sneaking around Archie's shop?" Katie asked.

"I am. If those blackmail pictures of Ben and Vanessa are in Seaside Gifts, then we need to find them. It shows strong motive for Ben to want Archie dead."

They were sitting on a boardwalk bench by the railing overlooking the beach. It was noon, and Katie had taken her lunch hour to meet Lucy on the boardwalk. It was also Lucy's parents' afternoon to watch Kebab Kitchen, and Lucy would return to run the dinner shift.

She breathed in the fresh ocean air and took in

the scene before her. Colorful umbrellas were spread across the beach, and sunbathers lay on towels and sat on beach chairs while people waded in the ocean. Children frolicked in the surf and built sandcastles with pails and shovels. The lifeguards watched from tall chairs.

"If we're lucky enough to find the compromising photos, then what? We can't just turn them in to the police. How do we explain how we found them?" Katie asked.

Katie had a good point. If they turned them in, then they would have to confess that they'd sneaked into the shop, rummaged through Archie's belongings, and found pictures of Ben and Vanessa.

"I guess we'd have to tell Bill," Lucy said.

Katie looked at her incredulously. "You're always the one who doesn't want to get Bill involved."

"I know." Bill had come to Lucy and asked her to help, or at least, listen and report any tidbits to him. She'd never told Katie about her meeting with Bill. "Well . . . um . . . Bill's been worried about you."

"He's always worried."

"He's voiced his concerns to me."

Katie's eyes narrowed. "What do you mean by 'voiced his concerns?'"

"We've met at the coffee shop to talk." Lucy flinched. She hated keeping anything from Katie, but she didn't want to betray Bill's confidence. Revealing that they'd had coffee to talk wasn't a betrayal, was it?

"He asked for your help, didn't he?" Kate's lips dipped into a frown.

"Don't be mad at him."

"He could have told me that he met with my best friend," she argued.

"He asked me to ask around. A lot of people come into the restaurant."

"He also knows you've been more successful lately than Calvin Clemmons's when it comes to solving crime," Katie said.

"He loves you."

Katie let out a slow breath. "I know. I love him, too. Stubborn man."

Lucy felt a stab of jealousy. She hadn't been blessed with a husband who loved her more than himself. Her relationship with Azad was rocky, at best. "You're lucky. I haven't been as fortunate in the male department."

"I think your luck is going to improve," Katie said.

Lucy didn't feel as confident. "I apologized to Azad, but I'm still not sure—"

"Maybe you need another visit with Madame Vega to boost your confidence."

Lucy burst out laughing. "I just might. I think she specializes in relationship advice."

In the distance, two boys tossed potato chips in the air and a swarm of seagulls swooped in. Their mother immediately scolded them. Lucy smiled as she watched the scene play out.

"Now, as for Archie's shop," Katie said, "I don't think Bill would want us to snoop inside."

"No, he wouldn't," Lucy said.

"But we're going to anyway, aren't we?"

Lucy stood. "All you have to do is distract Neil while I pretend to shop. I'll slip into the back room and see what I can find."

"Got it."

They passed the Sun and Surf Shop, Harold's store. Harold was flipping through a bin of boogie boards while a kid studied the design on each board.

They entered Seaside Gifts. Several tourists were inside, and Neil was behind the counter at the cash register. He was wearing a faded and frayed blue T-shirt. His long hair hung in his face and he looked like he'd just rolled out of bed—a far cry from how he'd presented himself at his uncle's funeral. Spray-painted canvases hung on the walls, dark splashes of color that gave off the vibe that the artist was angry or euphoric or both. Neil's latest artwork.

Lucy went to a rack of beach cover-ups near the back of the store and pretended to sort through each one while Katie headed straight for the counter.

"Hi. I'm looking for shorts for my husband," Katie said, her voice cheerful.

"All our shorts are at the front of the store," Neil said.

"He's picky. He only wears certain brands."

"Do you know what kind?" Neil asked.

"Not off the top of my head, but I think I can recognize them if I see them. Can you help me pick out a couple of pairs?" Katie asked.

"Sure." Neil stepped out from behind the counter and led Katie to a rack of men's clothing.

Smart Katie. She'd keep Neil occupied for a while.

Lucy didn't waste time. She slipped around the counter and headed to the back storage room. Boxes were stacked and labeled with everything from men's board shorts to bikinis to magnets, key chains, and bottle openers. A battered metal desk was in the corner, its surface crowded with papers and files. A computer and printer were on the desk. A large roll of duct tape and scissors sat next to the computer. A metal filing cabinet was to the right of the desk, and wooden shelves cluttered with more papers lined the wall behind the desk. A large canvas was propped against a squat box against the wall. The painting was of a woman looking over her shoulder as a shadow of a man loomed behind. The paint smelled fresh. It gave Lucy the creeps. It must be Neil's artwork.

She turned her attention back to the room. Simply put, it was a mess. She'd need hours to properly search.

Where to start?

Seconds were ticking by. Lucy sprinted to the desk and started searching. Invoices, order sheets, time slips, and old tax records were haphazardly scattered across the desk. She opened one of the side drawers. More papers. She shut the drawer and moved on to the next one.

Each desk drawer was just as cluttered. She was almost out of time. Katie could only hold off Neil for so long.

She had a strong suspicion that Ben had been the one to break into this shop in search of the incriminating photos.

She was sweating. There was no question. Lucy had to find a way to sneak back in here.

She closed the second drawer, and opened the slim drawer, which contained pens, pencils, erasers, and random-sized paper clips. Nothing.

Just as she was about to close the drawer, a

glimmer of sunlight from the window in the storage room door reflected off of something. A key.

She picked it up and looked at the key tag. It read SPARE.

Her heart kicked up a notch.

Could it be?

Her gaze flew to the back door. There was no dead bolt, just a lock in the doorknob. The burglar had pried open the rolling security gate in the front of the shop that led to the boardwalk. He didn't try to break in from the back door. She snatched the key and hurried to the door. The key slipped into the lock, turned, and the door opened.

Success!

Lucy closed the door and locked it with the key, then slipped the key into her back pocket.

She rushed from the storage room just as Neil and Katie were headed to the register. Heart thundering, Lucy ducked behind a shelf of sunscreen.

"Oh! I forgot one more thing. Bill wants a pair of new sunglasses, too. Can you just point me to where they are?" Katie asked.

"Over there." Neil turned to point to a wall on the store displaying a large selection of sunglasses.

Lucy darted to a rack of beach cover-ups she'd been pretending to shop for earlier.

Katie pressed a hand to her chest. "Thank you. I don't know how I could have missed that sunglass display."

"Neither do I," Neil muttered.

Katie paid and waved on her way out just as Neil noticed Lucy. "Can I help you?"

"No, thanks. I don't see what I'm looking for." She waggled her fingers and left the shop.

* * *

Katie waited for Lucy at the same bench where they'd met before they'd ventured into Seaside Gifts. Katie carried a bag from the place. Bill would be getting a few new items.

"Did you find anything?" Katie asked.

"No. I didn't have time to properly search. But I found this." Lucy held up the spare key.

"What's that?"

"A spare key to the back door."

Katie's blue eyes grew large. "How do you know?"

"The tag says SPARE. I also checked. It opens and locks the back door to the storage room. There's no alarm."

"Don't you think Neil will notice it missing?" Katie asked.

"No. The place was a mess. He won't notice for a while. At least, I hope he won't."

Katie eyed her warily. "What are we going to do with it?"

"We're coming back late tonight after everything is closed."

"You plan to break into the store?"

"I don't want to think of it that way. But yes. There's a good chance the blackmail pictures are inside," Lucy said.

"Can't we just tell the police?" Katie asked. "Clemmons can conduct a search."

"The police need probable cause to get a search warrant. We can't just tell them we snuck into an old boat and eavesdropped on Ben and Vanessa, then followed a tip and snuck into Seaside Gifts. Even if we did, I'm not sure that's sufficient to get a warrant and it will take time. We need to do it. I understand if you don't want to come," Lucy said.

"Don't be an idiot! I know it's not just the town festival that's on your mind. It's my neck you're trying to save. Of course, I'm coming with you."

Despite her resolve, Lucy was relieved to have Katie by her side. "Neil lives upstairs. We'll have to be very, very stealthy."

"I'll bring the flashlights."

CHAPTER 18

Fragrant aromas filled the kitchen later that evening. The lunch shift had long since ended, and they were preparing for their dinner service. Azad's marinated lamb chops and simmering lentil soup made her mouth water.

"We hope it's going to be busy this evening," Sally said. She was standing at the waitress station and filling small glass vases with irises for the tables.

"They're very pretty," Lucy said.

"Angela picked them up from the farmers' market earlier. She also purchased bunches of fresh parsley and left them in the kitchen. She wants you to remove the stems and wash the parsley. She said Azad needs it for the herb-stuffed bass he's preparing as a seafood dish for tonight."

"I assume my mother wants me to do it as soon as possible," Lucy said.

Sally smiled and planted her hands on her slim hips. "Sorry. I offered, but Angela turned me away and said, 'Properly preparing herbs is part of Lucy's cooking lessons and she needs to work at it.'" Sally mimicked her mother's accent and demeanor perfectly and they both laughed.

"She's getting out of hand," Lucy said.

"Getting?" Sally asked with a smile. "Angela hasn't changed in all the years I've been working here."

"Then I better go do my mother's bidding." Lucy had a long list of duties that included payroll in the office and inventory, but she knew better than to push her mother's work aside. Plus, if Azad needed it for tonight's seafood dish, then she'd best get to work.

Lucy turned toward the swinging doors that led into the kitchen, then halted as she remembered why she'd approached Sally in the first place. "Hey, before I go, where's the reservation book?"

"Raffi had it last," Sally said.

The thick, leather tome was like her father's bible. If they had switched to a computerized system, which Lucy wanted, then she wouldn't have to worry if her father misplaced it.

Sally trimmed an iris stem with scissors to fit in the short vase. "He did say we had six cancellations."

"Six? That's a lot. It must be the murder."

"Tourists are finicky."

"It's not finicky. I don't blame them. Who would want to put their families at risk? Not when there are other close Jersey shore towns. Plus, the beach festival was canceled."

Sally set the scissors down. "It's not your fault, Lucy."

"I know, but still."

"You had nothing to do with Archie's murder. A tragedy like that could have happened anywhere."

Sally placed the vases on a tray and started carrying

them to the tables. Lucy jumped into action and helped her. It wouldn't take long; then she'd head for the kitchen and tackle the parsley.

Each just-set table had a white linen tablecloth, sparkling glasses, a votive candle, and a vase of fresh-cut flowers. A handful of maple booths were tucked away in the corners like cozy couples. Cherry wainscoting gave the place a warm, family feel. The ocean shimmered beyond large bay windows, and seagulls soared above the water. Only a handful of lingering customers remained for a late lunch, and they drank coffee and ate baklava.

"The place always looks so beautiful right before a service," Sally said.

It was beautiful, but Lucy's thoughts were preoccupied. At her silence, Sally placed a hand on her shoulder. "You're really worried."

Lucy met Sally's gaze. "Kind of."

"You're investigating, Miss Sherlock, aren't you?"

Lucy set out a sigh. "You know me too well."

"Don't worry. I can keep a secret around here." Sally winked. "Unlike the rest of your family."

Lucy felt overwhelming gratitude. And friendship. "Thanks, Sally." Even when dealing with bad situations, Sally could always make her feel better. She'd also been waitressing at Kabob Kitchen for years and knew her family better than anyone.

"Now, about your investigation, anything I can do to help?" Sally asked.

Lucy didn't hesitate. Sally was a favorite with the customers. Tall and willowy, she was chatty and quick to smile and she had an incredible memory and could recall facts about all the locals. Wedding anniversaries. Kids' birthdays. High school reunions.

"Customers love you. Keep your ears open, and please let me know if you hear any gossip about Archie's death and the return of his mysterious wife, Kristin," Lucy said.

Sally gave her a quick hug. "You got it. Now go and prep the parsley before Angela gets back."

Lucy slipped back to the kitchen. Dozens of bunches of parsley sat on the wooden prep table. The mingled aromas of fresh herbs and Azad's lamb chops were redolent in the air. Her stomach grumbled. As soon as Azad finished cooking, she would tell him she had to taste the food before their first dinner customer walked in through the door.

It would take her a good amount of time to trim the parsley stems and wash the herbs. Lucy knew the parsley wasn't just used for the herb-stuffed bass, but for other dishes as well. Azad used parsley and mint to make the popular appetizer, tabbouleh salad.

"Lucy!"

She whirled to see Sally in the kitchen. She'd been so engrossed in her task, she hadn't heard her approach. "What is it?"

"There's someone here to see you. Mrs. Marsha Walsh."

Lucy frowned. "The prosecutor?"

"I believe so."

Before Lucy could formulate a response, the swinging kitchen doors opened and Prosecutor Walsh stepped inside. A slender woman with short cropped hair in a stylish bob, she was dressed in a crisp white linen suit. Her respectable heels clicked across the terra cotta tiles of the kitchen floor as she approached.

"Hello, Lucy."

"Hi, Prosecutor Wash. I wasn't expecting you."

That was the understatement of the year. This wasn't the first time the prosecutor had visited Kebab Kitchen. In the past, she'd questioned Lucy about a murder, then ordered food from the restaurant. What was her intent today?

Walsh also had impeccable timing. In the past, Lucy had returned from a run on the beach, and she'd been sweaty and underdressed when Marsha Walsh had barreled into her life like a steamroller. At least today Lucy was dressed in her work uniform—a white-collared button-down shirt and black slacks. As for whether she was prepared for Walsh's visit?

Never.

Sally must have sensed her distress. "Are you all right, Lucy?"

"I'm good," Lucy said.

Sally nodded and headed back into the dining room.

Prosecutor Walsh arched a well-plucked brow as she watched Sally leave. "She's quite protective of you."

Lucy wiped her hands on a towel. "She's a good employee and friend. What can I do for you?"

"I've never seen the inside of a professional kitchen," Walsh said as she scanned the kitchen.

Did she want a tour?

"What's that?" Walsh pointed to a large piece of restaurant equipment in the corner by one of the sinks.

"It's a commercial floor mixer. It can hold sixty pounds of dough." The mixer was used to make homemade pita bread and choreg, a delicious

Armenian sweet bread. The mixer was big, almost as tall as her five-foot-tall mother.

Walsh lifted her nose and sniffed. "What's that wonderful smell?"

"Lentil soup is simmering, and marinated lamb chops are on the menu for tonight's dinner service. Are you here to eat?" Lucy asked.

"No. I'm here to talk. I read Detective Clemmons's report, and I have additional questions."

Lucy would have preferred that Walsh send notice in advance so that she could mentally prepare. But showing up at the restaurant seemed to be a tactic of the wily prosecutor to catch her off guard. Lucy tried not to shrink beneath the cold gray of the woman's watchful gaze.

"You found Archie's body under the boardwalk." It was a statement, not a question.

"Yes. I called the police."

"Did you touch the body?"

"Only to check if he had a pulse. I told all this to the police and gave a detailed statement."

"I know."

"Then what else is there to ask?"

"You have a knack for finding bodies, Lucy."

"That's not fair," Lucy protested.

"You've been in town how long?"

"Since April."

"Hmmm. Five months and three bodies. That has to be a record."

Lucy decided to ignore the reference to the prior murders and focus on the current one. "I had nothing to do with Archie's death."

"Hmm." Walsh glanced at the prep table and the mound of fragrant parsley. "What are you doing?"

"Preparing parsley for one of tonight's specials, herb stuffed bass."

"I thought you said you're serving marinated lamb chops."

"We are. The bass is the seafood option. We always offer one."

"What were you doing under the boardwalk the day Archie was killed?" Walsh asked.

Lucy's mind whirled at the change of topic. She was catching on to the prosecutor's interrogation tactic—keep the subject constantly off guard.

Lucy cleared her throat. "I'm on the beach festival committee, and I was in charge of the food and wine tasting. It was a hot and busy day. After hours of running around, I needed a break, so I took a walk on the beach. That's when I found Archie," Lucy said.

"What's the food and wine tasting?"

"It's part of the weeklong beach festival that takes place at the end of the summer season. All the local restaurants, bakeries, ice cream parlors, and bars offer samples of food and drink on the boardwalk. I was in charge of organizing the restaurants and making sure they had what they needed."

"Did Kebab Kitchen participate?"

"Yes."

"What did you serve?" Walsh asked.

How was this pertinent to Archie's death? "Gyros, lamb shish kebab, grilled vegetable skewers, meat bulgur sausage, falafel, and date cookies," Lucy rattled off.

"Sounds delicious."

"It was."

"What about your friend, Katie Watson?" the prosecutor asked.

Alarm bells went off in Lucy's head. "What about her?"

"You're smart enough to know she is on the suspect list."

A cold knot formed in Lucy's stomach. "She shouldn't be."

Walsh arched an eyebrow. "Oh? Why is that?"

"Because Katie is not a murderer. Clemmons should know this and he should have moved on to other suspects by now," Lucy said.

"You mean because her husband is an Ocean Crest police officer? Or because she is your lifelong friend and you are living with her?"

Lucy tried to keep her heart cold and still. "Neither. Because she didn't kill Archie Kincaid." As a lawyer herself, she knew this wasn't a solid defense. It wasn't a defense at all. Just character testimony.

"I *know* she's innocent," Lucy added, as if rephrasing herself would make a difference.

"Well, then, I'll take your insight into consideration," Walsh drawled in a tone that said she didn't believe a word Lucy had said. "But what I won't accept is you meddling with a murder investigation."

"Pardon?"

Walsh couldn't know anything, could she?

She couldn't know that she'd met with Mr. Citteroni who'd tipped them off to soon-to-be mayor Ben. She couldn't know that Archie had blackmailed Ben with dirty lap dancing pictures with Vanessa, a stripper from the Pussy Cat. And the prosecutor certainly couldn't know that Lucy and Katie planned to use a stolen spare key to break into Archie's shop tonight.

"We spoke with Kristin Kincaid," Prosecutor Walsh said. "She told us you asked her pointed questions at her husband's funeral."

Oh, no.

Lucy thought fast. "She must have been mistaken. We were just expressing our condolences and reminiscing about Archie."

"We? Do you mean you and Katie?"

Way to put your foot in your mouth, Lucy. "Yes."

"How convenient. It seems you are both sticking your noses where they don't belong."

The stakes were rising, and her fears were stronger than ever. If Katie was still on the suspect list, then Lucy couldn't rest easy.

How could she not try to help her best friend?

Lucy was afraid of Walsh, and her stomach churned with anxiety every time the prosecutor showed up at Kebab Kitchen, but she was even more afraid of Detective Clemmons arresting the wrong person.

Walsh gave her a pointed look. "I expect you not to harass Mrs. Kincaid in the future. Meanwhile, rest assured that we are investigating all leads."

Lucy wanted to shout out, "What leads?" but held her tongue. They couldn't know about Ben and Vanessa. She needed solid proof before approaching Clemmons or Walsh.

Proof they would hopefully find tonight.

Walsh eyed her. "Stay out of it, Ms. Berberian. You may have gotten lucky in the past, but this time

Detective Clemmons and I are watching you. Do you understand?"

Lucy didn't hesitate. "I understand."

"Good. Now I'd like to sit in the dining room and order a bowl of lentil soup."

CHAPTER 19

Late that night, Katie parked her Jeep on Ocean Avenue, four blocks from Seaside Gifts. Dressed entirely in black, including black beanie hats, they each carried cross-body messenger bags containing flashlights.

"I feel silly, like one of the criminals from a *Columbo* episode," Katie whispered.

"Except we're the good guys," Lucy said.

At least the weather was cooperating. A crescent moon was hidden behind a thick blanket of fog, and the streetlights did little to illuminate the back alleys. They ducked behind parked cars, buildings, and an ice cream parlor that had closed for the night as they crept toward the boardwalk.

Katie joined Lucy in squatting behind a minivan as a car drove by. "I thought you'd back out after Walsh's surprise visit today."

Lucy had filled Katie in as soon as Marsha Walsh and eaten her soup and left Kebab Kitchen. The prosecutor was a mystery. She'd arrive unannounced, interrogate and frighten Lucy, then enjoy the food and hospitality of her family's restaurant.

It was maddening.

"I haven't changed my mind. In fact, I'm more convinced than ever that we need to find evidence. You're still on the suspect list. We need proof, and this is our chance to get it."

"All right. Let's do this," Katie said.

Each shop on the boardwalk had back stairs that led to storage rooms. This way, owners could receive deliveries and come and go without having to enter their businesses from the crowded boardwalk.

They reached Seaside Gifts, and Lucy glanced up at a two-story flight of stairs. The first flight led to the back door of the shop, and the second flight led to the apartment where Neil was currently living. They clung to the railing as they climbed up the first flight. The wooden stairs creaked beneath Lucy's feet, and her heart pounded.

"Could these steps be any louder?" Katie whispered.

"Try to tread lightly," Lucy said.

At last, they reached the landing. Lucy unzipped the pocket of her thin running jacket and pulled out the spare key. She inserted it in the lock and pushed open the door.

Lucy held her breath and, after she was certain there was no alarm, they stepped inside and closed the door.

It was pitch black.

They both turned on their flashlights, and two beams of light illuminated the room. It looked exactly as Lucy had described it to Katie—boxes scattered across the floor, a battered metal desk covered with papers, and a file cabinet pushed against a wall. An ashtray full of cigarette butts rested on of a stack of boxes by the door.

Katie sucked in a breath. "It's a mess. Where do we even start?"

"I already looked through the desk, but I was rushed and could have missed something."

"I'll take the desk. You search the file cabinet," Katie said.

"Good idea." Careful not to bump into anything, Lucy wound around boxes until she reached the file cabinet. The rusty top drawer squeaked as she opened it.

"*Shh,*" Katie said.

"I know."

From the look of the old filing cabinet, there was a good chance that the other drawers would be just as noisy. Lucy held the flashlight in her left hand and flipped through files with her free hand. Almost all the file folders were labeled.

Lucas novelties. Gilroy's boogie boards. Hoover's clothing.

Each file was filled with invoices and bills from the merchants Archie had ordered from.

She shut the drawer as slowly as possible to prevent the noisy squeak, then opened the second drawer. Same thing here. She moved onto the third drawer. The files weren't labeled here, and the drawer was only half-full.

She pushed the hanging file folders to the back of the drawer so that she could quickly flip through each one. That's when she noticed a large manila envelope lying flat on the bottom of the drawer beneath the hanging folders. Reaching inside, she pulled it out.

Lucy opened the metal clasp on the envelope and pictures fell out—glossy color pictures of Ben with Vanessa.

"Oh, my," Lucy said.

Katie spun around. "What is it?"

"Look and see."

Katie's eyes widened in surprise. "You found them!"

Together they flipped through the pictures. There were a dozen in all. Naughty pictures of Vanessa sitting on Ben's lap in a room decorated with red velvet sofas, fringe curtains, and an end table with a pair of pink fuzzy handcuffs resting on it. Vanessa was wearing short biker shorts, stilettos, and a bikini top. His hands were on her hips, and he was grinning from ear to ear.

"It must be the inside of the Pussy Cat. Vanessa is giving Ben a lap dance."

"Gross!" Lucy said.

Lucy kept flipping. The next set of pictures showed Vanessa and Ben kissing in his car. Others showed them walking into a house together. Lucy read the address above the door: 245 Mollusk Street. "That must be Ben's house in Ocean Crest."

The people of Ocean Crest wouldn't stand for a mayor who frequented a strip club and paid for lap dances. Even if Ben and Vanessa had since developed a romantic relationship, the pictures were damning. The town had a family-friendly reputation to uphold. Livelihoods depended on it.

"Archie must have followed Ben into the Pussy Cat, taken these pictures, and then followed them home."

"Ben's wearing different shirts in the pictures," Lucy pointed out.

"Then Archie had been following them for a while."

Lucy tipped the envelope over and a camera memory card slid into her palm. "Ben must have been searching for this as well when he broke into the shop."

"You're holding solid motive for murder. My bet is on Ben shooting Archie," Katie said.

"Mine, too," Lucy said. "We have to turn this over to Detective Clemmons. I just don't know how I'm going to manage it without telling him we broke in here and illegally searched the shop."

"We'll think of something. First, let's get out of here."

Lucy stuffed the pictures and the memory card back in the envelope and slipped the entire package in her messenger bag. Next, she returned the spare key to the slim desk drawer. If all went according to plan, Neil would never notice it missing.

"Open the door and turn the doorknob lock. It should lock behind us and no one will be the wiser that we were here," Lucy said.

Katie headed for the door, but before she reached it, she bumped into one of the boxes. The ashtray full of cigarettes that had been perched onto the stack of boxes fell and shattered across the floor.

The sound echoed ominously in Lucy's ears.

"Oh, no!" Katie turned, her eyes wide in the flashlight beam.

"Quick! Open the door."

Katie opened the door, then halted to turn the lock in the doorknob.

Lucy wanted to shout it didn't matter now. Neil would discover the smashed ashtray and figure out that somebody had been back here, and—

Voices sounded outside the storage room, and they quickly turned off their flashlights, then froze.

"I heard something," a gravelly female voice said.

"I didn't hear a thing," a masculine voice said.

Neil's voice.

Seconds later, the light went on in the front of the store.

"That's because you sleep like the dead."

"I still think it's your imagination."

"Did you already forget about the robbery?" The woman's voice rose an octave.

"I haven't forgotten. There's no one here. See?" Neil said.

"Let's check the storage room."

Crap! Lucy motioned frantically to Katie, and Katie got the message and flew outside. Lucy heard her footsteps on the wooden stairs.

Lucy didn't waste another second. Hurrying to the door, she bumped her hip on the edge of a box and knocked it to the floor. She was halfway through the door when the storage room light flicked on.

"Stop! Or I'll shoot!"

Lucy didn't think. She sprinted out the door.

The deafening *crack* of the gunshot resounded through the room and whizzed by her ear.

Panic speared through her, and she flew down the stairs. She was panting by the time she rounded the corner.

Had she been shot? She didn't feel any pain, but she was also in a full-fledged flight response. As she sprinted along the path they'd come by, Katie shot out of the darkness to grab her arm.

"This way!"

Together they ran around the ice cream parlor and headed for the residential area. They passed houses, the lights off at this late hour. Beach towels hung on laundry lines, and beach carts and boogie boards leaned against the sides of houses.

Halfway to Katie's car, sirens sounded down Ocean Avenue. Panicked, they ducked behind a hedgerow of bushes as a cop car streaked past. The gunshot had been loud. Either Neil reported an intruder or his neighbors had.

"We need to keep moving," Lucy said, her heart pounding like a drum in her ears. Sweat beaded on her brow and trickled between her breasts.

At last, they made it to Katie's car, and ducked inside as two more cop cars whizzed by.

"I can't believe Neil has a gun!" Katie said, wild-eyed.

"I think the bullet just missed me," Lucy said, panting.

Katie moved swiftly to unzip Lucy's running jacket and scan her for injury. "Are you hurt?"

"No. I don't think so."

Katie sagged in her seat. "My God! That was a close one."

"Too close," Lucy said.

"Neil wasn't alone. Who was the woman?" Katie said.

"She could be Neil's girlfriend. Jose mentioned that Neil was arguing with a woman when he was working at the shop. If she was sleeping over, it makes sense that she was his girlfriend," Lucy said.

"Who shot at you? Neil or his girlfriend?"

Lucy shivered as she recalled the harrowing moment. "It was Neil who shouted for me to stop or he'd shoot."

"Did they recognize you?" Katie asked.

Lucy shook her head. "I don't think so. It was dark, and I never fully turned around to face them. Plus, my hat covers my hair."

"You still have those pics and camera card?" Katie asked.

Lucy reached into her messenger bag and pulled out the envelope. "Right here."

"How are we going to get them to the police?" Katie asked. "You can't just stroll into the police station and hand them over to Detective Clemmons. And I can't just give them to Bill. He's a great husband, but he'd flip his lid if he learned we stole a key, illegally searched the shop, then were shot at as we fled."

"It does sound bad, doesn't it?"

"It sounds worse than bad," Katie said. "What are we going to do?"

Lucy pursed her lips in thought. "I'm going to deliver them anonymously to Clemmons."

"Don't you think the police will put two and two together and figure out whoever broke into the store tonight also stole these pictures?" Katie asked.

"If Neil does not know about the pictures, then he wouldn't know to report them missing."

"And if Neil knew about the blackmail pictures and discovers they're missing?" Katie asked.

Lucy's mind spun with the possibility. "If Neil knew his uncle was blackmailing Ben, he wouldn't tell the police about the pictures. Either way, the police won't know the pictures were stolen from Archie's store."

"If the police don't know the photos came from Archie, then how will they connect them with a motive for murder?" Katie asked.

"I'll include an anonymous note and tell Detective Clemmons that Archie was blackmailing Ben Hawkins. Clemmons will have to question Ben as a suspect."

"You think that's enough?" Katie asked.

It was a troubling thought. Lucy slid the pictures from the envelope, turned on her flashlight, and studied them more closely. Her eyes widened. "I think we're worrying for no reason. Archie will tell Clemmons for us."

"What do you mean?"

"Look here. Archie wrote on the back of each picture. He even initialed some with 'AK.' Lucy flipped over the lap dance picture and read out loud, " A lap dance to doom. " Next, she turned over the picture with the fuzzy pink handcuffs, and read, "'You're in a cash bind.'" Others showed Ben kissing Vanessa, and Ben and Vanessa making out in his car. Lucy read the hand-written notes, " This one is worth a couple grand. And so much for your political career. "

Katie snatched the pictures from Lucy. "I don't believe Archie had the gall to initial any of them. "The pictures, combined with your anonymous note, is enough to make even hardheaded Detective Clemmons question Ben."

"Good."

Katie shook her head. "We didn't escape unscathed. Our plan of stealthily breaking into the shop and returning the spare key without anyone knowing we were there has been blown out of the water. Someone called the cops. Whether Neil called the police, or his neighbors who heard the gunshot, it doesn't matter. The police will think there have been *two* burglaries at Seaside Gifts." Katie's gaze dropped to the envelope in Lucy's hands. "At least you found the pictures. They're proof Ben was being blackmailed and are his motive for murder."

"True. But I think we're overlooking something even more important."

"More important than the pictures?"

"Yup."

"What?"

"The gun. What if it's the same one that shot Archie?"

"You two did what?" Bill asked as he looked at Lucy and Katie in what could only be described as a combination of horror and anger.

They were in Katie's kitchen the following morning after their narrow escape the night before. Katie had waited until Bill had drunk a cup of coffee before they'd confessed everything.

"We know you're upset, but we hadn't planned on things happening as they did," Katie said.

"You mean getting caught illegally breaking and entering, then dodging a bullet as you fled?" A muscle twitched at Bill's jaw, and he set down his coffee mug with a thud on the laminate countertop.

"It's not Katie's fault," Lucy piped up. "It was my idea." She felt horrible; she had never intended to cause a rift between her best friend and her husband. Lucy couldn't let Katie take the fall—not when last night had been her brainstorm.

Bill's gaze turned on Lucy. "That's nice of you to say, Lucy, but Katie's a cop's wife. She knows better."

"I stole the spare key, not Katie. I convinced her to tag along," Lucy argued.

Katie opened her mouth to argue. "Lucy—"

"It's no excuse," Bill snapped.

At Bill's uncharacteristic harsh tone, Lucy's gaze flew to him. He shouldn't be this hard on Katie. Not when he had initially come to Lucy and asked for her assistance. "You wanted me to help, remember? You were worried Clemmons was upset about your seeking a promotion and that he would take it out on you somehow."

"It's not the same," Bill said.

"Yes, it is. As long as Katie remains on Detective Clemmons's suspect list, I can't stand by and do nothing. Especially since he still holds a grudge against my family, and he knows Katie is my best friend."

Bill ran a hand through his brown hair. "I did ask for your help." He held up a hand before Lucy or Katie could interrupt. "But I never meant for you to do anything *illegal.* I asked you to keep your eyes and ears open at Kebab Kitchen, and maybe ask a few questions. I didn't ask you to pin a deputy star on your chest and immerse yourself in a full investigation. And I definitely never asked you to break into a store."

"What about what we found?" The manila envelope with the camera card and pictures of Ben and Vanessa rested on the counter. "It's motive for murder."

"It is. Clemmons needs to see it."

"You're not suggesting I hand it over to him? He'd ask where we found them," Lucy said.

"We may not have a choice," Bill said.

"I already had an idea. What if I anonymously mail them to him? I'll include a typewritten note saying the pictures came from Archie. Detective Clemmons can verify Archie's handwriting on the back of the pictures if he needs to. Either way, he will have to question Ben and the truth will come out."

Bill was silent for a moment, and Lucy knew he was thinking about it. "It's a solid idea. Except I'm duty-bound to tell the truth."

"You're also duty-bound to protect me first," Katie said.

Bill frowned at his wife. "All right. I'm not happy with either of you, but I don't have much of a choice. It's not like I'd turn my wife or her best friend in to be arrested." He pointed a finger at them. "But no more stunts. You're both lucky you weren't shot."

After last night's scary episode, they were both quick to agree.

CHAPTER 20

"Guess what, *Mokour* Lucy?" Niari said. "We won our soccer game!"

Lucy smiled brightly as her niece stepped out of Emma's parked car outside Kebab Kitchen. *Mokour* meant mother's sister in Armenian, and Lucy loved hearing it as much as spending time with her niece.

Niari ran to Lucy and they hugged. Niari was a lovely mix of Emma and her father, Max. Niari's olive complexion and dark hair were from her mother's side, but her blue eyes were from her father's Irish heritage. Today, she was wearing cleats, shin guards, and her soccer uniform. A red glitter headband read GO STRIKERS!

Gadoo peered from behind a bush, then padded forward to wind around Niari's feet. She swept Gadoo into her arms and scratched behind his ears. The cat immediately began to purr. Gadoo loved Niari. Of course, he also knew treats were forthcoming whenever the girl visited.

"Who'd you play today?" Lucy asked.

"Cape May."

"What was the score?" Lucy asked.

"Four to two. I scored a goal."

"That's great! How about some cookies to celebrate?"

Niari eyed her with suspicion. "Not those date cookies?"

"You thought they were chocolate."

"Yes, but now I *know.*"

Lucy grinned. "How about some sugar cookies from Cutie's Cupcakes that I picked up?"

"Sure!" Niari darted for the door of the restaurant with the cat in her arms.

"Wait," Lucy said. "Your grandmother will throw a fit if she sees Gadoo inside."

Niari pouted. "I thought you were the manager now."

"I am," Lucy said. "But I know better than to challenge your grandmother." Angela was a stickler for cleanliness in the restaurant and, as a rule, Gadoo wasn't allowed inside.

"She's not in there," Emma said as she joined them.

"You sure?" Last time Lucy had checked, her mother was in the office in the storage room.

"I called her cell to let her know we were coming. She said she left ten minutes ago to wake up Dad," Emma said.

Her mother had never mentioned to Lucy she was leaving. Angela must have gone out the back door. Lucy eyed her niece and the cat. "In that case, I keep Gadoo's special treats in the storage room. Want to feed him some?"

"Yes!"

Niari traipsed into the restaurant carrying Gadoo,

and they walked through the swinging kitchen doors. The heat of the kitchen engulfed them as they passed through, and Butch and Azad looked up from simmering pots and waved. "Hi, Niari."

She waved back. "Gadoo wants treats."

Gadoo purred in her arms as Niari continued to stroke his soft fur. Once they were in the storage room, Lucy reached for a bag of cat treats on one of the shelves. "Only Holloway's carries the organic treats that he loves."

Niari set the cat down and Lucy poured some treats into her niece's hand. "Go ahead and feed him."

Gadoo's yellow eyes looked up as if to say, "Thanks," then his tail swished as he devoured the treats.

"Can I take him home with me?" Niari asked.

"I think your grandmother would get upset." So would Lucy. She'd gotten quite attached to the cat and looked forward to his welcoming meow when she arrived at work each morning. Lucy also wanted to take Gadoo with her when she moved out of Katie's home and into her own apartment. Her plans always seemed put off by Katie's protests and her own lack of time to look for an apartment. She'd have to talk to Max about finding a place. After all, he was the king of real estate in Ocean Crest.

"There you are," a male voice said.

Lucy and Niari turned to see Max enter the storage room. Handsome, with light brown hair and blue eyes, he was quick to smile. His charming personality helped him sell houses and occupy shore rentals.

"Hi, Dad," Niari said. "*Mokour* Lucy said I could feed Gadoo."

Max planted his hands on his hips. "I think he needs to go outside. No cats inside a restaurant, remember?"

"He's right. Gadoo can't stay," Lucy said.

Disappointment flashed across Niari's features. "Oh, okay."

Lucy opened the back door a few inches and Gadoo, who realized there would be no more treats, headed out.

Niari waved. "Bye, Gadoo!"

Max chuckled. "That cat has your entire family wrapped around his paw." He ruffled Niari's hair. "My daughter's, too."

"He's a good cat," Niari said. "I want to adopt him, but Lucy said Grandma would be upset."

"She's right. Heaven forbid we upset Angela," Max drawled.

Niari didn't look convinced, but Lucy wholeheartedly agreed. "Niari, your mom's waiting for you with cookies in the dining room."

"Thanks!" Niari traipsed out.

"Hey, Max. Did you ever look into finding me an apartment?" Lucy asked.

"I did. But your price range is difficult to find in Ocean Crest. Most people don't want to rent out all year. They live in their homes during the winter and rent out for the summer. It's more lucrative that way."

"Oh, so I guess there's nothing—"

"I did find something. Mrs. Lubinski is an elderly widow, and she is looking to rent out the second floor of her home. It fits your price range, and the second floor has its own entrance and privacy."

"Let me think about it." It wasn't what she'd hoped for, but she was on a tight budget and knew property rentals in the shore town could be sky-high, especially during the summer.

They joined Emma and Niari in the dining room where Niari was enjoying a plate of sugar cookies and a glass of milk.

Lucy turned to Max. "I forgot to ask. How's work?"

"Slow."

"Slow? Isn't it your busy season?" Lucy asked.

"It should be," Emma said before Max could answer.

Max leaned back in his chair. "Tenants have backed out of late-summer rentals, some even willing to lose their deposits. As for sales, it's very slow, and I've only had one potential buyer all week. The you-know-*what*"—he glanced at Niari, who was busy stuffing her face with a cookie—"has definitely affected sales."

Niari looked up from her plate. "You mean the murder, Daddy?"

Emma looked upset. "Niari, honey. What do you know about the murder?"

Niari rolled her eyes. "All the kids are talking about it, Dad. Madeline Newton started a text group about who did it."

"Niari!" Emma admonished. She looked at her husband. "Max, I told you to check her cell phone."

"I do, but not every day," Max countered.

Emma glowered at her daughter. "When did this text group start?"

"A while ago, right after Mr. Kincaid was shot," Niari said.

"You shouldn't talk about a man's death like it's entertainment."

"We're not. Madeline is upset that the beach festival is cancelled. Her mom is the balloon artist and she needed the money from the festival," Niari said.

"Archie's death has affected the entire town. Business at Kebab Kitchen is slow, real estate sales too, and the canceled beach festival has upset the kids and chased away tourists," Lucy said.

Max shook his head. "It couldn't have happened at a worse time."

"What about the second break-in at Seaside Gifts?" Emma clucked her tongue. "Crime is on the rise. Whatever happened to our safe, small town?"

Lucy struggled to keep an impartial expression. Had she unwittingly made things *worse?* A murder and *two* burglaries. She felt guilty for not confessing the truth to her sister and brother-in-law, but the less people that were involved, the better.

Niari set down a half-eaten cookie and looked at Lucy. "You solved a crime before. Can't you do it again?"

CHAPTER 21

Angela Berberian often preached that food was the best way to show all types of human emotion. A shish kebab platter loaded with rice pilaf, grilled vegetables, hummus, and pita was perfect for congratulating someone on an accomplishment, offering condolences, or apologizing for a wrongful act. Lucy was taking her mother's advice today, and she planned to apologize to Bill by offering a platter.

Lucy parked her Toyota in front of the Ocean Crest police station. Across from the library, the station was located in the center of town in a redbrick building that also housed the town hall and municipal court.

The station was a hubbub of activity. It was three days after Lucy's and Katie's harrowing escape from Archie's shop. During that time, Bill had been busy at work, and when he'd been home, he'd ignored them. It was obvious he was still angry, and Lucy felt horrible. She'd never meant to cause trouble between husband and wife. She'd botched everything.

Meanwhile, Lucy had anonymously mailed the photographs to Detective Clemmons. She'd typed his name and address on a computer label, adhered it to the manila envelope with the proper postage, then dropped the package in the mail. She'd also typed and included a one-line note, that said:

These pictures belonged to Archie Kincaid. Looks like blackmail to me.

From a concerned citizen.

Lucy knew town mail was delivered quickly, and Clemmons would have received the pictures by now.

A young, brown-haired officer, whom Lucy didn't recognize, buzzed her inside the station doors and sat behind the front desk. His name tag read ZIMECKI. She suspected he was one of the summer season's rent-a-cops.

Lucy carefully placed two stacked take-out containers on the counter. "Hello. I'm here to see Officer Bill Watson. I'm a friend, and I have lunch for him."

Officer Zimecki licked his lips. "It smells good."

"It's shish kebab and baklava straight from the oven. There's extra. I'm sure he'll share."

"I hope so. Watson sits at the fourth desk on the right."

"Thanks." Lucy knew which desk was Bill's. She also knew which office belonged to Detective Clemmons. She'd been summoned here by Clemmons on more than one occasion.

Don't think of those unpleasant visits now.

Two rows of metal desks lined the room. Officers sat behind their desks, typing reports on their computers, answering phone calls, or chatting at the water cooler. Bill was busy sifting through paperwork on his desk. He looked up when she approached.

"Hi, Bill. I thought you could use some lunch." She placed the containers on his desk. "Shish kebab and baklava for dessert. Katie said lamb is your favorite."

He eyed her suspiciously, but then his gaze slid to the take-out containers. "It is. Thanks. You want to sit?"

She occupied the chair beside his desk and lowered her voice. "It's a peace offering. I feel guilty, and I know Katie does, too. I'm sorry about our escapade."

He opened the top container and glimpsed inside. "As far as bribes go, I rate this pretty high."

"Does that mean you forgive us?"

"I do. I know you meant to help and"—he leaned forward in his chair and lowered his voice—"you did."

"You have info?"

"I do."

She drew her lips in thoughtfully. He wasn't being very forthright, but could she blame him? "I know you can't talk in-depth right now, but can you tell me *anything?*"

"Your pictures and note arrived this morning. Let's just say, it caused a ruckus."

"That exciting?"

"Exciting enough for Clemmons to jump out of

his seat and spill his coffee all over himself," Bill said, a glint of humor in his eyes.

Good. She wanted Clemmons to take the pictures seriously. As for the spilled coffee, well, Lucy couldn't help but grin along with Bill.

"What about both burglaries, including ours?" she whispered.

"We're no closer to finding the first burglar, but Clemmons has a theory. He believes the same person was responsible for the second break-in of the store."

"He does?"

"He thinks the criminal was after something specific. After his first failed attempt at prying open the security gates, Clemmons's theory is that the same person returned to break in the back door."

"And the pictures?" she whispered.

"So far, Clemmons doesn't believe the pictures are related to either burglary and that your anonymous envelope is unrelated."

This was good news. "Who does Clemmons think sent the pictures?" Lucy asked.

"Someone who hates Ben Hawkins and will do anything to ruin his credibility and prevent him from becoming mayor. According to Clemmons, what better way to do that than to send the pictures to the police?"

"Easy. The 'burglar' could have sent them to Stan Slade." Lucy knew firsthand how the town newspaper reporter loved juicy gossip and didn't always fully investigate the facts before reporting stories that were splashed across the front page of the *Town News*.

"True. But Archie's handwritten notes on the back of the pictures sealed the deal. Now there's evidence *and* motive," Bill said.

"You mean motive for Ben to want to shoot Archie?"

"Exactly. Ben will be brought in for questioning. His ladybird, Vanessa, too. If Ben is arrested, the pictures will come out eventually."

"So Detective Clemmons doesn't think it was Ben who first broke into the shop?" Lucy asked.

"Not as of right now."

She supposed it made sense from Detective Clemmons's point of view. Why would Ben send scandalous pictures of his affair with a stripper to the police?

Lucy, who knew the full truth, was convinced Ben *had* tried to break into the shop the first time to find the blackmail pictures, but he was interrupted before he could begin his search. Who knew if Ben would have found the pictures even if he had time? They were well hidden in the bottom of the file cabinet. Lucy thought it was dumb luck that she'd found them.

"What about the gun that Neil fired to chase away the burglar? The locals have been buzzing about the break-in and the gunfire. Was it the same gun that was used to kill Archie?" Lucy asked.

If it was, then Neil would be in big, big trouble.

"The weapon was sent to the State Police lab. Forensics is analyzing it as we speak."

Just then, one of the office doors opened and voices sounded from inside.

"Just remember that we demand justice!" a gravelly female voice said.

"We are looking into all angles. Meanwhile, don't leave town anytime soon, Ms. Smithfield," Detective Clemmons said.

Neil stepped out of the office, followed by a woman of average height with green eyes and poker-straight blond hair that fell to her waist. She looked to be in her mid-twenties, about the same age as Neil. Lucy thought the woman was attractive, but the unpleasant voice did not match her pretty face.

Trepidation traveled down Lucy's spine as she stared. The woman's voice was unmistakable. She'd heard it before. Seconds before a gunshot had whizzed by her head.

"How dare you accuse us! *We* are the victims," Ms. Smithfield said, pointing to herself. "The weapon was legally registered, and we used it to protect ourselves from an intruder. We want it back."

"As I explained, you'll get it after the forensics team has analyzed it," Clemmons said.

The woman huffed. "Come along, Neil." She turned on her heel and headed for the exit. Her gaze met Lucy's as she strode by, and for a pulse-pounding moment, Lucy feared she'd recognized her, but then she turned away and kept walking. Neil trailed behind like an obedient dog.

"Who was that?" Lucy asked Bill.

"Sharon Smithfield, Neil's girlfriend. Her father owns Smithfield's Surf Shop in Bayville."

She'd heard of the surf shop. Bayville was only a few towns north of Ocean Crest, and Smithfield's

Surf Shop was well-known for selling high-end surfboards and a large selection of pricey beach attire. Lucy also remembered seeing Neil's fancy surfboard when she'd talked with him on the beach.

Jose had told Lucy that he'd overheard Neil arguing with a woman with a distinct gravelly voice. Neil must owe Sharon Smithfield money for his surfboard.

Neil remained a suspect in his uncle's murder, and if forensics showed the gun was used to kill Archie, then he was most likely a killer.

Meanwhile, Ben had just as strong a motive.

Clemmons spotted Lucy and his narrow face pulled into a deep frown. "Ms. Berberian. What are you doing here?"

"I'm delivering food. Would you like a piece of baklava?" Lucy asked.

His eyebrows rose as if he was seriously considering her offer, then lowered. "I'd like a word with you in my office, if you don't mind."

I do mind, she thought. *I mind very much.*

But how could she not go? She looked at Bill, and he nodded. "I'll come in in fifteen," he murmured.

She stood and walked into the detective's office. She'd been summoned here twice before. It was a spacious room with a large desk with a computer and two faux leather chairs. A coatrack stood in the corner, a suit jacket hanging on one of the arms. Clemmons was an avid fisherman, and he'd added another picture of himself holding up big fish behind his desk. He was a fan of taxidermy, and stuffed fish hung on the walls. A bluefish and trout stared down at her with a mixture of sympathy and accusation as if to say: *We know what you did.*

Ugh. Lucy took a seat, crossed her legs, and folded her hands in her lap.

Clemmons glared down his long nose at her. "Funny how we keep meeting like this."

Lucy forced herself to meet his eyes. "I don't know how I can help you."

He opened his desk drawer, removed a large manila envelope, and placed it on the desk. She recognized the address label on the file, and her anxiety increased a hundredfold.

He leveled his gaze at her. "Did you send this to me?"

"No."

"Are you sure?"

"Yes. What is it?"

He leaned back in his chair. "Evidence."

"I see."

"Do you?"

"No. Not really. I can't see unless you open the envelope," Lucy said.

He stayed silent and watched her face for the slightest crack in her demeanor. Her nervousness grew. Was he a human lie detector who could tell she was lying?

No way. She'd gotten better at this. Years of experience at the Philadelphia law firm had taught her a few things about how to confront an adversary.

Never let them see you sweat.

She raised her chin and met his eyes.

"All right," he said. "I needed to be sure. This was delivered soon after the burglary at Seaside Gifts."

"Which burglary? The first or the second? The town has been all abuzz about both."

"The second," he said. "I received this envelope this morning, three days after the second burglary."

"So?"

"I'm wondering if they are connected," he said.

She masked her surprise. This wasn't what Bill had said. He'd told her Clemmons didn't believe the anonymously sent pictures were related to either burglary.

"Are you saying whatever is inside that envelope was sent from the burglar who broke into Seaside Gifts?" she asked.

"It's a possibility."

Clemmons was simply fishing for information. She believed what Bill had told her. Lucy also knew Clemmons wouldn't open the envelope. He couldn't. He just wanted to see her reaction when he'd pulled the envelope out of his desk drawer, see if she'd break down and admit to sending it to him, and there was no way she was confessing to *that.*

"I couldn't help but overhear the woman with Neil as they left your office," she said. "It's a small town and gossip runs like wildfire. People heard the gunshot. It's all everyone is talking about. Is it the same gun that killed Archie?"

"I'm asking the questions."

"Sorry. It's just customers are talking at the restaurant and if the murder is solved, then everyone wants the beach festival to resume."

His look was grim. "No festival. Not yet, anyway."

Disappointment settled in her chest. The beach festival wasn't resuming anytime soon. Not until

Archie's murderer was behind bars. Only then would the residents and tourists feel safe.

Her thoughts spun. While she was in his office, she could ask a question of her own. "What about Archie's wife, Kristin?"

"What about her?" he asked, his mustache twitching with annoyance.

"Isn't the spouse always a suspect?"

"Not that it's any of your business, but I confirmed that she was in her New York City office. I spoke with three witnesses who saw her at work on the day of the shooting. She wasn't in town when her husband was killed."

It's what they'd suspected, but knowing Clemmons had confirmed it made it one step more legitimate in Lucy's mind.

"Is there anything else, Detective?"

"That's it for now."

She stood and pushed back her chair. She couldn't leave fast enough. She opened the door, stepped outside, and ran smack into Sharon Smithfield.

"Oh!"

"Watch where you're going, lady!" Sharon said, as annoyance crossed her pretty features and turned them into something much less attractive.

"Sorry. I didn't see you," Lucy said.

"Is there a problem, Ms. Smithfield?" Detective Clemmons stood and walked to the entrance of his office.

"I forgot my sunglasses." Sharon strode inside the office and fetched a pair of Ray-Bans that she'd left on the corner of Clemmons's desk. Then, on her way back out of his office, she met Lucy's eyes.

"Have we met before?" the woman asked Lucy.

Lucy froze, aware of Detective Clemmons right behind her. "No."

"Are you sure?"

"Yes. But I have a familiar face. Lots of people have told me they thought they'd seen me before. Must be the curly hair. Or height. Or whatever." She was rambling, and she felt her composure cracking.

Get a grip, Lucy!

She'd just survived an interrogation by a detective. How could she get so flustered now?

Bill came to her rescue as he approached, holding one of the take-out containers. "This baklava is amazing. You have to try a piece, Calvin." He lifted the lid to show two large remaining pieces of the walnut and cinnamon-filled pastry. "I'm afraid I've already devoured the shish kebab." He winked at Lucy. "She knows lamb is my favorite."

Sharon glanced at the container in Bill's hand in disgust, then turned and walked away. Neil was waiting for her at the exit.

Lucy breathed a sigh of relief. The last thing she wanted was for Sharon to recognize her from the night she'd snuck into Seaside Gifts. "Thanks, Bill. I'm glad you enjoyed the food." She turned to Clemmons. "How about you, Detective? Would you like to try the baklava?" It was a test of sorts. Did he believe her story? Or did he think she was somehow involved and had sent him the envelope?

Seconds passed, then Clemmons reached for the box. "I think I will."

CHAPTER 22

After leaving the police station, Lucy changed into running gear and headed for the boardwalk. She needed to clear her mind and think. It was her afternoon off and Angela and Raffi were managing the afternoon lunch shift. Azad and Butch were in the kitchen, and Sally and Emma were waitressing.

She motored down Ocean Avenue and ran up the ramp that led to the boardwalk. It was a beautiful, August afternoon at the Jersey shore. Humidity was down (unusual!) and a breeze blew wisps of hair that escaped from her ponytail. She breathed in the fresh ocean air.

Picking up her pace, she ran the length of the boardwalk, down the stairs, and then on the beach. Her running shoes picked up sand and it sprayed the back of her calves. She glanced at her watch, happy to see that she'd made the distance faster than last time. It had taken weeks, but her endurance had improved.

Sunbathers lay on beach towels and sat beneath colorful umbrellas. Children splashed in the surf.

A Windsurfer with a brightly-colored, rainbow sail coasted across the water. A single-engine, propeller airplane pulled a banner advertising the early-bird dinner at the Crab House, the seafood restaurant just outside of town that had catered the funeral, across the sky.

She made it to her favorite lookout—the jetty. Here, the spectacular Atlantic Ocean was spread out before her. The isolation, combined with the vastness of the sea, helped keep her problems in perspective.

She sipped from her water bottle as the ocean breeze cooled her heated skin. Her thoughts turned to Archie's murder. He'd certainly had his fair share of enemies in town and the list of suspects was growing.

The first suspect that came to mind was Ben Hawkins. Ben had political aspirations, and the pictures Lucy had found were enough to dash any hopes for his would-be career as mayor. Archie's blackmail scheme would have ensured that Ben stay in his back pocket and help influence the Ocean Crest zoning board to approve any future businesses Archie had in mind. Ben certainly had motive and opportunity. Had Ben killed him in order to silence his blackmailer? Or had Vanessa done the dirty deed for her lover?

Then there was Archie's girlfriend, Rita Sides. Rita certainly had motive to want her boyfriend dead. Archie had lied to her about his marital status and had added insult to injury when he'd purchased Rita an engagement ring with a fake diamond. Rita admitted she'd found out about his wife, Kristin, and was angry and hurt, but she adamantly claimed that she didn't kill him. Was she lying?

Harold Harper, Archie's business neighbor on the boardwalk, was also on her list. The two men had hated each other and had been fierce rivals. Archie's cutthroat pricing tactics to put his rival out of business could have pitched Harold over the edge. Harold had gone so far as to say whoever had killed Archie had done the town a favor. Harold had also been beneath the bandstand when the winner of the sand sculpture competition was announced. He had opportunity and motive. But did he go so far as to shoot Archie in cold blood?

And then there was Neil. Archie's nephew had a lot to gain from his uncle's death. He received Seaside Gifts, the lucrative shop. It was more than Neil had earned in his lifetime so far. Plus, Neil had big dreams of competing with professional surfers. If he'd borrowed money from his girlfriend, Sharon, to buy an expensive surfboard, he needed the cash to pay her back. He'd certainly had opportunity. Lucy had spotted him at the back of the bandstand with Archie that day. His aspirations to leave the tiny town of Ocean Crest and head to Hawaii to surf with the pros, combined with his debt to Sharon, were enough motive to shoot his uncle.

Last, there was Archie's wife, Kristin . She didn't seem like a loving wife or a grieving one at the funeral, but Lucy knew appearances could be deceiving. Had she learned of her husband's affair with Rita? Had she seen red and killed him? It wouldn't be the first case of a wife disposing of her husband, except Kristin had a rock-solid alibi. She'd never been to Ocean Crest before the funeral. She couldn't have killed him.

So who had pulled the trigger?

Frustration roiled in her gut. She was missing something, but what? Lucy stood and brushed the sand off her shorts. She had come here hoping for answers, but her time on the jetty had only resulted in more questions.

She carefully picked her way off the jetty and was about to run back when she spotted Kristin on the beach. Dressed in a yellow bikini and wearing a large white sun hat with a black band, the widow was sitting in a beach chair and reading a glossy fashion magazine.

Lucy was surprised the woman was still in Ocean Crest and hadn't fled back to New York City. Never one to miss an opportunity, Lucy jogged over to the woman.

"Hello, Mrs. Kincaid," Lucy said as she stopped by Kristin's beach chair.

Kristin lowered the magazine and peered at Lucy above the rim of her large sunglasses. "Oh, hello. I remember you from the funeral."

"I'm Lucy Berberian. I was with my friend Katie Watson when we met you at the funeral."

"A sad day."

"Again, I'm sorry for your loss."

Kristin's lower lip quivered. "I still think Archie is going to call me. I haven't erased his voice mail messages on my cell phone. I listen to them at night."

Was the woman going to cry? Lucy didn't know if she was sincere or acting. "The beach is a good place to think of loved ones and to relax. Will you be staying in Ocean Crest for a while?"

"I'm sifting through Archie's belongings. It's a tedious task. Everything reminds me of him." Kristin reached into her beach bag, pulled out a tissue, and began dabbing the corner of her eyes.

"Is Neil helping you go through Archie's belongings?"

Kristin scoffed and dropped the tissue. "Hardly. Neil spends all his free time on the beach and has unrealistic dreams of becoming a pro surfer. I give Seaside Gifts six months before it closes because of his incompetence."

Wow. Harsh words from the widow. Lucy also couldn't help but notice that Kristin's tears had quickly stopped flowing.

"Aren't you Neil's aunt?" Lucy asked.

"In marriage only. Neil was Archie's brother's son. After Ralph died, Archie took Neil under his wing. I was against it. Neil had a drug and alcohol problem."

"I understand Archie volunteered at a teenage drug clinic," Lucy said.

"He did. The in-town clinic helped Neil. He no longer does drugs, but he's still a deadbeat in my opinion. His artwork is mediocre at best, and he used to complain about working in the boardwalk store."

Lucy's suspicions had been correct. Neil had attended the clinic. Archie had then taken Neil into his home. It was the most redeeming quality she'd learned about Archie so far.

Kristin pulled out a bottle of sunscreen and

began to apply it to her neck and chest. "The sun is strong. I don't want wrinkles or sunspots."

She'd probably have them surgically removed. Lucy pondered how to ask her about Archie's death, then decided to be forthright. "Do you know who would want to harm Archie?"

Kristin froze, a dollop of sunscreen on her neck. "There are quite a few people who come to mind. But why ask? I already talked with a Mr. Clemson from the police."

"You mean Detective Clemmons?"

"Yes. That's it."

Once again, Lucy was grateful that Clemmons had followed up and questioned Kristin. "Well, I'm staying with a friend. Her husband is an Ocean Crest police officer. Anything you can think of that you forgot to mention to Detective Clemmons would be helpful in finding Archie's killer," Lucy said.

"I already told the detective about Archie's business neighbor, Harold. Archie complained about the man all the time. Archie claimed that Harold threatened him and said one of them had to go."

"You think Harold shot Archie?"

"Why not? It would solve Harold's problem. I'm aware Archie could be difficult."

This wasn't new information. "Anyone else you can think of?"

"My husband's girlfriend."

Lucy blinked. "Pardon?"

"Oh, I know it's bound to come out if it hasn't already. Archie had a girlfriend, a younger woman who worked at a hair salon in town," Kristin said, her voice laced with distaste.

"I'm sorry."

"Archie and I had a long-distance relationship. It was bound to happen."

"You aren't angry?"

"Now I am. I think the woman killed my husband when she realized Archie wouldn't leave me for her."

"I'll be sure to pass on your concerns to my friend's husband," Lucy said.

"You do that." Kristin leaned back in her chair and reached for her magazine. Clearly, Lucy had been dismissed.

"Enjoy the beach," Lucy said, then headed back toward the boardwalk. Kristin had not revealed new suspects, but their talk *had* revealed more of Kristin's personality. She was not affectionate or warm, and under any other circumstances, she would rank high on Lucy's lists of suspects.

But she hadn't been in town when Archie was murdered.

The boardwalk stores were a colorful blur as Lucy's mind raced along with her feet as she picked up her pace.

"Lucy!"

She turned to see Madame Vega standing at the entrance of her psychic parlor. "Oh, hello!" Lucy called out, then she jogged over. "I've been meaning to stop by for another reading."

"Come in. I haven't been busy." The medium adjusted her turban.

Madame Vega's comment was another reminder of how business in town was slow, especially on the boardwalk.

"I can't right now. I have to shower and be at work," Lucy said.

"Another time then."

"Yes. I promise. I need more advice in the . . . the romance area." Things with Azad had heated with a date and a kiss, then gone chilly when he'd grown jealous over her friendship with Michael, and now they were back to lukewarm after she'd apologized.

"Ah, I'm not surprised. You are young and single. You will need advice for a long, long time."

"Not that long, I hope," Lucy said. Her mother's nagging wouldn't cease. Angela wanted grandchildren and fast.

"What else is troubling you?"

Lucy shook her head regretfully. If only Madame Vega had a special deck of tarot cards that showed the faces of the suspects of Archie's murder and could predict the killer. If only it were that simple. "I'm not sure the answer to that question is in the cards either."

Madame Vega dipped her head. "Visit soon. One never knows with tarot."

Azad was hard at work in the kitchen, stirring a large pot when Lucy showed up in the kitchen before the dinner service. He looked good, dressed in a short-sleeved chef's shirt and black-and-white checked pants.

"What are the dinner specials?" Lucy asked. She'd showered and changed and showed up early.

"Taste this," he said as he poured a ladle full of soup in a bowl and handed it to her with a soup spoon."

"What is it?"

"It's Swiss chard lentil soup, a traditional Lebanese dish." A dark curl rested on his forehead and her fingers itched to reach up and push it back.

"It smells delicious." She slurped a spoonful. The hearty soup was a wonderful blend of lentils and greens. "Yum. It's sooo good."

"I also prepared beet salad with goat cheese, baked chicken in tomato sauce, and shrimp kebabs for the seafood option."

"I love beet salad. What's the dressing?"

"Wine vinegar, extra virgin olive oil, and my secret—a dash of sugar."

Lucy's stomach rumbled. "When can I taste everything?"

"As soon as it's ready, I'll prepare you a plate." He smiled, and the sexy dimple in his cheek drew her eye.

It was hard for her to tear her gaze away. This wouldn't do at all. As casually as she could manage, she smiled back. "I better make sure the dining room is ready."

"Lucy, wait," he said, reaching out to touch her sleeve. "That cover band, the Beach Bums, is playing at Mac's Pub tomorrow night. It's much more casual than Le Gabriel, but the band is fun. Are you free?"

Her heart skipped a beat at his light touch on her arm. All wasn't lost between them, was it? He was asking her on a second date. "I'd like that a lot."

"Great. We can head there right after work. I'll drive."

Perhaps she didn't need to visit Madame Vega for romantic advice after all.

CHAPTER 23

That night, Lucy locked up the restaurant and headed out the back door. Gadoo appeared right on time as Lucy filled his food dish. "Sorry, Gadoo. I'm out of treats. I have to make a run to Holloway's."

Gadoo twitched his tail and glared at her.

"I promise to go straight there tomorrow morning."

He meowed loudly, expressing his dissatisfaction.

"Spoiled rotten kitty."

A loud rumble sounded and, seconds later, a motorcycle pulled up in the restaurant's parking lot. Gadoo took off like a shot across the asphalt and then down the street.

Lucy had a different reaction as she approached the leather-clad motorcycle rider. Michael parked his bike, lowered the kickstand, and removed his helmet.

"You're not headed home already, are you? It's the perfect night for a ride," he said.

"Depends if you'll let me drive." She was teasing, of course. She hadn't had proper lessons. Though she promised herself that one day she would learn how to safely drive a motorcycle.

Michael rubbed his chin with a thumb and forefinger as if seriously considering her request. "Not yet, but I have a gut feeling that you'll learn soon."

She laughed. Michael was attractive enough to draw any woman's eye, but Lucy felt a strong kinship with him. She supposed she was a one-man gal, but that didn't mean she couldn't have friends. Even sexy, Italian ones who radiated a bad-boy persona with his motorcycle.

She also enjoyed riding with him on his Harley-Davidson. For someone who'd always been afraid of the roller coaster on the boardwalk pier, that turned out to be a surprise.

"I'm game to ride tonight. Where do you plan on heading?" she asked.

"I never have a destination in mind. I just ride."

It sounded good to her. She'd been too tense lately. Archie's murder was never far from her thoughts. Then there was an uncertainty about her relationship with Azad. They may have veered off course, but Azad had asked her to Mac's Pub and, once again, their relationship seemed to have gained traction.

Still, she was always happy to see Michael. "I'm glad you stopped by," she said.

"Ready?" he asked.

She noticed he had a spare helmet attached to the saddlebag on the side of the bike.

"How did you know I'd say yes to a ride?"

He studied her thoughtfully for a moment. "I didn't. I was just hopeful."

She knew all about hope. She hoped Detective

Clemmons had removed Katie from his suspect list. She hoped they'd find the murderer soon. And she hoped the beach festival would resume and business would return to normal for everyone in town.

She locked her purse in her car, then climbed on the back of the motorcycle and held on to Michael's leather-clad sides.

He pushed back the kickstand and the Harley purred beneath her like a contented beast. They headed down Ocean Avenue and out of town.

It really was a perfect night for a motorcycle ride. It was warm, but an ocean breeze cooled her heated cheeks.

"Boardwalk?" Michael asked.

"Yes."

They'd often stopped at the boardwalk. Tonight they sat on a bench overlooking the ocean. The Atlantic Ocean always looked different to Lucy at night. More foreboding. Ominous. But beautiful in a dark way.

Michael had brought a bag of peanuts and they shelled them and ate while sitting back on the wood bench and resting their feet on the railing. Michael pointed to a spot near the jetty. "There's going to be a party with a few of my biker friends on the beach tomorrow night. Nothing formal, just a fire pit, music, and some beer. I know you have to work, otherwise, I'd invite you."

"Too bad. I haven't been to a beach party in ages."

"Next time."

"How's your father?" she asked.

Michael shrugged. "The same. I haven't seen him much since we went to dinner together."

"The evening was well worth the Italian food

and the information." Lucy shelled a peanut and popped it into her mouth. It was perfect—salty and crunchy.

"I never had a chance to talk with you about the information my father provided. Did it help?" he asked.

She didn't plan on hiding what she'd discovered from Michael. He was her confidant, and she knew he would keep what she said secret.

"It did. Your father was right. Politics is a dirty business. It turns out Ben is in a relationship with an employee at the Pussy Cat."

Michael arched an eyebrow. "By employee do you mean stripper?"

"Yes. Her name is Vanessa."

"Okay. Knowing my dad, I assume this has something to do with Ben running for mayor. Probably Archie had dirt on Ben about his relationship with the gal. I'm assuming pictures."

She looked at him in surprise. "How did you know?"

Michael reached for another peanut. "Like I said, I know my father."

She felt a stab of sympathy for him. Michael was nothing like his father and they'd often been at odds with each other.

"You're right. It turns out Archie was blackmailing Ben with naughty pictures."

Michael held up his hands. "I don't get it. In today's day and age, who would care?"

"More than half of the town. It's a family-friendly tourist location," she argued.

"I suppose you're right." He looked at her with renewed interest. "But how did you know about the pictures, or that they were naughty?" At her silence, his lips thinned. "Oh my God. You broke into Seaside Gifts, didn't you? Talk about the second break-in has been all over town. Neil fired a gun at you!"

Lucy glanced around. "*Shh,* I don't want anyone to hear."

"I can't believe it. You're going to give me a heart attack."

"You? I was the one who had a bullet whiz by my head."

He rolled his eyes heavenward. "Good God, Lucy. I feel responsible. If I didn't arrange for you to have dinner with my father, you would never have known about Ben and wouldn't have put yourself at risk."

Clearly, he was getting upset. Some kind of male overprotectiveness. "It's okay. I'm fine."

"Are you still investigating the murder?" he asked.

Lucy turned her attention to cracking the peanut shell in her hands. It was sealed tight and stubborn. "I'm not breaking and entering anywhere, if that's what you're asking."

"You are, then."

"I'm just keeping my eyes and ears open," Lucy said. It was exactly what Bill had asked her to do in the first place.

His blue gaze locked on her. "Be careful. There's a murderer on the loose. How many lives do you think you have?"

"I haven't been keeping track."

"One more question. How are things with that hot-tempered chef?" he asked.

It was unusual for Michael to ask about Azad. It was also an uncomfortable topic of conversation between them. How was she supposed to answer the question? She cleared her throat. "Azad and I have had a few rough patches, but we're making a go of it."

"Well, if he keeps screwing up, I'm happy to step in."

Wow. She wasn't sure how to answer. They'd flirted in the beginning, but since then, they'd shared a different type of bond. Both of them had strong families with unreasonable expectations. They understood each other, sympathized together, and she valued his friendship.

"Thanks," she said.

"I mean it."

"So do I. I won't forget the offer."

Lucy arrived at the restaurant early the following morning to see Jose's truck parked out front. She'd been expecting him and was pleased to see he was prompt.

She approached him with a smile. "Hi, Jose. Are you ready to do some more work?"

"I am. I hope to install half the ceiling fans today, and the second half in a few days."

"The fans are in boxes in the storage room."

She'd asked him to arrive early before the restaurant opened. This way, he could work undisturbed. She held the front door open as he carried in a ladder and then his toolbox. He set up the ladder to reach the electrical box he'd previously installed, then ran back to his truck. Lucy assumed he'd forgotten a tool.

Jose returned with a plastic container. "I almost forgot. Maria made you *pollo guisado*—braised chicken. She said to thank you for the baklava."

"Please tell her thanks. She didn't have to do that." Lucy peeked inside the container. If the chicken was as good as the flan, then she knew it would be exceptional. Maria Alvarez certainly knew how to cook.

"Maria believes food is the best way to show gratitude," Jose said.

She sounded just like Lucy's mother. The two women should get together and swap recipes. "Maybe Maria can give me a cooking lesson."

"She'd like that."

"How's the pregnancy?" From what she'd remembered, Maria was almost eight months pregnant by now.

"Good. Little Enrique is getting big."

"You know it's a boy."

Jose's face broke into a wide smile. "We weren't going to, but we asked the ultrasound technician to write the baby's sex on a piece of paper and seal it in an envelope. We agreed to wait to open it after the baby was born, but aren't as disciplined as we thought."

"Emma and Max found out as soon as they could." They'd known Niari was a girl as soon as the technician squirted the ultrasound gel on Emma's stomach. Lucy had helped Max paint the room pink and she'd shopped with Emma to pick out pink bedding with ballerinas at Babies Galore.

Jose's cell phone rang and he unclipped it from his belt. The phone's blue cover was embellished with a gold cross.

He glanced at the screen. "Excuse me. It's Maria."

"Of course."

Lucy carried the container into the kitchen and opened the lid. It was still warm, and she inhaled the delicious aroma of braised chicken. Reaching for a fork, she took a taste. The combination of spices—onions, garlic, celery, peppers, and olives—was divine and the chicken was so tender it melted in her mouth. The chicken rested on a bed of fluffy white rice. She stuffed another forkful in her mouth, then another. Maybe Azad could introduce this into the menu. It may not be Mediterranean cuisine, but he could put a spin on it, couldn't he?

She was still sampling the chicken when Jose passed through the swinging kitchen doors with his toolbox. "This is delicious!"

"I'll be sure to tell Maria. Mind showing me where the fans are stored?"

She reluctantly set down her fork and walked him through the kitchen into the storage room where the boxes of fans were stacked in a corner. Jose picked up two. "I should be finished before your first lunch customer arrives."

A thought crossed Lucy's mind. She knew he'd worked in Archie's shop. She'd already questioned him about it, but now that she knew the identity of Neil's girlfriend she wondered if there was more Jose could recall.

"Jose, remember when you said you'd last worked

in Archie's shop and you overheard Neil arguing with a woman?" Lucy asked.

"Yes."

"I met her. Her name is Sharon Smithfield. She's pretty and blonde."

"I didn't see her, but I remember her voice. It was irritating."

"By 'irritating' you mean gravelly, right?" Lucy asked.

"Yes."

"And you said they were arguing over money?"

"He owed her money for a surfboard. She asked when he would pay her back for it. Like I said, I never saw them. I just overheard their conversation while I was working on the electrical box. I wasn't purposely eavesdropping. They were arguing loudly."

"Don't worry. I believe you. Sharon's father owns Smithfield's Surf Shop in Bayville."

Jose set down his toolbox. "Smithfield's? Wait a minute. Now that you mentioned it, I remember her saying her dad wouldn't be happy when he noticed the surfboard missing."

Lucy contemplated this news. If Sharon was worried about her father, did that mean they'd taken the surfboard from the store without paying for it? Had Neil promised Sharon he'd pay for it and then not made good on his promise?

It certainly raised the stakes. Neil hadn't just borrowed money for his surfboard, he'd *stolen* it.

CHAPTER 24

Mac's Irish Pub was packed with locals. The pub was a hometown favorite and known for its large selection of microbrews and beers on tap. The smell of beer and fried bar food always lingered in the place. A long mahogany bar, polished but nicked from years of use, ran the entire length of one wall. A large flat-screen TV was mounted above the bar and neon signs advertising beers were scattered on the walls. Two pool tables, which were in use every time Lucy visited, were in the back, and a low stage was in the corner. Tonight, a number of tables had been moved to face the stage.

A band was setting up their equipment on the stage when Lucy and Azad walked inside. The front of one of the drums read THE BEACH BUMS in bold block letters. The Beach Bums were a wildly popular local cover band, and they played everything from Bon Jovi and Mötley Crüe to Green Day and Pearl Jam to current pop music.

Azad pulled out a seat for her at a table. "The band warms up in a half hour."

A waitress approached with an empty tray in one hand. "What can I get you to drink?"

They ordered two beers and sat close together so they could hear each other above the din of the already-busy pub. A table occupied by men drinking beer and watching a baseball game on the large-screen television called out to Azad and waved.

Azad waved back. Another couple passed by and the man slapped Azad on the back to greet him.

"Do you know everyone here?" Lucy asked.

"A lot of folks. I wasn't the one who left town for eight years."

"Not fair. I was working."

He squeezed her hand. "I didn't mean to offend you. I only meant that Kebab Kitchen has a funny way of drawing you back in, doesn't it? After working at the restaurant in high school, I never thought I'd end up back there as head chef. The place calls to you, just like Ocean Crest. They are both like old friends that you can't let go."

Like old friends.

It was true. Kebab Kitchen was in her blood. Her father had often used the phrase, but she'd discovered the truth behind his words when she'd returned home and discovered her parents had wanted to sell the restaurant. Unthinkable, was her first reaction. It took a couple of months for her to sort it all out, but she realized she wanted to stay and manage the place. She couldn't bear the thought of her parents selling it.

As for real-life friends, Ocean Crest was the place to find them, or at least, return to them. She'd never replace Katie, Sally, or her own sister, Emma. She'd even grown close to Lola from the coffee shop and Susan from the bakery.

During all the years she'd spent in Philadelphia, she hadn't made a lot of friends. Lawyers weren't very social, as they worked long hours. Sure, she'd made some friends, but those acquaintances couldn't compare with what she had with Katie and the others.

The tug to return home had been strong, and she hadn't regretted the decision.

As for Azad, he'd shown her that people could change, and she had changed as well. She was no longer a lovesick teenager or college student; she was a mature woman.

"I suppose you're right about the restaurant. It does suck you back in," she said.

"And us?" he asked.

She bit her lip. "I wasn't the one who broke us up."

He reached across the table to tuck a curl behind her ear. His touch lingered and his gaze captured hers. "You're right. But I won't make the same mistake again."

There it was. His ability to make her pulse pound in her throat, and a sizzle to zing through her veins as if she'd touched a white, hot electric wire.

"Azad, I—"

The loud thump of a drum and the screech of an electric guitar interrupted her as the Beach Bums started warming up. The waitress returned to the table, carrying a tray full of drinks. She plucked two beers in frosted mugs from the tray, set them down on cardboard coasters advertising domestic brews, and then sailed off to deliver the rest of her drinks.

Lucy sipped her cold beer and sat back to enjoy the music and the company. It was an entirely different date from the quiet, romantic ambience of Le Gabriel, but enjoyable in a different way.

The band began to play a Dave Matthews Band song and she tapped her feet to the beat. Azad was attentive, and he soon had her singing and laughing along with him. People started to crowd the dance floor, and Azad pulled her to her feet. They moved to the rhythm and clapped. His arms encircled her as they danced and he twirled her once or twice.

They returned to their seats, laughing. She hadn't had this much fun at a bar in a long time. They ordered more drinks, and soon Lucy needed to visit the little gal's room. She motioned to Azad above the noise and headed for the back of the bar. Male and female stick figures indicated the right doors.

Lucy was washing her hands, when a woman approached next to her and reached for the automatic soap dispenser. Lucy looked up in the mirror and froze.

Vanessa.

She wore a tank top with sequin stars, skintight jeans that looked painted on, and high-heeled wedge sandals. Her brown hair was pulled back in a braid that revealed perfect cheekbones and heavily lined eyes.

What on earth was she doing here? Just as that question crossed Lucy's mind, another followed. Was she here with Ben?

No one else was in the ladies' room. She would never get a better chance to talk with the woman.

"Hello," Lucy said.

"Hi." Vanessa never even bothered to glance at her. She dried her hands and reached in her bag for a tube of lip gloss and started applying it to her big lips.

Lucy wasn't easily deterred. "I've seen you before with Ben Hawkins."

Vanessa's hand froze in midair, the tube of lip gloss in her hand. Her eyes flew to Lucy's in the mirror. "You must be mistaken."

"I don't think so."

Vanessa put the cap on the lip gloss, shoved it into her bag, and turned to face to Lucy. "I've never seen you before in my life."

"I've been to the Pussy Cat," Lucy lied.

Vanessa arched an eyebrow, and her gaze swept up and down Lucy. "You?"

"That's right. I saw you together in the club, and then when I was leaving, I saw you get into Ben's car. You kissed him."

Vanessa's face paled, a feat Lucy didn't think was possible with all the heavy makeup she was wearing.

"Who are you?" Vanessa asked.

"An acquaintance."

"Of Ben's? *I* sure as hell don't know you."

"Yes, I know Ben," Lucy said. "I also know he's running for Ocean Crest mayor."

A dim flush raced like a fever across Vanessa's face. "I know what you think. That Ben paid me to . . . to get into his car with him. But it's not like that."

"I didn't think that at all. I assumed you were in a relationship."

"Yes," Vanessa said, her tone hopeful. "We are. I care for Ben."

"Still?"

"Of course. We happened to meet at the club,

but that's all. We have feelings for each other, but we are forced to keep it secret."

Lucy tilted her head to the side. "That must be difficult for you. If news of your relationship leaked out, I know a lot of town residents who wouldn't be as understanding. Chances are Ben's political campaign would suffer."

"I know! That's why we don't go out in public."

Just how far would the two lovebirds go to keep it secret? Did Vanessa encourage Ben to break into Archie's boardwalk store to try to find the blackmail pictures? Did they shoot Archie?

"I won't tell a word, if you tell me what I want to know," Lucy said.

Vanessa's eyes narrowed. "And what's that?"

"Did anyone else find out about you two?"

Vanessa opened her mouth, then shut it.

"If I know, then I can only assume other people know as well," Lucy said.

Vanessa shifted on her wedge heels. "There was someone else. But he's not a problem anymore."

No, Archie wasn't. He was six feet under. But he'd left behind pictures. Very vivid and telling pictures. But Lucy couldn't reveal that to Vanessa.

"Who?"

"Archie Kincaid."

"The dead guy who was found shot under the boardwalk?" At her silence, Lucy pressed. "How convenient."

Vanessa's eyes flashed in outrage. "What are you suggesting? That I shot him? Well, I didn't. Ben didn't either."

Lucy wasn't convinced. As far as she was concerned, Vanessa and Ben ranked high on the suspect list. She couldn't admit she knew about the blackmail pictures. That was going too far and would raise a slew of questions. But she could ask about what was public knowledge.

"Archie's shop was broken into twice. Did he have something on you two? Were you responsible?" Lucy asked.

Vanessa's eyes widened. "No! We'd never do anything against the law."

The band started a new song, something that involved a drum solo. The walls nearly shook from the pounding. Azad was waiting for her, probably wondering what was taking so long. She'd gotten everything she could out of Vanessa. She wasn't sure she believed her denials, no matter how fervently they were delivered.

"My lips are sealed." Lucy said.

"Thanks." Vanessa looked deflated as she worried her bottom lip. "I'm with friends and need to get back." She opened the door and sailed out.

Lucy waited a minute, her thoughts turning. She didn't need to speak about Vanessa's affair with Ben. Detective Clemmons had the incriminating envelope. She only hoped he'd do his job, thoroughly investigate Ben and Vanessa, and drop Katie from the suspect list.

Or was that wishful thinking?

CHAPTER 25

"I had a great time," Lucy said.

"Me, too."

Azad had driven her back to Kebab Kitchen where her car was parked outside. He guided her forward, and the mere touch of his hand on her lower back sent a warming shiver through her.

They stood awkwardly for a moment, then Azad gathered her into his arms and held her snugly. His breath was warm against her face, and her heart raced. She wound her arms inside his jacket and around his back. He lowered his head and captured her lips. His mouth slanted over hers as she parted her lips in a sigh.

He pulled back to gaze in her eyes. "I'm glad we're together. I'm sorry if I acted like a possessive jerk."

The tenderness in his eyes made her heart turn over in her chest.

She wanted to kiss him more. It didn't matter that they were standing in the restaurant's parking lot beneath the lights. She inched closer, parted her lips, and pressed them against his.

He groaned, then finally met her in a hot kiss. Her palms moved to press against his chest, not to push him away, but to feel the pounding of his heart and the tantalizing muscles through his shirt. Her fingers traveled upward to caress the strong tendons in the back of his neck as she kissed him back.

"Hey, Lucy!"

They broke apart at the sound of the male voice. It was coming from behind the fence that separated the restaurant from the bicycle rental shop next door. She recognized the owner before Michael stepped around the path and came into view.

He stopped in his tracks when he spotted Azad with Lucy.

"What the hell does he want now?" Azad mumbled under his breath.

Lucy shot him a glare before waving Michael over.

"What is it?" she asked him.

"Sorry. I didn't know you were with someone. I heard a car and assumed it was yours." Michael glared at Azad.

Azad glared back.

Lucy lost her patience. "It's okay. What is it?"

"I found the gun."

"What gun?" As soon as she asked the question, she knew the answer. "The gun that shot Archie? Where?"

"I was setting up the fire pit on the beach when I spotted it under the jetty. It must have washed ashore. I called the police and they collected it. They couldn't say for certain if it's the actual murder weapon, but I overheard Detective Clemmons say to another cop that it's the same caliber. I thought you'd want to know."

"Yes! Thanks for coming over."

If the gun Michael found was the same weapon that had killed Archie, then that meant the gun that Neil fired at her the night she'd broken into Seaside Gifts wasn't.

She couldn't jump to conclusions until both guns had been tested by the State Police forensics lab, but she had a feeling in her gut that Michael had found the murder weapon.

"Sorry to disturb you," Michael said, then turned and disappeared behind the fence.

"I guess our evening is over?" Azad asked.

"I'm sorry. I want to get home and talk to Bill and see what they've learned," Lucy said.

Azad looked frustrated. She couldn't blame him. Michael had interrupted them in the past when they were about to kiss. She gave Azad a quick kiss on his lips. "Thanks for tonight. I had a lot of fun."

That night, Lucy and Katie waited up for Bill to get home from his shift at the station. Lucy had informed Katie all about the evening including her confrontation with Vanessa and Michael's surprising announcement that he'd found a gun beneath the jetty. Of course, she'd omitted her heated kiss with Azad.

No need to talk about *that* in detail.

Katie had brewed a pot of green tea and handed Lucy a steaming mug. Lucy sipped the tea and they sat at the kitchen table snacking on homemade chocolate chip cookies. Lucy was on her third cookie when they heard the key slide in the front door. They both jumped out of their seats as Bill strode into the kitchen.

"We heard they found a gun that had washed up on the beach. Is it the murder weapon?" Katie asked.

Bill halted in the process of removing his hat. "Well, as far welcomes go, that was pretty bad."

"Sorry," Katie said as she approached and gave him a brief kiss. "Michael told Lucy he found the gun."

"What can you tell us?" Lucy asked.

Bill placed his hat on the counter and ran his hand through his cropped brown hair. "Thankfully, Michael had the good sense not to touch the gun. It's in police custody and will be sent to the State Police lab for testing. But the salt water has made it difficult, if not impossible, to test for fingerprints. And the serial number had been filed off. Nine times out of ten this means the weapon was illegally purchased."

"But it's the same twenty-two caliber," Lucy said.

"Yes."

"And if you had to guess?" Katie asked.

"I don't like to guess," Bill said.

"But if you had to?" Katie asked.

"I'd place my bet on it being the murder weapon. The killer tossed it into the ocean from the jetty, but it looks like it was stuck in a fisherman's netting," Bill said.

Lucy took a deep breath. "Then that means the gun Neil fired at us isn't the murder weapon."

"That's right," Bill agreed.

"What about the pictures of Ben with Vanessa? Has Clemmons questioned either of them?" Lucy asked.

"He's spoken with both of them, but he hasn't made any arrests," Bill said.

"What's he waiting for?" Katie asked.

"He's in close contact with Prosecutor Walsh. If she was certain she had sufficient evidence, then I don't doubt one or both would have been charged by now," Bill said.

Clemmons was one thing. Prosecutor Walsh was another entirely. The woman was smart as a whip and, a while back, Lucy had looked up her professional record. The prosecutor rarely lost a trial. Which meant if she didn't give Clemmons the green light to arrest Ben or Vanessa, then that could only mean one of two things: either they were innocent or the prosecutor required more evidence of their guilt.

A heaviness centered in Lucy's chest. "Then we're back to the beginning, and no closer to finding the killer."

CHAPTER 26

The doors to Kebab Kitchen opened to a lunch rush. Lucy was pleasantly surprised at the increase in business, but as she helped seat the customers, she realized they were mostly locals. News of the murder had chased many tourists away.

"The mayor is at table three."

Lucy turned at the sound of Emma's voice at her side. "Is he alone?"

"No. He's with Ben Hawkins. They were talking about politics when I seated them," Emma said as she righted a pile of menus at the hostess station.

Lucy glanced at her sister. Did she know something was going on between the two? She felt a bit guilty for not confiding in Emma about her involvement in Archie's murder.

A flicker of apprehension coursed through Lucy. She'd had a nightmare last night about gunshots zinging past her head. No doubt it was due to learning that a gun, most likely the murder weapon, had been found under the jetty.

Emma pulled a waitress pad out of her apron

pocket. "Sally's busy with a large table. I'll wait on them."

"No. Let me," Lucy said.

"Why? You're the manager. You're not supposed to be the waitstaff."

"I know. But I'd like to talk with the mayor and the mayor-to-be." At Emma's questioning look, Lucy was quick to add. "It's about the canceled beach festival."

"Okay," Emma said hesitantly, then handed Lucy the waitress pad.

Lucy halted as Emma touched her sleeve. "I forgot to tell you—Jose came by early this morning to check on the wiring for the fans he installed. Dad was here and let him in. Everything looks good, and Jose left some tools in the storage room. He'll be back to finish the job later."

"Okay. Thanks for letting me know," Lucy said.

She headed for the mayor's table, pad in hand. "Hi, Mayor Huckerby. Mr. Hawkins. What would you two like?"

The two men looked up. "Hi, Lucy," the mayor said.

Ben smiled. "What do you recommend?"

"The hummus bar as an appetizer. The pita is served hot from the oven and I'll get that for you. Lamb gyros with homemade tzatziki sauce are our lunch special for today, and grilled cod is our fish option."

"The gyros sound delicious," the mayor said. "I'd also like coffee."

"I'll take the same," Ben said as he handed Lucy their menus.

Lucy tucked the menus under her arm. "Are

either of you getting nervous about the upcoming election?"

"No," the mayor said.

"A bit," Ben admitted.

"But you are running unopposed. Has someone stepped up to run for the position?" Lucy asked.

"No. But things can change," Ben said.

"What things?" Lucy asked.

"Nothing is a hundred percent guaranteed in politics, is it?" Ben asked.

"That's true," the mayor said. "But Ben is an upstanding citizen of Ocean Crest. I have no doubt he will be good for this town. Don't you agree, Lucy?"

Lucy gazed from one man to the other. "Of course."

If you don't count a possible burglary, blackmail pictures with a stripper, and murder.

She left to get their drinks, tucked their order in the cook's wheel for Butch, and watched the two men from behind the waitress station. It wasn't the first time she'd seen them together. They were talking at Archie's funeral reception. Did they have more in common than a political agenda?

They could be friends but was there more there?

Did the mayor know about Ben's relationship with Vanessa? If he did, was the mayor a customer of the Pussy Cat, too? She couldn't imagine Thomas Huckerby at a strip joint, but then again, she'd never place Ben there either. Ben appeared straitlaced with his blue, button-down shirt, khakis, and neatly clipped hair. He'd owned the barbershop in town since she was a teenager.

If there was one thing she'd learned since returning to town and stumbling upon a body . . . or two . . . is that not everyone was as innocent or guilty as they appeared.

Could Ben be a cold-blooded killer?

Lucy's thoughts continued as she strode into the kitchen to fetch a pot of coffee. She noticed the coffee urn was low. They were also out of coffee filters. She hurried to the storage room where a large box of coffee filters was stashed on a low metal shelf. Jose's toolbox was directly in front of the shelf. She started to push it aside when she noticed his cell phone on top of the toolbox. He must have accidentally left his phone when he'd stopped by this morning.

Lucy had wanted to visit his home and personally say thanks to Maria for the flan and the braised chicken and to deliver some food as well. Now she had an excuse. She'd visit and deliver the food right after the lunch shift. Slipping the cell phone into her back pocket, she grabbed the box of coffee filters and went back to work.

After a successful lunch shift, Lucy placed dolma, stuffed tomatoes and peppers in meat and rice, in a container, then searched for her father. She planned to tell him she was running an errand and would be back soon.

"I'll stay," Raffi said when Lucy found him in the office. He was sifting through time sheets, and a pencil was tucked behind his ear.

"You sure, Dad?"

"I want to work on payroll."

"I'm supposed to do that now."

Raffi swiped a hand across his balding pate. "I know. But I don't want to go home just yet. It will give me something to do."

Lucy sucked her cheeks in and studied him. "Are you fighting with Mom?"

"She's nagging me."

"About what?"

"She wants me to drive her to Philadelphia for another one of Cooking Kurt's book signings. He's also doing a cooking demonstration."

Lucy struggled not to smile. Lucy had taken her mother to one of the celebrity's chef's book signings at Pages Bookstore not long ago. It seemed he had another cookbook out and was capitalizing on his fame.

"I think you should take her," Lucy said.

"That man is a fraud. I've never believed he's written a recipe in any of his cookbooks."

Her father was probably right. But what harm could it do to take her mother? Her dad could score big points with her by driving her. For all her fierce independence, her mother had never learned how to drive.

"You could make a day out of it in the city and please Mom at the same time."

"I don't like driving that far and I don't like the city," he grumbled.

Lucy knew that all too well. Her parents had rarely visited her for the eight years she'd worked in Philly. Even though Center City Philadelphia was only ninety miles—one and a half hours—from Ocean Crest. Crossing the Delaware River via the Ben Franklin Bridge was like traveling to another country for her parents. They'd always expected her to come home.

"If you don't want to drive you could take a bus. I think you should go," Lucy said.

"What about you?" he asked.

"I took her to his last book signing because you wouldn't. It's your turn."

He sighed. "Fine. I suppose we could make a day of it in the city. It's been years since we've toured Independence Hall, and I want to visit the new Constitution Center." Raffi's gaze dropped to the take-out box in her hands. "What have you got there? Food for Katie and Bill?"

"No. It's for Jose's wife, Maria. She's sent me flan and chicken. Both were delicious. Jose left his cell phone behind so I figured I'd return it and deliver this food as a thank-you," she said.

Raffi nodded in approval. "Go on. I'm happy to finish here," he said, indicating the time sheets in his hand.

"Okay. Thanks, Dad." She placed a kiss on his cheek, grabbed a bag of cat treats, and headed out the door.

She shook the bag. It didn't take long before Gadoo showed up. "Hello there. I told you I'd get more treats." He wound a figure eight around her legs and meowed. She scratched him under his chin and he purred. She poured out a handful of treats, checked his food and water bowls, then headed to her car with the take-out containers. She started her car and headed north, to a small development where Jose lived. She'd pulled his address from one of his invoices. Turning down a narrow street, she parked in front of a tan Colonial with blue shutters. The lawn was well-kept and a large flowerpot with pink and white begonias added a splash of color. Jose's truck was in the driveway.

She parked in the street, then headed for the front door with the food. She knocked and waited.

No answer.

Maybe they were in the backyard on this pleasant evening, she thought, heading around the side of the house to the back door. No one was in the backyard. The delicious smell of burgers wafted from the grill. A clothesline full of laundry blew in the breeze. She stepped around the clothesline and pushed aside a red hoodie, then froze.

Something caught her eye. The hoodie had a torn pocket and piece of fabric was missing. Her mind spun back as she recalled the piece of fabric she'd found under the rolling security gate of Seaside Gifts the night of the first burglary.

The police had never found the first burglar.

Her breath stalled in her throat as her mind raced.

Was Jose the burglar, not Ben?

But why?

Why would Jose break into Archie's shop? Jose had been doing electrical work for Archie. Had he accidently torn his hoodie while working at the shop? Or was there more?

Was he desperate for money, and he'd discovered an easy way inside? It didn't make sense. Jose had a good job. He was in demand. It had to be something else. But what?

Had Archie been blackmailing Jose?

It wasn't a far stretch. Archie had already been blackmailing Ben. Archie had wanted Ben in his pocket as mayor in order to approve his mercantile licenses.

But what could Archie have wanted from Jose? Her gut told her Jose was somehow involved, and her instincts had never led her wrong in the past.

Whatever the reason, she was holding evidence that could prove that Jose had broken into Archie's shop. If he was the burglar, then he'd lied to the police. He'd lied to her.

Another thought followed, even more frightening.

Could Jose be the murderer?

The sound of the back door opening made her jump. She dropped the red hoodie and whirled around. She should have expected it, but the sudden, male voice frightened her just the same.

Jose loomed on the back step. "You figured it out, didn't you?"

CHAPTER 27

"It was you, wasn't it? You broke into Archie's shop," Lucy said.

Jose's eyes lowered to the red hoodie at her feet. "I should have tossed that out."

"Is that a yes?"

Jose stepped down from the back steps. "It's not that simple. You know I worked in Archie's store."

"Yes, I know. But the security gates would have been open, not closed. If you snagged your clothing, then the gates would have had to have been lowered almost all the way."

His features screwed into a painful twist. "I never meant for it to happen."

"For what to happen?" she pressed. Would he confess to burglary, murder, or both?

"I told Neil I had to check on the electrical box I'd installed for Archie, and I jammed the lock on the rolling security gate. I returned that night and used a jack to raise the rolling gate, crawled inside the store, then unjammed the lock."

Lucy felt as if her breath was cut off. It made sense. She'd wondered how the burglar had managed to get past the locked security gate. Even a jack wouldn't have worked to raise the heavy rolling gates if the gate had been properly locked from inside.

She wanted to flee, but she also knew she didn't stand a chance if he decided to pursue her. He was much bigger and faster. She wouldn't make it around the corner of the yard.

Instead, she looked him square in the eye and asked the question that had been pestering her. "Why?"

"Archie had something on me. I needed to get it."

"What was it?" she asked.

His brow furrowed, and something flickered in his eyes, something deep and disturbing. His voice lowered, and she strained to hear. "I'm illegal."

Oh my God.

He was an illegal alien. His words were like a punch to the gut. She knew Jose was from the Dominican Republic and his wife, Maria, was from Mexico. She'd always assumed they had green cards or work visas.

"Archie was holding that over you?" she asked.

"It's not what you think. I didn't walk across a Texas border or swim here from a leaky boat. I arrived with a legal green card years ago. When Archie moved to Ocean Crest, he hired me to do some electrical work. One day, he overheard me talking on my cell that my green card was up for renewal. Archie told me he'd helped a relative not only renew his green card but apply for permanent citizenship. He said he'd help me renew mine as well. I believed him."

"He lied?"

"He claimed he filled out the forms to renew my green card, but he said the renewal was denied based on a technicality. No big deal, he'd said. More documents were needed, and I supplied them. Archie was supposed to reapply, but he never did. All the notices were sent to him."

"He set you up?"

"I had no idea. Months later he showed me an order to be removed by Immigration Services. I'm to be deported."

She couldn't imagine how he'd felt. Betrayed. Frightened. Desperate. "What did you do?"

"Things got worse. Archie started blackmailing me. He demanded I work for him for free. In exchange, he claimed he wouldn't turn me in as an illegal alien. He grew bolder over time, too. Soon after, he insisted I work for free for his 'friends,' who turned out to be Archie's out-of-town suppliers. His suppliers provided discounted merchandise for Archie's store. The electrical work took up most of my time, but I had no choice. I live in fear of being deported."

Jose's story was heartbreaking. Archie had been a true cad. "Why break into Seaside Gifts? What were you after?" Lucy asked.

"My expired green card and all the denied paperwork, including the final notice with the deportation date. I had to retrieve the documents before someone else found them. As far as I know, Archie's nephew, Neil, doesn't know. No one must know."

"Did you find what you were looking for?"

"No. As soon as I heard the police sirens, I ran."

"What about Maria? Does she know about this?" Maria was far along in her pregnancy. Was she illegal as well?

"She has no idea. Her green card is up to date, and she has a good job at the school."

"Why haven't you told her?"

His face fell and he shoved his hands into his jean pockets. "I can't bring myself to tell her the truth. Maria's due in less than a month, and she's been so happy. She's been picking out paint colors and linens for the baby's room and cleaning out the house. She calls it nesting. How can I destroy her happiness? And worse, I know that if I tell her she will get very upset. How might that affect the pregnancy, and our baby?"

Lucy didn't want to think about those kinds of possibilities. Maria would be devastated. Her husband and the father of her child could be deported. What then?

Archie had to know about the baby, but that hadn't stopped him from hurting Jose. Could Archie have been so mean-hearted?

Yes. If it meant lining his pockets.

Archie had been blackmailing the mayor-to-be Ben for potential political favors. He'd used Jose as a source of income. The electrician provided unpaid services for Archie and Archie's business associates. In exchange, Archie had received extremely cheap merchandise for his store. The more she discovered about Archie, the less likable he seemed.

But still, the man didn't deserve to be shot under the boardwalk.

"Getting the immigration papers was the only reason you broke into Archie's store?" Lucy asked.

Jose's eyes blazed. "Yes! I didn't want to steal anything."

"It worked out for you that Archie was shot," she said. "You were on the boardwalk for the beach festival that day. I also remember you'd said you had work to do in Archie's store." She could be facing a killer. Jose had motive and opportunity.

"I swear I didn't kill him." At her silence, he stepped forward. "Are you going to tell anyone?"

How could she not? How could she? She'd promised to tell Bill everything. Heck, she'd promised not to do anything risky, only to keep her ears and eyes open.

But this didn't count. She hadn't come here intending to stick her nose in someone else's business. She'd come here to return Jose's cell phone that he'd left behind at the restaurant and deliver a meal. Facing a possible killer hadn't been her plan.

So what should she do now?

"Lucy?"

They both whirled to see Maria through the back door screen. She stepped outside, and Jose rushed over to hold out his hand and help his wife down the back steps. She wore a maternity dress and held her swollen stomach as she walked.

She smiled, her pretty brown eyes warm with welcome. "It's so nice to see you again, Lucy! It's been a long time," Maria said.

Relief swept through Lucy. Jose wouldn't harm

her in front of his wife. "Hi, Maria. It's good to see you."

Maria smoothed her brown hair. "I wasn't expecting you. I would have put on some makeup and prepared something to eat."

"You look lovely, and I was just stopping by to return this to Jose." Lucy pulled a cell phone out of her back pocket and handed it to him. "He left this at the restaurant on top of his toolbox. I also wanted to thank you for the flan and braised chicken. It was delicious. I have *dolma* for you both. It's tonight's dinner special." Lucy handed Maria the take-out containers.

Maria's face beamed. "A day I don't have to cook is a treat. Would you like to come inside?"

Lucy's gaze darted to Jose's. "No, thank you. I have to return to the restaurant. Another time? I'd love to catch up. Jose says the nursery is coming along."

"It is. And another time would be lovely. My maternity leave starts next week and it would be good to have company."

Lucy forced a smile and waved. "Next week then." As she hurried to her car, her mind raced with what she'd learned. She didn't think Jose was a killer, but could she be sure? He had the strongest motive so far.

Deportation.

Leaving behind a pregnant wife.

Even Lucy might be driven to kill a blackmailer under those circumstances.

Telling Bill was difficult. Lucy knew he was obligated to act on the information, but a part of her wanted to protect Jose and Maria. On her drive home, she'd argued the pros and cons with herself and had come to the conclusion that she trusted Bill as much as Katie. He would know what to do with the information.

"Thank you for telling me, Lucy," Bill said.

"Poor Maria," Katie said.

Katie had brewed fresh iced tea and had carried out a pitcher and glasses to her back deck. Katie joined Lucy on a two-seater deck swing, and Bill was in a patio chair across from them. It was his afternoon off, but Lucy knew he'd have to go into the station soon and reveal what she'd discovered to Clemmons.

"Will they arrest Jose?" Lucy asked.

Bill let out a slow breath and picked a stone out of the tread of his shoe before answering. "It's likely. Clemmons will have to call immigration today as well."

"Today?" Lucy's stomach bottomed out. She didn't think it would happen that fast. Poor Maria. She couldn't imagine her distress and hoped it wouldn't affect her pregnancy.

"They can't deport Jose that quickly, can they?" Katie asked.

"I'm sorry," Bill said. "I don't know how it works, especially if Jose's charged with murder. I promise to keep you both updated."

CHAPTER 28

"Lucy? Are you paying any attention?" Sally asked.

Lucy blinked. "I'm sorry. Did you need something?" It was the following day, and Lucy was at the hostess stand seating customers for lunch service. There had been a steady flow of business, but her mind wasn't on work. Instead, she kept reliving her visit to Jose's home, and despite debating whether to tell Bill what she'd learned, she knew she'd done the right thing.

Bill had left for work hours ago. He must have told Detective Clemmons everything by now, and the police would have to act. Would they arrest Jose for murder or for evading deportation or both?

She felt ill, like a corkscrew was slowly twisting in her stomach.

"I asked you if you could deliver the food to the table by the window with the baby in the high chair. I need to take an order for a large table of ten and I don't want their food to get cold," Sally said.

"Oh, sorry," Lucy said.

"Hey, what's wrong?"

"Nothing. It's just . . ."

Sally lowered her voice. "Murder business? I know you, and I know that look."

Lucy met Sally's eyes. "You're right. It is murder business. Only my conscience is bugging me."

"How?"

Lucy lowered her voice. "I wonder if I made a mistake by telling the police something . . . something that could ruin a lot of lives."

Sally squeezed her arm. "Go with your gut, Lucy. It's hasn't failed the town in the past. I believe in you."

A warm glow flowed through her. She was reminded time and time again what good friends she had in Ocean Crest. "Thanks, Sally."

Sally gave her a nudge. "Now go fetch my table's food."

Lucy let out a deep breath, and loaded a tray with plates. She hurried to deliver the food and was rewarded with a giggling baby in the high chair. She was happy the restaurant was running smoothly. Butch and Azad worked in harmony. Sally and Emma took orders and delivered food seamlessly. Customers were content. But Lucy couldn't shake off the feeling that something was very wrong.

The restaurant's phone rang. Lucy hurried to answer the landline by the cash register. "Kebab Kitchen."

"It's Katie."

She could tell by her friend's voice that it was bad news. The knot in her stomach returned.

"Jose's been arrested for murder."

Oh, no. It was what she'd feared. "What about

the others? Ben? Harold? Neil? Even Rita?" Had Clemmons overlooked the longtime locals and gone for the illegal immigrant? Nothing would surprise her.

"Ben had an alibi that checked out."

"Who?"

"He was seen at the Pussy Cat picking up Vanessa by one of the club's workers."

"By 'one of the club's workers' do you mean a fellow stripper?" Lucy asked.

"A lady who goes by the name of Pinky Pie."

Good grief. "And Clemmons believes her?"

"Yes. There's one more thing. The State Police lab forensic results came in. Neil's gun, the one that he fired at you, is not the murder weapon."

That would help clear Neil as a suspect. It was looking worse and worse for Jose. Lucy's eyes closed and she recalled Maria's happy expression when she'd seen her and talked about the baby.

Baby Enrique. He wouldn't know his father now.

It was all so confusing. She should be happy if she'd provided the information that resulted in finding the murderer. That's what she'd wanted all along, wasn't it? For the killer to be arrested, for everything to return to normal, and for the beach festival to resume.

Then why did she feel like she'd done something terribly wrong?

Lucy's running shoes pounded on the boards. There was only one place she could think clearly and without interruption. Her jetty overlooking the Atlantic Ocean.

To avoid questions from her parents and the rest of the staff at Kebab Kitchen as to why she needed to leave before lunch service was over, she'd claimed she had to run an important errand. She'd changed into her running clothes in the storage room, driven to the boardwalk entrance, and had headed out from there. She motored at a slow pace as her mind kept turning to Jose's arrest. Suspects ran through her mind in pace with her feet.

Ben and Vanessa's alibi, Pinky Pie. Neil's gun and his dreams of surfing grandeur and his debts to his girlfriend for his expensive surfboard. A spurned Rita who not only discovered her engagement ring was a fake, but that her fiancé had been married. A longtime business rivalry with Harold. She felt like she was missing something, but she couldn't put her finger on it.

Two seagulls squawked and fought over the remains of a hot dog that had missed the trash can. The shops blurred by. The custard stand, the two pizza shops, the tattoo parlor. The bright yellow-and-blue boardwalk tramcar passed with its speaker blaring, *"Watch the tramcar, please!"* On the beach, people made the trek with their beach carts and chairs toward the ocean to find the perfect spot. Children frolicked in the surf and built sandcastles. She even spotted Kristin sunbathing in her beach chair.

"Hello, Lucy!" Madame Vega called out and waved from outside her psychic parlor as she puffed on a cigarette.

Lucy jogged over. "Hello. Busy day?"

The woman sighed and shook her head. "It's not in the cards. Are you coming for the reading?"

She wasn't, but because the hopeful expression on the woman's face, Lucy didn't want to disappoint her. She *had* promised to stop by for another tarot card reading, but she'd never had the time.

Maybe she can help.

Lucy didn't know where that thought came from. It's not like she believed in the tarot cards, but her first visit had been eerily close to the truth.

"Sure," Lucy said. "I can use some advice."

Madame Vega put out her cigarette in a soda bottle that had been cut in half to serve as an ashtray. Lucy followed her inside the room and sat at the velvet-draped table. Candles burned low and cast shadows on the tablecloth. The woman reached for her blue turban with its large fake sapphire, covered her graying curls, then started shuffling the cards.

"What is your question?" Madame Vega asked.

Lucy had half a dozen, but she knew the one that was troubling her the most. "My conscious is troubling me. Did I do the right thing, even if it means a man will go to jail?"

Madame Vega's brown eyes snapped to hers. "A big burden."

"Yeah. A big one."

"Let's see what the cards say." She shuffled the cards and spread them out in a fan on the tablecloth. "Just like last time. Put your hopes, feelings, and desires into the cards."

Lucy ran her hands across the cards and thought about her troubles and the nagging questions that she hoped could been answered. She stacked the cards and handed them back.

"Last time you had your cards read you had questions about Archie's death. I assume that's whom you are asking about?" Madame Vega asked.

"It is."

Madame flipped over the Nine of Pentacles card—a woman holding a bird in a garden with ripe fruit for picking—and her lips drew in thoughtfully. "The past card is not a surprise," she said. "Your hard work has paid off and you've accomplished a lot in life. You are an attorney, after all. But you must keep up the hard work and focus." Madame Vega tapped the card.

What Madame said could pertain to almost anyone. It didn't help Lucy with her guilt over Jose's arrest or answer the nagging questions that still persisted.

"Let's see your present. The Page of Wands." She flipped over a card to show a man gazing up into the sky. "A critical decision awaits you. Perhaps it involves a man? Perhaps a burgeoning romance awaits on your horizon? You are receiving messages, but will you listen? Will you balance impulse with practicality and take a risk?"

The medium's words hit Lucy square in the gut. This advice was closer to the truth, was similar to what had happened at her last reading. It was as if Madame Vega had crawled inside her head and read her mind.

Yes, Azad was definitely in her present. Lucy was receiving messages from him—clear messages if she considered their heated kiss. She was also at the crux of making a big decision, and balancing logic with her hormones was a part of it. Could she take a leap of faith and encourage their burgeoning romance?

"Your future." She flipped over the final card. "Goodness. The Death card. It doesn't always signify loss of life, but perhaps it does in this instance. Archie's murder was a tragedy for the town. I vividly remember the day. Do be careful."

Lucy had already asked the medium about that day. Madame Vega had been working on the boardwalk, but she'd said she'd been busy with customers and hadn't seen anything. Still, Lucy felt compelled to ask again.

"You didn't see anything suspicious the day Archie was shot?" Lucy asked.

Madame Vega shook her head and the gem in her turban glinted in the candlelight. "No. I was sitting here reading palms. It was a busy day with the tourists. But the murder has troubled everyone. I feel bad for his wife."

Lucy's head snapped up. "His wife? You mean Archie's wife, Kristin?"

"Yes."

"Have you met her?"

"I have."

Lucy struggled to recall if Madame Vega had been in the church for the funeral or the reception that had followed, but she came up blank. "You mean at the funeral?"

Madame's wrinkled brow furrowed even more. "Oh, no. I hate funerals and avoid them. The spirits of the dead may harm my ability to read palms or draw the right cards."

A slight hum ran through Lucy. "Then when?" According to Kristin, she hadn't stepped foot in Ocean Crest until the funeral.

"She is a big believer in the cards and she came to me to have her cards read."

"When?"

"About two weeks before her husband was killed."

Two weeks.

Oh my God. Had Kristin lied about her indifference regarding Archie's affair with Rita? Had she discovered that her husband had proposed to another woman, purchased an engagement ring, while he was still married to Kristin?

Had that sent her over the edge? She'd had the perfect alibi so far. Even Detective Clemmons had confirmed it.

Until now.

Kristin could have slipped out of her city office. New York City was just shy of a three-hour drive from Ocean Crest in South Jersey via the Garden State Parkway. It was possible to appear in both locales within the same day. It would have been easy to sneak into Ocean Crest unnoticed when the entire town was busy with an influx of tourists for the beach festival. Easy to call Archie on his cell and convince him to meet her under the boardwalk, shoot him, then blend into the crowd and disappear back to New York with no one the wiser.

It was the perfect crime. Except for one glitch. A quirky boardwalk medium.

Lucy leaned forward and clasped Madame Vega's hand. "Please don't tell anyone what we've discussed." Not until she could get a hold of Bill and tell him everything.

"Have I helped ease your conscious and answered your question?"

"Oh, yes." Lucy released her hand and reached for her purse.

Kristin was the killer, not Jose. "You said she first had her cards read two weeks ago. Have you seen her since?"

"No, but she has an appointment for today."

"Today?"

Madame Vega pushed back her voluminous sleeve to glance at her watch. Lucy thought it odd that a woman who claimed she could predict the future even had one.

"At one o'clock," Madame Vega said. "She should be here any minute."

Lucy gasped. "Any minute?"

Someone cleared their throat, and Lucy spun around in her seat just as a shadow blocked what little sunlight lit the darkened room.

Kristin stood in the entrance. Dressed in a white beach cover-up, shorts, and high-heeled flip-flops, she must have just left the beach.

"Come inside, Mrs. Kincaid," Madame Vega said. "Lucy and I are finished here."

Madame Vega had no idea how critical her information was. She hadn't attended the funeral where Kristin claimed she'd never set foot in Ocean Crest before the funeral. She didn't know.

Lucy swallowed hard. She needed to tell Bill. She also needed a poker face now more than ever. "Hello, Mrs. Kincaid," Lucy said.

For a pulse-pounding moment, both women stared at each other. In that split second, comprehension dawned on Kristin's face as she realized that Lucy had just learned the truth. Kristin's eyes narrowed, then she turned and made a beeline out the door.

CHAPTER 29

Kristin took off like a shot down the boardwalk. First shocked by learning that Kristin was the murderer, then from having her suddenly appear, Lucy stepped away from Madame Vega's table only to have the velvet tablecloth snag on the Velcro pocket of her running shorts. The tablecloth crashed to the floor followed by a flurry of tarot cards.

"Stop!" Lucy yelled after Kristin.

"What's going on?" Madame Vega asked, her voice taking on a high-pitched tone.

"Kristin killed Archie! Call the police!" With that final statement, Lucy took off running.

Panic rioted within Lucy. She couldn't let Kristin out of her sight. Not until the police arrived, cuffed her, and read her her Miranda rights.

Lucy sprinted out of the medium's room, then halted, momentarily blinded. It took precious seconds for her eyes to adjust from the dim lighting inside Madame Vega's enclave, to the bright sunlight on the boardwalk. Looking left, then right, she didn't see Kristin anywhere through the throng of people and bicycles on the boardwalk.

How could she move so fast in those ridiculous high-heeled flip-flops?

Then she heard an outraged cry as a man picked up a woman off the boardwalk. Kristin apparently had rammed into the couple and without stopping to check on her casualties, teetered away fast. She was at least a block away.

Lucy had the advantage of running shoes and adrenaline, and she took off in hot pursuit. Legs pumping and chest heaving, she gained on Kristin.

Kristin glanced back, noticed Lucy was catching up, and kicked off her flip-flops. Head down, she picked up her pace, barging recklessly through the crowd. She crashed into a family leaving a refreshment stand carrying armfuls of popcorn and french fries. Popcorn and hot fries flew everywhere. The couple's child cried out at the lost food.

Other people shouted in anger, but Kristin ignored them, her arms and legs flying as she kept going.

Lucy slipped on a french fry, fell, and banged her knee on the boardwalk. She ignored the pain, sprang to her feet, and kept going. She raced past the Gray sisters' shop, Harold's store, and spotted Neil smoking outside Seaside Gifts. The custard stand flew by, followed by a burger joint and a large, flashing neon root beer sign.

"Stop!" Lucy shouted.

Kristin didn't stop. She barreled her way into a group of bicycles. A surrey, with a child in the front, swerved to the right and almost ran into the side rail to avoid a collision. The child repeatedly rang the surrey bell. A bicyclist cursed as he caught himself just before crashing his bike into another rider.

Kristin kept going and knocked over a trash can in an attempt to stop her pursuer, but Lucy hurdled over the obstacle like a high school track star.

All down the boardwalk, people yelped and shouted as Kristin ran wild. But Lucy was determined.

As she neared a street exit on the boardwalk, Lucy could tell that Kristin was starting to struggle. She grasped her side and slowed to catch her breath.

Lucy, on the other hand, felt good. The weeks of jogging the boards and the beach had paid off. She could keep running, whereas Kristin looked winded and exhausted. The color had drained from her face and she had a wild panicked look in her eyes.

I've got her now, Lucy thought.

What would Kristin do next? Head for the street and her car? She had to know the police would pursue her. If they couldn't stop her in town, the Ocean Crest police could radio the next town and she would eventually be caught and . . .

What the heck!

At the last moment, Kristin darted inside a fudge and salt water taffy shop. As soon as Lucy set foot inside, she heard the screeching. "Are you crazy, lady?!"

A candy maker in a stained apron who'd been wrapping taffy, stood with her hands on her hips staring at the candy scattered across the floor.

"Sorry! Which way did she go?" Lucy asked.

The woman pointed to the side door.

"Call the police!" Lucy shouted as she sprinted out the door.

Rather than leave the boardwalk, Kristin had turned and headed back the way Lucy had chased her.

Where was she headed now? Were they going to run up and down the boardwalk until the cops showed up or until one of them collapsed in exhaustion?

Then she saw it. Or rather, she heard the recorded message blaring from the speakers.

"Watch the tramcar, please!"

Lucy registered Kristin's next move a second before Kristin hopped onto the back of the moving tramcar.

Crap.

Lucy pumped her legs and ran after the tramcar. She could see the young, rear attendant arguing with Kristin, but Kristin ignored the girl. Clutching the seats, Kristin made her way to the front.

Lucy reached the back of the tramcar and grabbed onto the metal frame with her right hand. Her legs pumped double-time to catch up to the running vehicle, and for a moment, she was suspended—one leg on the floor rubber mat, the other dangling in midair.

"Watch the tramcar, please!"

The attendant finally noticed Lucy, and started shouting just as Lucy gained a foothold and pulled herself up to stand inside the tramcar.

"Miss! You can't do that. You have to board at a stop!" the attendant called out, her face pale.

"Call the police!" Lucy shouted, heading down the aisle after Kristin.

Passengers stared agape. Kids chattered and pointed in excitement.

Reaching the front of the car, Lucy clutched the

back of Kristin's beach cover-up. "Stop! There's nowhere left to run."

"Get off me!" Kristin screamed, then wiggled out of the robe. Lucy was left with a fistful of beach cover-up, and Kristin was left with a bikini top and skimpy jean shorts. The driver finally noticed the disturbance and the tramcar came to a grinding halt. Lucy, holding on to nothing but Kristin's cover-up, lost her footing and crashed to the rubber floor mat, reinjuring her already-skinned knee.

Kristin took advantage of Lucy's fall and leapt off the tramcar.

Gritting her teeth, Lucy sprang to her feet. She wasn't about to give up. Not after she'd chased Kristin all this way. She spotted Kristin running down the boardwalk stairs and onto the beach.

"Miss, you have to pay three dollars," the driver said as he looked at Lucy like she'd lost her mind.

"I'll mail it in," Lucy said, then jumped off the tramcar in pursuit.

Running on the beach was harder than the boardwalk. Kristin, already winded, started to stagger. Lucy's daily jogs on the boards and the beach really paid off now. Her knee stung and blood ran down her leg, but she wasn't out of breath and felt she could run another half hour.

Kristin plowed into a sandcastle, knocking it over. Kids screeched in protest. One even threw an empty bucket at her, but missed.

She can't keep going. Now I have her!

Kristin veered right and headed under the boardwalk. If Lucy didn't stop her soon, Kristin could make it to the street and then to her car. In her panicked state, she could run into pedestrians and hurt people. Lucy couldn't let that happen.

It was several degrees cooler under the boardwalk and the sand was damp. Lucy's legs pumped and she gained ground until she was only an arm's length away from Kristin.

In one last-ditch attempt, Lucy launched herself onto the woman and knocked her to the ground. They struggled, skidding across the sand. Kristin screeched in outrage, kicking and biting, but Lucy grasped her wrists and pinned them to the sand.

Lucy grit her teeth. "It's over. The police are on their way."

Kristin sagged as she panted to catch her breath. A seagull landed a foot away from her head to peck at a piece of popcorn that had flown from her hair.

"You shot your husband? Why?" Lucy asked.

"Archie deserved it."

"No one deserves to be murdered."

"Like hell! I knew about his affair to that . . . to that hair salon tramp."

"Her name is Rita, and she's not a tramp."

"Whatever. She had the audacity to call me and tell me that he'd proposed to her . . . that he'd purchased an engagement ring for her. He deserved to die. I did both of us a favor."

Her cold words caused a shiver to course down Lucy's spine. Kristin was the spurned wife, but she turned out to be just as manipulative as her cheating husband.

Lucy thought of Jose stuck in a jail cell. He faced murder charges and deportation. Maria must be in a frenzy of worry. "You would let an innocent man take the fall for your crime?" Lucy asked.

"I did this town a favor. I suspected Archie was blackmailing more than one person. He was also worth more to me dead than alive," Kristin said.

"Life insurance?"

"No. His businesses."

Confusion creased Lucy's brow. "Archie had only one, the boardwalk shop. He left it to his nephew, Neil."

She laughed, a high-pitched sound. "One in Ocean Crest. He has businesses out of state. I get them all."

This was news to Lucy, but it made sense. Revenge and greed. Two motives for murder.

"You won't get anything now." It was fitting that Kristen was caught under the boardwalk—the same place she'd shot Archie.

Lucy looked to the beach to see children jumping up and down and pointing to where she had Kristin pinned under the boardwalk. Bill, followed by Detective Clemmons and two other officers in uniform, came running.

"Lucy! Are you okay?" Bill asked.

Lucy released Kristin and stood. Clemmons pulled Kristin to her feet and cuffed her. Kristin shot daggers at Lucy the entire time.

"I'm fine. She murdered Archie."

"We heard," Clemmons said. "Numerous phone calls came into the station." He glared at her. "Just in case you forgot, Ms. Berberian, you are a civilian and not permitted to chase down criminals."

"I understand, Detective. But I have to say, it was my best workout yet," Lucy said.

The detective shot her a cold glare before dragging Kristin away.

"You're bleeding," Bill said with a frown.

"It's only a skinned knee."

Bill leaned close to whisper in her ear, "Good work, Lucy. I'll drive you home."

"Not yet. I have one more stop in mind."

"Where?"

"The police station."

"I'm sorry, but we can't release Jose Alvarez. We already called the proper authorities about his status as an illegal alien and they are expected shortly," Detective Clemmons said.

Lucy faced Detective Clemmons at the police station. Bill stood beside her. "You have to wait. Jose should have an attorney present," Lucy said.

After Lucy had explained everything to Bill, he'd taken her straight to the station where they'd run into Maria as she was leaving from visiting Jose in his cell. She'd been distraught and her eyes were puffy from tears. Lucy had been concerned for the baby and had asked her to sit in the waiting room.

"Why are you here, Ms. Berberian? Are you representing Mr. Alvarez?" Clemmons asked.

"No. Ms. Clara Rose is on her way from Philadelphia," Lucy said.

"Who?" Clemmons asked.

"I called a professional acquaintance at my former Philadelphia firm. Clara Rose specializes in immigration law and she has agreed to represent Mr. Alvarez."

Clemmons rubbed his mustache with his thumb and forefinger. "An order for removal has already been issued. I don't see how she can help."

"She's filed a motion to reopen Jose's case." Once the extenuating circumstances were presented along with any missing documentation, Clara was hopeful Jose's green card would be renewed. "Blackmail," Clara had said, most likely qualified as an extenuating circumstance. Clara was even hopeful that Jose could become a United States citizen one day.

Her words were a huge relief.

Jose would have needed *two* attorneys—a criminal defense attorney and an immigration attorney—but no longer. Kristin had been arrested for killing her husband, and the murder charges against Jose would be dismissed.

"I think you should listen to her," Bill told Clemmons.

Detective Clemmons nodded curtly and, to everyone's surprise, he cracked a smile. "For once, I'm happy to agree with Mrs. Berberian's suggestion."

Maria was summoned from the waiting room and told the news. A cry of relief broke from her lips, and she rushed forward to embrace Lucy. "How can we ever thank you?"

"Your flan was the best I ever tasted," Lucy said.

Maria wiped tears of joy from her eyes and smiled. "Then you will have a lifetime supply."

CHAPTER 30

Kebab Kitchen closed early that night. Everyone was gathered around a table full of Angela's favorite meze—or appetizers—of hummus, tabbouleh, olives, and feta cheese. Raffi had brought out his favorite cognac, and Niari was drinking sparkling grape juice.

"Did *Mokour* Lucy really chase a killer down the boardwalk and end up tackling her on the beach?" Niari asked, her blue eyes wide.

"Where did you hear that?" Emma asked.

"I heard Azad say it to Butch in the kitchen," Niari said.

Azad and Butch exchanged a glance. "You shouldn't eavesdrop," Azad admonished.

"Well, it's true. Isn't it?" Niari asked.

"Yes," Lucy said. "But it wasn't as glamorous as it sounds and you should never do anything like that."

Niari rolled her eyes. "That's what grown-ups say about *everything*."

Lucy chuckled, then caught Azad's gaze. He was frowning, definitely not finding anything amusing.

"Lucy, will you help me bring the baklava trays from the kitchen?" Azad asked.

She followed him through the swinging doors into the kitchen. Azad didn't wait long before he pulled her behind the big industrial mixer. "You promised me not to do anything dangerous."

"It wasn't dangerous. I was chasing Kristin on the boardwalk, a very public place."

Azad frowned. "Lucy," he said, his voice full of exasperation as he said her name. "Kristin shot and killed someone. She could have been carrying a gun."

"But she wasn't. And I'm fine. I couldn't just let her get away."

"How about calling the police?"

"I told other people to call the police."

He let out a huff, then hugged her. "I can't change you, can I?"

She melted into his arms. It felt too good to fight, and despite her words, it had been a harrowing day. "You wouldn't want me to."

"True."

He lowered his head and kissed her. The touch of his lips sent the pit of her stomach into a wild swirl. This felt right and she knew deep in her bones it was meant to be between them. Their past was as entwined as her parents' grapevine, and their future was an offshoot of the vine. He'd come back into her life, not just as the head chef, but as a grown man who'd changed.

Just like she had.

Her heartbeat throbbed in her ears. They still

had a long way to go, but she believed Madame Vega's advice was sound. The cards didn't lie.

A burgeoning romance awaits on your horizon. Will you balance impulse with practicality and take a risk?

Yes. Absolutely. She could.

Pulling back, he gazed into her eyes. "Amazing. When can we do that again?"

"How about tonight?"

He flashed a sexy grin. "Absolutely. But first, let's go out there and celebrate with everyone."

Lucy followed Azad back into the dining room and was surprised to see more people had arrived. Bill and Katie. Sally and Butch. Michael and Mr. Citteroni from next door. Even Detective Clemmons stood by one of the tables with a plate in his hand. Her mother had been quick to serve him.

Clemmons finished chewing before he said, "Kristin confessed to killing Archie. She had a double motive—at first she just wanted his businesses, but then she learned about his affair with Rita. Archie had five out-of-state businesses, dealing in everything from clothing stores to shoes to sports equipment. Kristin arranged to be seen in her office by coworkers before she left unnoticed from a back door, drove a hundred and fifty-five miles—just under three hours—from New York City to Ocean Crest. She called Archie, lured him under the boardwalk, then shot him."

"Did she admit to anything else?" Katie asked.

"She claims she didn't break into Archie's shop.

I believe her. She had the keys and could have taken anything she'd wanted at any time," Clemmons said.

"Oh? Then who do the police think was responsible?" Katie asked.

"Jose confessed to the first break-in after Lucy discovered his torn sweatshirt matched the piece of fabric caught beneath the rolling security gate," Clemmons said. "Neil decided against pressing charges after learning his uncle had intentionally failed to properly renew Jose's green card. The prosecutor has agreed."

That was even more good news. Lucy could only imagine both Jose's and Maria's relief.

"What about the second break-in?" Katie asked, her blue eyes innocent.

Bill coughed and sputtered as he lowered his drink. Katie absentmindedly patted her husband on the back. Lucy didn't think Bill's coughing fit was from the cognac.

"We still don't know. We changed our theory and now think the second burglary wasn't related to the first break-in or the murder. It's not uncommon for criminals to believe that a business is uninhabited and easy pickings after reading an obituary in the newspaper," Clemmons said.

Lucy met the detective's eyes and forced herself to stay calm. If the police believed that to be true, then she wouldn't enlighten them.

"Well, I'm relieved the murderer was arrested," Lucy's mother said.

"Amen to that," Raffi said.

The door opened and Neil stopped by the hostess stand.

"Hello, Neil," Lucy said as she hurried over to greet him. "Can I help you?"

He ran a hand through his shaggy hair. "I heard about Kristin. I can't believe she killed him."

"I'm sorry."

He shuffled his feet on the tile and lowered his eyes. "Don't be. I stopped by to thank you for catching my uncle's killer. And to let you know that I'm closing the shop."

"To go to surf in Hawaii?"

He shook his head. "No. I'm working in my girlfriend's father's surf shop. I owe him some money for a surfboard. I guess all this craziness has convinced me to do the right thing and start over."

She was surprised and impressed. "Well, good for you. Would you like something to eat?"

His gaze met hers and he cracked a smile. "Sure." He joined the group and Angela handed him a plate with a large piece of baklava.

Neil took a bite and chewed. "This is awesome."

Angela beamed.

The door swung open again and Ben and Mayor Huckerby stepped inside. For a small celebration, it was quickly turning into a town event.

"Hello, Mayor. Hello, Ben," Angela said, greeting the two men.

"We wanted to stop by in person to announce that the beach festival is set to resume tomorrow morning with a beach volleyball competition."

Lucy clasped her hand to her chest. "Wonderful!"

"We want to thank you as well, Lucy. You put yourself at risk by figuring out Kristin was the real killer and chasing her down," Ben said.

"I wouldn't have known if it wasn't for Madame Vega," Lucy said. "She deserves to share the credit."

"We'll have to thank her then," the mayor said.

Ben accepted a glass of cognac from Raffi, then motioned for Lucy to speak privately. "I want to personally thank you. Vanessa told me you spoke with her at Mac's Pub. She said you saw us together at the Pussy Cat, but I suspect you learned about our relationship in an entirely different fashion."

Trepidation traveled down Lucy's spine. If he knew she'd never visited the Pussy Cat, then he had to know that Lucy learned of his relationship with Vanessa another way. Did he suspect she was the one who broke into Archie's shop, found the pictures, and mailed them to Detective Clemmons?

Ben must have sensed her unease. His expression eased. "Don't worry. I'm grateful. My lips are sealed if yours are. Everything that has happened has shown me what is truly important. I've decided not to run for mayor, but to continue to run the barber shop with Vanessa by my side. I truly care for her.

"Who will run for mayor instead?"

"Theodore Magic, of Magic's Family Apothecary, has expressed interest."

Lucy's lips eased into a smile. "I'm sorry about the election, but if Vanessa makes you happy, then you should introduce her to the town. I'd start at Lola's Coffee Shop. Good coffee has a way of bringing out the kindness in others."

Ben's eyes brightened with gratitude. "Good advice. Thank you."

Lucy's heart danced in happiness as she watched

the group of people in Kebab Kitchen's dining room.

The beach festival had resumed. Their small town would be all right. And best of all, her inner circle of family and friends was growing.

Author's Note

This mystery series is straight from my heart. For almost thirty years, my Armenian-American family owned a restaurant in a small town in South Jersey. My mother was a talented cook and the grapevine in our backyard was more valued that any rosebush. I'd often come home from school to the delicious aromas of simmering grape leaves, stuffed peppers and tomatoes, and shish kebab. Lunch at school would be hummus and pita instead of peanut butter and jelly at a time when hummus wasn't as popular as it is now. It wasn't always fun as a teenager to have an eccentric, ethnic family, but I've grown to value my roots and my own colorful cast of family members. In contrast, my husband is like Katie's family—they can almost trace their roots back to the Mayflower. We have two young daughters who have the best of both worlds, and yes, they both know how to make hummus and baklava and like them.

I loved writing this book, and I'm happy to share my own favorite family recipes with you. Enjoy the food!

RECIPES

Heat olive oil in saucepan over medium heat. Add celery, carrot, potato, garlic, and onions. Sauté until onions are transparent. Add chicken broth and lentils. Cover and simmer for about an hour until lentils are tender, but not soft. If soup is too thick, add ½ cup water to thin the broth. Add salt and pepper to taste. Serves four.

Butch's Greek Salad with Feta Cheese

Greek Dressing

juice of one lemon
2 tablespoons of red wine vinegar
1 clove minced garlic
1 tablespoon granulated sugar
1 teaspoon honey
½ cup extra virgin olive oil
¼ cup crumbled feta cheese
salt and black pepper to taste

Greek Salad

1 head romaine lettuce chopped
1 cucumber, sliced
1 green or red pepper, sliced
½ pint cherry tomatoes or 1 large tomato sliced
½ cup Kalamata olives (pitted is best!)
½ cup crumbled feta cheese
salt and black pepper, optional
Parmesan cheese, shaved, optional

Whisk together lemon juice, vinegar, garlic, sugar and honey. Slowly add olive oil and whisk until well combined. Add feta cheese. Add salt and pepper to taste. Dressing can last in the refrigerator in an airtight container for five to six days.

For the salad, combine all the ingredients and toss with how ever much dressing you prefer. Add salt and pepper or shaved Parmesan cheese to the salad if desired. Enjoy!

ACKNOWLEDGMENTS

I am very grateful for everyone who has encouraged me on my path to publication, especially my supportive husband, John, and my wonderful girls, Laura and Gabrielle.

A very special thanks in memory of my parents, Anahid and Gabriel. Sadly, they have passed away, but this series would never have come to fruition if it wasn't for them. They owned a restaurant for nearly thirty years in New Jersey, and I grew up in the business. They taught me to work hard and reach for my dreams. I miss them every day.

Thank you to Jeannie and Fran for watching the kids so I can travel to writing conferences.

Thank you to grammar queen Maryliz Clark for her guidance and longtime friendship.

To my Violet Femmes friends, and all my friends from Sisters in Crime, NJ Romance Writers, and Liberty States Fiction Writers—thank you for your support and encouragement.

Thank you to my wonderful agent, Stephany Evans, who makes every page shine.

Thank you also to my fabulous editor, Martin Biro, and everyone at Kensington Publishing for their hard work on my books.

Last, thanks to readers, booksellers, and librarians for reading my Kebab Kitchen mysteries and spreading the word. I hope you enjoy this one!

"Did you see who's at table three?"

Lucy Berberian set down a tray of wrapped silverware and looked where her sister, Emma, pointed from behind the waitress station.

"Isn't that Scarlet Westwood?" Lucy asked. The attractive blonde was a famous Philadelphia socialite and the daughter of a hotel mogul. Her picture was splashed across tabloids at the checkout counter of Holloway's, the sole grocery store in the small Jersey shore town.

"In the flesh!" Emma's voice rose an octave and she dropped the towel she'd been using to wipe down tables.

"Who's the older woman with her?" Lucy asked.

"Probably her personal assistant. Socialites don't go anywhere without them." Emma nudged Lucy. "They asked for you when they came in."

Lucy blinked. "Me?"

"That's right. They want to talk to the manager. That's you now, Sis."

Less than two months ago, Lucy had quit her position as an attorney at a large Philadelphia law firm, packed her bags, and returned to her small hometown of Ocean Crest, at the Jersey shore. She'd only planned for a temporary visit home until she could get back on her feet and find a new job, but she'd ended up staying and having a go at managing Kebab Kitchen, her family's Mediterranean restaurant. Her semiretired parents continued to work part-time, but Lucy was taking on a bigger role each day.

Lucy toyed with a cloth napkin on the tray. "Did they say what they wanted?"

Emma shook her head. "No. But don't keep Scarlet Westwood waiting. I don't think the celebrity types have a lot of patience."

Lucy snatched an order pad from the counter and headed for table number three, the best seat in the house, which overlooked the Atlantic Ocean and the Ocean Crest boardwalk. The table was also tucked away in a corner, semiprivate, and often requested by romantic couples. It was a hot and humid June afternoon, and sunlight shimmered on the ocean like shards of glass. Umbrellas and towels were scattered across the beach like a colorful quilt. Children frolicked in the surf and played in the sand while sunbathers reclined on beach chairs. In the distance, Lucy could see the amusement pier with its old-fashioned wooden roller coaster and Ferris wheel.

Lucy took a breath as she approached the table, wondering why they'd asked for her. Did wealthy socialites expect to be served by the manager and not the waitstaff?

"Good afternoon. My name is Lucy Berberian. How can I help you?"

Both women looked up. Scarlet Westwood removed her sunglasses and tucked them into a slick, black Chanel purse. She was stunning, just as she appeared in the celebrity photographs. She was in her late twenties with long, blond hair that brushed her shoulders and sky-blue eyes. Her makeup was expertly applied, and her trademark lips were big and glossy. Lucy had read that Scarlet liked her Botox, and her full lips were a result of a skilled doctor's injections.

"I was told you are the new manager here," the older woman said.

Lucy turned to the woman seated across from Scarlet and studied her for the first time. She appeared to be in her midfifties, old enough to be Scarlet's mother, with a brown bob and shrewd, dark eyes. Dressed in an elegant champagne-colored suit, she drummed long red fingernails on the pristine white tablecloth.

Lucy tucked the order pad back in her apron. "Yes, that's right."

The woman shot her a haughty look. "We're here on business and don't have much time today."

"Of course. Our kitchen is quick. Would you like to hear our lunch specials? Or if you prefer there's a hummus bar that offers a variety of hummus and vegetables for dipping. Pita bread is served warm from the kitchen and—"

"Not that type of business."

Then what? From what Lucy had read in the gossip rags, Scarlet liked to party and enjoyed expensive food, wine, and couture clothing. Kebab Kitchen was a pleasant family establishment, certainly nothing as trendy as the upscale establishments to which Scarlet was accustomed.

Scarlet flipped an errant blond curl across her shoulder. "I'm getting married at Castle of the Sea in Ocean Crest. I want Kebab Kitchen to cater my reception. This is my wedding planner, Victoria Redding."

Lucy's insides froze for a heart-stopping moment. Her first thought was that it would be a once-in-a-lifetime opportunity to cater the socialite's wedding. Her second thought was how would she pull it off? She was still learning the business, and she'd recently hired her ex-boyfriend, Azad, as the new head chef to take her mother's place. Things were as sticky as baklava syrup between them and Lucy was taking it day by day.

Which led to a bigger question: why would someone of Scarlet Westwood's status want to have a small, family-owned Mediterranean restaurant cater her reception?

"I'm flattered that you chose us, but I have to ask—"

"Why?" Scarlet finished for her.

Lucy shrugged. "Well, yes."

"I've vacationed at the Jersey shore since I was a child, and I recently purchased a summer home in Ocean Crest."

"I see." But that still didn't explain it.

"I plan to film my first movie, and a scene will take place on the beach here. My fiancé is Bradford Papadopoulos, the show's director. Bradford has

Mediterranean roots and he loves the cuisine. He also raved about the food when he last ate here."

That made more sense. Lucy remembered hearing about a possible movie being filmed on the beach from her best friend, Katie Watson, who worked at the Ocean Crest town hall. And if the groom preferred Armenian, Greek, and Lebanese food, then Kebab Kitchen was the best in all of South Jersey.

Lucy cleared her throat. "Congratulations on your engagement, and I'm honored you want us to cater your wedding."

"We realize this is a big opportunity for you," Victoria said, her voice stern. "And we have certain conditions."

Lucy may have been taken aback at Victoria's caustic tone, but she schooled her expression. The business would be great for the restaurant's catering arm. She could put up with a bridezilla, or in this case, an aggressive wedding planner, if it meant helping the business and proving her worth to her family.

"First, we intend to have two hundred and fifty guests. Have you ever catered for that large a number?"

"Of course," Lucy lied as her pulse pounded like an overloaded food processor.

She'd never catered at all. Her mother had handled the catering end of the business, and as far as Lucy knew, the largest order she'd filled was for a hundred people. But Lucy was stubborn and determined. Azad was an experienced chef, and together with their line cook, Butch, and her parents' part-time help, she was confident they could handle two hundred and fifty guests.

"Second, the wedding will take place in two weeks."

Only two weeks to prepare? The pressure tightened in her chest, and her mind whirled with all the details that would be required. The labor would be a problem, but she'd come up with something. Katie was always willing to help out, and there were college kids looking for summer jobs.

"And most important, news of the wedding must be kept as secret as possible, understand?" Victoria said.

Now this posed a different type of challenge. Gossip in Ocean Crest traveled as fast as greased lightning. It didn't help that the *Town News* was run by Stan Slade, a former New York City reporter who was always hungry for a story. Lucy recalled how hard it had been to keep things under wraps two months ago when the town's new health inspector had been murdered. It had been pretourist season then and Ocean Crest had been quiet, but now that it was late June, the town swelled with tourists and it was impossible to find a vacant parking spot. Talk was sure to start if anyone spotted Scarlet on the street or the boardwalk.

"I'll do everything in my power to keep it quiet. Only my staff will know, and they can be trusted. But what if you're seen in town? Surely people will ask questions."

Victoria cleared her throat. "Yes, but like Ms. Westwood said, she now owns a shore home in town. People have no reason to suspect she's getting married."

Both women stood. Victoria handed Lucy a

business card. "Here's my personal cell number. I'll be in touch to go over the menu for the cocktail hour and the reception. Some of the guests have dietary restrictions that must be accommodated."

"Of course," Lucy said.

Scarlet reached into her purse and slipped her sunglasses back on. Lucy thought the disguise did little to conceal her true appearance. "You must wonder why I would want my wedding kept a secret when I live in the limelight."

"No." *Yes.* Scarlet's escapades and lavish lifestyle were blasted weekly in the tabloids and television celebrity shows. Bad publicity only served to add to her impressive number of young fans.

"A large part of my life is for public display," Scarlet said, "but my wedding is different. I want that one day for myself."

Good luck, Lucy almost slipped, then bit her lip. It would take a small army of personal bodyguards to keep a wedding of that size secret. Even the guests could leak details of the wedding to the press. Nothing was off limits when it came to Scarlet and publicity. Did she plan on blindfolding two hundred and fifty people and driving them in large buses to the wedding? On an off-season day, that felt like much of Ocean Crest's entire population.

As soon as the women left, Emma and Sally, a longtime waitress at the restaurant, rushed over. Both wore their uniforms—black slacks, button-down white shirts, and red aprons—and their faces were anxious with anticipation.

"Well? What did Scarlet Westwood want?" Emma asked.

"She wants Kebab Kitchen to cater her wedding." Lucy still couldn't believe it.

"That's fantastic!" Sally said.

"It's for two hundred and fifty guests. We only have two weeks to prepare." Lucy felt a bit light-headed.

"You're kidding?" Emma asked.

"Nope. That's what she said."

Emma pursed her lips. "Well then, you'd best talk to Azad."

Lucy's gut tightened at the mention of her ex. *Really, Lucy. He works for you now.* She had to keep things in perspective. It was just a wedding, and so far, she'd insisted on maintaining a professional working relationship with Azad, the restaurant's new head chef.

It wasn't as if *they* were getting married.

Her legal training would kick in to full gear. Lucy had always excelled at organization, and she just needed to come up with a battle plan for Azad, her parents, and the rest of the staff to efficiently tackle each task. She'd give Scarlet Westwood a perfect reception.

After all, with organization and hard work, what could go wrong?

"You're doing it wrong."

Lucy turned at the masculine voice to see Azad Zakarian looking over her shoulder. Tall, dark, and good-looking, the sight of her ex-boyfriend still made her heart pound a bit too fast.

She straightened her spine and wrinkled her nose. "How? There is no wrong way to chop garlic."

Lucy knew the basis of Mediterranean cuisine was garlic, onions, and olive oil. It may give you killer breath, but it was one of the healthiest diets around.

Over the past two weeks, everyone at Kebab Kitchen had been working overtime to prepare for Scarlet Westwood's wedding. The kitchen had been a whirlwind of activity—the ovens heated the kitchen, the constant whirling of the industrial-sized mixer never seemed to end, and the delicious smells of freshly baked pastry and breads floated through the restaurant.

Lucy eyed the bowl of unpeeled garlic cloves soaking in cold water on the kitchen worktable. The garlic was needed for several of the dishes that would be served at the wedding reception, and Lucy had thought to peel and chop the garlic to relieve Azad from the menial task. But from the tense look on Azad's face, it was clear he didn't want her assistance.

"Yes, there's a wrong way," he said. "You're going to slice off the tips of your fingers. That chef's knife is wicked sharp and dangerous in the hands of an amateur."

In the hands of an amateur.

How many times had she heard similar comments over the past weeks? Her mother, Azad, and even their line cook, Butch, all seemed to remind her of her culinary shortcomings on a daily basis. She knew she wasn't a chef. When she'd worked as a city lawyer the extent of her culinary talent was to memorize the take-out numbers of all the restaurants within a two-mile radius of the firm. But since returning to Ocean Crest and deciding to take a stab at running her family's restaurant, she'd been determined to learn how to prepare basic Mediterranean dishes.

Lucy frowned up at him and set the knife on the cutting board. "Fine. Show me, then."

Azad plucked a clove of garlic from the bowl, efficiently peeled the skin, and placed it on the cutting board. "First, keep the tip of the blade on the cutting board at all times, then press downward and use the full length of the blade to slice your food."

He took the knife and began deftly to mince the garlic. His knife worked at breathtaking speed, and Lucy could barely follow his movements. Her gaze moved to his muscled forearms and rose to his chest. His broad shoulders strained against his shirt. She could see the day's growth of stubble on his chiseled cheeks and the sexy dimple in his chin. He wore his dark hair a bit long and it brushed his collar. Despite her determination to maintain a working relationship, she couldn't help but acknowledge that there was something irresistibly sexy about a competent male in the kitchen.

"There are five ways to mince garlic. Knife-minced, garlic-pressed, mortar and pestle, knife-pureed, and microplaned," he rattled off as he continued to work. "Each has different qualities and unique tastes for dishes."

"What about the jars you can purchase from Holloway's grocery store? The garlic comes perfectly minced."

Azad's knife halted in midchop and he gave her an incredulous sidelong glare. "You're kidding, right? Your mother would have a fit."

It was true. Everything was made from scratch at the restaurant. Her mother, who had been the head chef before Azad took over, even insisted on grinding her own meat for her dishes. *"It's never as fresh if you don't do it yourself. Fresh is everything,"* Angela Berberian had often said.

"I never said I was a chef. That's why I hired *you*, remember?" The words came out a bit harsher than Lucy wanted.

He flashed a grin, and the dimple in his cheek deepened. "Don't get all bent out of shape. I'm just showing you proper technique."

Lucy felt her face grow warm. They'd dated back in college, and when they'd graduated, their relationship turned serious. Or at least, *she'd* been serious. Azad had broken her heart when he'd suddenly ended things and they'd gone their separate ways—Lucy to law school and Azad to culinary school. She was older, wiser, and now his boss. So why did she let him get under her skin? One charming grin and she felt like a hormonal teenager gazing longingly at the star quarterback at a high school football game.

Ugh. She'd have to try harder to hide her emotions.

Only a few months ago, Azad had wanted to buy Kebab Kitchen. But Lucy's "temporary" visit home, after quitting the firm, had turned into a permanent stay, and she'd come to realize how much she'd missed her family, her friends—and surprisingly—how important Kebab Kitchen was to her. So Lucy had stepped up. Her parents were more than happy to teach her the business as they worked part-time and eased into retirement.

At least it had seemed the perfect arrangement for her. Azad may not view it that way. He'd left his sous chef job at a fancy Atlantic City restaurant to become head chef of Kebab Kitchen. She knew he'd initially wanted to buy the place from her parents and make it his own, but he'd changed his mind after Lucy had stated her intentions to remain in town.

Azad set the knife aside and wiped his hands on a dish towel. "Now do you remember how to knife-puree it?"

"Sure. Start by crushing it with the back of the blade."

Determined to show him she could do something, Lucy picked up the knife, pressed the back of the blade flat on a clove, and slammed her fist down to squash the garlic on the cutting board. But instead of cooperating, the finicky garlic clove shot from the board and flew across the kitchen like a smelly projectile.

Oh, no. Her eyes widened in dismay. What the heck went wrong? He made it look so simple.

She was saved from another culinary lecture by the sound of footsteps on the kitchen's terra-cotta floor.

Her mother, Angela, appeared behind an industrial mixer almost as tall as her five-foot frame. Her signature beehive, which had gone out of style decades ago, added a few inches to her height. The gold cross necklace she never left the house without caught a ray of light from an overhead kitchen window.

Angela frowned as she bent down to pick up the wayward piece of garlic from the floor. "You're doing it wrong, Lucy."

"She forgot to add salt," Azad said.

Salt! That was it. Lucy resisted the urge to smack her forehead with her palm. Salt made it easier to crush the garlic.

Angela's face softened as she looked at Azad in approval. She tossed the clove in a trash can and approached to pat Azad on the arm. "Listen to Azad, Lucy. He knows how to cook."

Lucy fought the urge to roll her eyes. If her mother had her way, Lucy would be baking her own baklava to celebrate her nuptials with Azad. It was no secret Angela Berberian wanted more grandchildren. Lucy had turned thirty-two and Angela firmly believed that her daughter's biological clock was set to explode. It wasn't enough that Emma was married to Max, a real estate agent in Ocean Crest, and they had a ten-year-old daughter, Niari. Lucy's mother wanted more grandkids, and fast.

"Now, do you have everything planned for that woman's wedding?" Angela asked, her tone a bit chilly.

"Her name is Scarlet Westwood," Lucy pointed out.

Angela folded her arms across her chest and arched an unamused brow. "Hmph. I know her name. I don't have to like her. She's done nothing to earn her fame except to be born into a wealthy family."

Lucy set aside the knife. "I know, Mom, but think of it as great publicity for the restaurant."

"Bah! Kebab Kitchen has done just fine for thirty years. Plus, that woman is a home wrecker."

Her mother was referring to several of Scarlet's past relationships with engaged or married men. Almost all were older and wealthy. Lucy wondered how much of what was reported was true and how much was sensationalized. "Since when do you watch the celebrity news channels? I thought you only liked the cooking channel and that good-looking chef."

Angela looked affronted. "What's wrong with Cooking Kurt? At least he's honest and single."

Lucy couldn't help but smile. One of the things she'd discovered since returning home was that her mother liked watching cooking shows while she worked. But she wasn't as interested in the new recipes as she was in watching the hot, sexy star of one of the shows.

"What's this about Cooking Kurt?" her father's voice boomed.

Lucy and her mother turned. Raffi Berberian stood between the swinging doors leading into the kitchen. Arms crossed over his thick chest, her father was a large, heavyset man with a balding pate of curly black hair and a booming voice. He held a stack of papers.

Her mother waved her hand dismissively. "We've been over this. You won't take me to Cooking Kurt's book signing at Pages Bookstore," Angela said. "Now I have to ask Lucy to take me."

Raffi's brow furrowed. "The man is a fraud. I doubt he even wrote one recipe in that cookbook."

Her mother planted her hands on her hips. "Of course, he wrote it. Isn't that right, Lucy?"

All eyes turned to her, and Lucy squirmed beneath her parents' gazes. "I guess so, Mom. If he didn't, his name wouldn't be on the cover."

A glimmer of satisfaction lit her mother's face, and her gaze returned to her father. "See? Lucy would know."

"Harrumph," her father said, dismissing the subject in his own way.

Lucy coughed to hide a smile. Despite their bickering, she knew her parents loved each other.

Her father sifted through the papers in his hand. "I double-checked the remaining wedding invoices you prepared. Everything looks good." He'd been in charge of the finances and the day-to-day business aspects of running a restaurant. Her mother had been in charge of the cooking.

"Thanks for double-checking, Dad," Lucy said.

"Is everything ready to be loaded into the catering van?" her father asked.

Two tall, rolling, catering carts with Dutch doors stood ready in the corner. One was heated to keep prepared food warm, the other was refrigerated for the cold items. The meat kebabs and vegetables had been marinated and would be grilled at the reception.

"We're ready to go," Azad confirmed.

"Do not forget that everything has to be served minutes from the grill." Her mother's laser-like gaze landed on Lucy. "I don't know who the servers will be, so it's up to you, Lucy, to be sure the food arrives hot to every table. The reputation of Kebab Kitchen is on the line."

Lucy swallowed as her nervousness slipped back to grip her. Her mother, despite her five-foot frame, could be quite intimidating. The wedding was a test and she was determined to prove that she had what it took to be a successful restaurateur.

At Lucy's nod, her mother continued. "Good. I'll stay behind with your father, Emma, and Sally and run the dinner shift. You go with Azad in the van and take all the food. Butch will meet you there."

"Katie is helping." Her friend didn't normally work weekends and had agreed to help Lucy oversee the reception. They didn't need any more staff. Castle of the Sea had a full staff of servers, dishwashers, and bartenders. Kebab Kitchen was responsible for the *mezze*—or appetizers—for the cocktail hour, the main course, and baklava for dessert. The wedding cake was made by Cutie's Cupcakes bakery, and Lucy knew that anything Susan Cutie made would be a stunning and mouth-watering confection. The lemon meringue pie was Lucy's favorite.

Her mom shook a finger at her. "Remember what I told you. Don't interfere with Azad while he's cooking. I know how you two can be at times. You need to oversee the servers and make sure the dinner hour runs smoothly. Don't argue with him or get in his way."

"Why would I argue with him or—"

Angela clutched Lucy's chin and lowered her face to place a kiss on her forehead. "I'm proud of you, Lucy. Now go give that home wrecker a perfect wedding. If her marriage goes bad, it will be her fault, not ours."